Blind
Ambition

Also by Lutishia Lovely

LUTISHIA LOVELY
Blind Ambition

www.kensingtonbooks.com

DAFINA BOOKS are published by

Kensington Publishing Corp.
119 West 40th Street
New York, NY 10018

All Kensington titles, imprints, and distributed lines are available at special quantity discounts for bulk purchases for sales promotion, premiums, fund-raising, and educational or institutional use.

Special book excerpts or customized printings can also be created to fit specific needs. For details, write or phone the office of the Kensington Sales Manager: Kensington Publishing Corp., 119 West 40th Street, New York, NY 10018. Attn. Sales Department. Phone: 1-800-221-2647.

The Dafina logo is a trademark of Kensington Publishing Corp.

ISBN-13: 978-1-4967-2445-8
ISBN-10: 1-4967-2445-3
First Trade Paperback Printing: June 2021

ISBN-13: 978-1-4967-2446-5 (e-book)
ISBN-10: 1-4967-2446-1 (e-book)
First Electronic Edition: June 2021

10 9 8 7 6 5 4 3 2 1

Printed in the United States of America

Blind
Ambition

Chapter 1
Mama

Two short years ago, Chantel Scott's life was normal. At least by Midwestern, middle-of-the-road, ordinary folk standards. Married, good job, family. Her name was Chantel Wallace back then. She and her husband Art went to work. Paid their bills. Attended church on Sundays. A little partying on the side. Then Hurricane Karen blew in and threw her life into chaos. Not the tropical cyclone with thunder, lightning, and seventy-mile-an-hour winds. No, this storm had blond hair, brown eyes, a little money, and no morals. Their son Artani was almost three before Chantel realized Art was cheating. It was another six months before she discovered what Art and Karen had in common—another girlfriend named cocaine. Only after filing for divorce did Chantel learn that while he and Karen romped at a casino hotel near their home in Kansas City, he started gambling. Drained their joint savings account and maxed out their credit cards. The divorce was almost final when Uncle Sam came knocking with a bill for over twenty thousand dollars in unpaid taxes and fees. Turns out Karen won a jackpot and told Chantel's brilliant husband to claim the winnings and get half the prize. Chantel never saw a penny of that money. The IRS never saw a cent either and came to collect. A year and a half later, on top of the credit card payments she faithfully made to maintain a good credit rating, her check was being garnished. Artani was the only good that came out of her marriage. Seeing his big brown eyes or feeling his scrawny arms around her neck almost made her forget that the boy's daddy had put her through hell.

Shortly after her divorce finalized, Chantel decided she needed to shake up her life. She moved back to her hometown, a place with a population of less than ten thousand people. Instead of living her life to please others, as she'd done for Art, she decided to do what made her happy. That meant downsizing from the three-bed, two-bath home she'd enjoyed with Art to a two-bedroom, two-bath rented condo, and taking a pay cut to work at the local newspaper, the *Marquette Monitor*. Being an hourly-paid copy editor wasn't quite the same as becoming an author like her favorites Bernice McFadden and Zuri Day, but it proved all those journalism and creative writing classes weren't completely in vain.

Two months ago, while working against a looming deadline, she noticed an article about a new club opening in the city and an ad looking for a singer to headline at said club. Few knew that Chantel had serious chops. Along with her dream of being a best-selling author, singing was her secret passion. Knowing she didn't have a chance in Hades of being selected was one of the main reasons Chantel decided to audition. That and the egging on of good friends Rita and Terrence. They told her she was as good as if not a better singer than Jett, the famous sister she hardly knew and the other reason Chantel mostly kept her singing to herself. No one was more floored than her when she was called back for a second audition with the house band two weeks later and selected to headline the live music venue on Friday and Saturday nights. She thought it was an inside job, that maybe her friend Terrence had influenced the decision, since he'd been hired to manage the club. He assured her that the club's owner, King Richardson, had made the final decision because, in the owner's words, "that chick can blow!"

He'd named the club Diplomat, probably because King had thrown his hat into the political ring and was running for mayor of Kansas City, Missouri. The main room held two hundred tops, a far cry from the arenas her sister performed in at the peak of her fame. But that didn't stop Chantel from feeling like she'd won the lotto. Or from putting 150 percent into every practice and every show. Each night showcased a different genre. Hip-hop. Blues. Gospel. Spoken word. Chantel loved the classic jazz and adult R&B theme designed to satisfy the grown and sexy crowd on Friday and Saturday nights. Still, the bundle of nerves in her stomach during the club's opening weekend made her almost throw up. The crowd was her saving grace. About half of them were friends of hers or people she worked with. A few had grown up with her sister, Jett, and in her opinion came down to see if talent ran in the family. Her mother Anna was in the audience, of course, along with Anna's neighbor and best friend, Blanche. They'd come ready to party and had cheered her on. She felt like a star. By the second weekend she'd conquered the jitters, all ready to settle into the pleasurable part-time job that paid a Benjamin every night plus tips, enough for her to have a smidgeon of discretionary income to spoil Artani a bit and not have to pinch a penny so hard that it erased Lincoln's face.

Tonight, though, the nerves were back, a roiling in her stomach that had been there throughout her entire first set. In fact, the unsettling feeling had been with her all day, a subtle unease just below the surface, like the calm before a thunderstorm. The last time she felt this nauseous, Artani arrived nine months later. But unless she was going to make like Mary and experience an immaculate conception, being pregnant was most definitely not the issue tonight.

"Are you okay?"

Chantel looked over to find Terrence casting a concerned eye in her direction. It had been that way off and on all night. She knew why. The nerves. He'd noticed. They'd known each other practically all their lives, from when his family moved from St. Louis to their block in Marquette when Chantel was eight and he was thirteen. She'd been immediately smitten by his dark good looks and athletic prowess. He'd treated her like a kid sister. Continual teasing and one getting on the other's nerves grew into a solid friendship, as close as two of the opposite sex could be without being intimate, even though lately Terrence had grown generous with the compliments and flirted around. Rita swore Chantel had to have let that "fine thang" hit it at least once. Unfortunately, nobody had hit, bit, licked, or stroked anything since Art left. Since he'd taken away what little trust in men she'd had in the first place, it might be a while before anything that wasn't battery operated hit that thang again.

"My stomach's upset," she admitted, pressing a hand against her stomach in an effort to quell the butterflies. "I thought I was over being nervous."

"You've had your fortifier?"

Chantel held up the now half-empty glass of wine she allowed herself before the show and during the break.

"Well, tip it up, girl! You've got the second half of a show to do." Terrence peeked out of the small curtain that separated them from the paying crowd. "In case you need motivation, the boss just arrived."

Chantel's stomach flip-flopped. "Great."

"With a few of his shot-caller business associates."

"Lucky me!"

"Exactly."

"I was kidding, Terrence."

"I know."

In Marquette, Missouri, the club's owner King was a favored

son. He'd grown up in Kansas City but had roots to the area since it was where his well-heeled grandparents had been born and raised, and where he'd spent many summers until his early teens. By giving the adults in Marquette a social outlet, the handsome and popular attorney had made his already beaming star shine brighter. In every encounter, he'd treated Chantel with kindness and respect, but his prestige-and-power persona was intimidating. Simply put, he made her nervous. Given the knots her stomach was already in, his timing to visit the club he owned sucked. She wished for more time to settle herself, but the band kicked into her second-half intro.

Terrence walked over and gave Chantel a brief hug. "Go be amazing."

The second set intro hit its stride. Chantel bobbed her head to the beat while finishing the glass of wine and trying to convince herself that the night wasn't unusual. She berated herself for acting foolish, entertaining feelings of dread for no good reason. Anybody who knew Chantel knew that her life now looked better than it had in quite a while. Relocating back to Marquette had felt like a fresh start, and now her mother was talking about moving back, too. Anna was born in Texas, grew up in KC, and had moved to Marquette shortly after Chantel was born. She moved back to the city after Chantel graduated high school, but was about to retire and wanted to be near her one and only grandchild. Artani was good, adjusting to a new daycare center and pre-school, and the shuffling back and forth, two-household kind of life. Chantel had lost ten pounds. The divorce from hell from baby daddy became final just last month. She had every reason to celebrate, every reason to go out there and kill it for the crowd.

"Come on, girl," she whispered to herself. It was time to pull her act together and take it to the stage. Chantel placed the wine-glass on the small table beside her, then stood and straightened the form-fitting silver number on the toned, curvy figure she managed to offer the audience courtesy of the intermittent fasting craze and a pair of Spanx that should have been labeled *sausage casing*. Closing her eyes, she rolled her head around to further loosen up while tapping out the beat with her hand against her leg.

"Ladies and gentlemen," her bass player Walter drawled over the smooth, steady beat of the drum and bass guitar, "coming back to the stage with a voice of pure perfectly pitched rhythmic poetry, Marquette's own full-grown diva of jazz . . . Chantel Scott!"

Chantel walked out with her back straight and head high, smiling to the crowd and even managing a small wave and head nod to club owner King and his wife Tamela. She reached the stand, removed the microphone, and slid her voice in between the rhythm guitar and keyboard and over the saxophone and drums.

> "On the wings of your heart, let love flow.
> Soar high like the arrow from love's bow.
> Give it time, ease your mind, it will grow,
> If you let go and let love flow."

She settled onto a stool placed front and center, closed her eyes, and sang the song she'd penned with a heartfelt fervor, like someone swimming in their own happiness. By the time the song ended, she almost believed the words herself. Emphasis on *almost*. Still, her mood lifted. The uneasiness shifted. "Let Love Flow" was a crowd favorite. Their enthusiastic reaction and the couples two-stepping on the dance floor pushed back the nerves again.

"Let Love Flow" slid into an up-tempo Anita Baker cover and jazzed-up versions of recent R&B faves. Chantel paid homage to the greats: Ella and Sarah. Billie and Diana. Forty minutes later, as the closing number's funky instrumental intro played behind her,

Chantel had conquered the beast of nerves she'd fought with for most of the day. She grooved with the guys—hips swaying, fingers popping, a winning smile on her face—and hit the final note with all of the gusto it deserved. The crowd was appreciative. She acknowledged their applause with a slight bow, her hands brought together in a humble pose.

"Thank you, Marquette, my homegrown fam. Me and the guys really appreciate your support. Stay safe out there. See you next week. Until then, God bless and good night!"

Chantel disappeared behind the velvety red curtain that separated the backstage and office areas from the main floor. Terrence walked over with a bottle of water. She took it from him, unscrewed the top, and took a large drink.

"Thanks."

Kayla, one of the waitresses, walked up to Chantel, hand raised for a high five. "You did your thing tonight, girl!"

"Thanks, sis."

"What you did with that Phyllis Hyman number was beautiful. I thought Papa was going to come onstage and help you sing!"

Rita, the head waitress, walked by and heard that comment. "Papa needs to be put on a two-drink maximum. One day that man is going to embarrass us all."

Terrence shook his head. "Ah, leave the man alone, Rita. He ain't hurting nobody."

"Not yet," Chantel replied, easing her protesting size nines out of five-inch heels. She'd known Papa since childhood, before losing his wife and child in a botched home invasion and robbery drove him to drink. "Somebody had better make sure he's not driving home."

Terrence waved off the comment as the club phone rang and he walked down the hallway to answer it.

"He's got Uber on speed dial, and if he doesn't, we sure as hell do."

Kayla rolled her eyes. "Uber on speed dial? He needs AA on redial!"

Rita watched Papa stumble toward the door. "Let me make sure this man gets home safely. Ain't nobody trying to get sued!"

"Y'all are both wrong," Chantel said with a chuckle. "And so is the way this girdle is cutting into my midsection." She turned toward the closet-sized office that doubled as her dressing room. "I'm on my way to freedom."

"It's called belly bliss!" Rita said. Everyone burst out laughing.

Terrence burst back through the curtain. His countenance had done a one-eighty from the devil-may-care attitude he'd shown only moments ago.

"Chantel. Hold up." The severity of his voice stopped her in her tracks.

"What's wrong?" Chantel asked, though the look in his eyes and the knots that immediately formed in her stomach told her she didn't want to know.

"Let's go in your dressing room." Terrence took her arm and gently guided them both into a room barely big enough for one. As soon as the door was closed he took a breath and said, "That was Trinity Medical."

The Kansas City hospital where Anna was about to retire from after working there almost fifteen years? What did they want? Chantel frowned. "And?"

"Your mom was in an accident."

Chantel's hand flew to her stomach, now roiling double-time. The other hand gripped Terrence's arm like a vise. "What? When? Is she okay?"

"She's in surgery. They want you to get there as soon as you can."

Exactly eighteen hours, thirty-four minutes, and seven seconds after Terence uttered those words, Chantel's mom, Anna Michelle

Scott, took her last breath and exited stage left. She never awoke from the coma doctors induced before surgery, but Chantel was there when she died. Later, Chantel would realize that a little part of her died that day, too, even as another virus assailed her. This one was called grief, a high form of sadness for which Chantel saw no cure.

Chapter 2
Escapade

Just as Beyonce, Mariah, Alicia, and others were one-name wonders known around the globe, Jeanetta S. Scott Williams Dickerson Jones Scott (for the second time following her third divorce) was known to America and much of the world by Jett, the nickname coined by her Hollywood handlers when she was sixteen. Just Jett. No last name needed. Like Janet, Brandy, or Whitney, her fave. She'd never been crazy about Jeanetta but thought Jett sounded sexy. It was a fitting moniker for other reasons. One, back in the day, the older women had labeled her "fast." That meant she knew and was doing more than her young age should have allowed. "Five going on twenty-five," her mother used to say. The words were prophetic, as by the age of fifteen, for better or worse, Jett had experienced more than some women twice her age.

The events in Jett's life moved even faster than she did. After being heard belting out a Whitney tune outside a fast food joint, she was approached by a man who said he had connections, and introduced to a producer shortly after her sixteenth birthday. Turned into a singing sensation before hitting seventeen. Idolized as a leading TV star by the time she was eighteen. Named a triple threat and Grammy winner just shy of twenty-one. She'd experienced a pregnancy, three marriages, and three divorces by the time she was thirty-five. Today at forty-nine, thanks to reality television and a popular talent show, her career was making a much-needed comeback. Its second wind had given her a second chance. That she planned to make the most of it was the only reason that before most Angelenos had had their first cup of java she half lay, half sat, half sprawled, pushing it up and crunching it out—tired, sweaty, sore, but determined—on her patio's cool concrete floor.

"Come on, now. Let's make these last ten count." Randall, her superbly chiseled full-time trainer, part-time lover, hovered above her, cheering her on. "Ninety-eight. Ninety-nine. One hundred! Great job! That's what I'm talking about!"

Jett allowed the weights she held to fall beside her. "Whatever." She lay back with an arm slung over her eyes to block out the early morning sun.

"No, not time for that now." Randall softly slapped her thigh. "We need to stretch out those muscles we just worked."

Jett felt Randall's talented hands grasp her arms. She allowed herself to be pulled up and into his embrace and knew just how to distract him from further physical punishment that he had the nerve to define as a cooldown.

"I can think of a few other muscles that need stretching," she murmured against his ear.

"All in good time, my lovely," he easily countered, traces of his Caribbean heritage creating a melody that caused her yoni to clench. He knelt beside her, lowered his voice. "On your knees."

"Ooh, yeah." She turned over, raised to her knees, and wiggled her butt.

Randall swatted it before instructing her to ease her body forward to elongate her frame and stretch the core muscles she'd just strengthened with a hundred crunches while holding ten-pound weights. She shifted backward into a modified doggy-style, dropping her head and allowing the blood to refresh her brain. A few more moves, grunts, and sexy, calculated groans and the session ended. Jett got up and walked over to the patio table that held a bottle of water and her towel.

Randall's eyes then swept her body in that slow, sexy, languid way his hands would do shortly. "Damn, I'm good. My baby's body is tight!"

That Randall communicated better with his dick than his mouth was only one reason that after losing a few remaining, stubborn pounds their little tête-à-tête would be over. The other was that he was beginning to make the same mistake as most men she dated—get needy and possessive, catch feelings and stuff. Their session was over. She should have shown him the door. But she didn't.

"Join me for a shower?"

Randall smiled, full of himself, totally unaware he would soon be "to the left."

"Absolutely."

Jett's body reacted. She reached for his hand and led him through the patio doors, across the open-concept living/dining/kitchen area, down a hall, and through the master suite's double doors. Once there she shimmied out of her gym shorts, pulled off her sports bra, and watched as Randall shed his boxers and released the snake she adored.

"Come here, you . . ."

She pulled him into her arms, her lips searching for and finding Randall's cushy landing spot. Their tongues dueled, danced, deliciously devoured as naked bodies, relieved of fabric, engaged in an intimate get-to-know. Jett crawled onto the bed bench, adopting a position much like the doggy down used to stretch her core. She was ready for action and then . . .

Her cell phone rang.

Jett barely noticed. That's what voicemail was for. Randall had assumed the position behind her and introduced his tongue to particular body parts that were more than happy to make the acquaintance.

Her landline tinkled. Ignored again.

Seconds later, notes of a Ladymac jazz tune drifted through the sensual haze surrounding Jett and Randall. Whoever called had circled back to her cell phone.

"Maybe you'd better answer," he finally suggested, his stiff soldier poised at the point of entry and ready to strike.

Jett's head swung from side to side in anticipated ecstasy. She wrapped perfectly manicured fingers around the python he offered. "Ignore it."

Randall tried to, Jett would later recall. His tip touched her core as she raised up to greet him. But instead of a welcome home from his sizable shaft, the ringing that had stopped only seconds ago started again. Someone was calling back to back.

"It'll probably keep ringing." Randall moved from his hovering position and fell back on the bed.

Jett cursed. "I'll turn off the ringer."

"Answer the call, baby. It could be important."

Jett sighed as she reached for her cell phone. Only now did she remember Chantel's repeated calls from the day before. Between the photo shoot for the reality talent gig, last night's guest appearance at a club frequented by A-list celebs, and this morning with Randall, she'd forgotten all about them.

Must need money. That had been the case three months ago, the last time they'd talked. Then, Jett hadn't been able to help her much. Since the news was out about her getting the judging gig, she assumed her sister was back for an increase.

Tapping the screen, she engaged the speaker button. "What?"

A hesitant pause. "Jett, it's Chan."

"I know who it is." Randall slid out of bed and Jett swatted his ass, admiring its tautness as he walked into the en suite bath.

"You've been blowing up my phone for almost twenty-four hours. Obviously, I'm busy. What do you want?"

"You didn't listen to any of my messages, even the last ones marked urgent?"

"I'm listening now." Jett knew Chantel couldn't see the attitude on her face, but she hoped the message that this call was an inconvenient interruption came through loud and clear. "What. Do. You. Want?"

"Mama was in a car accident."

Jett jerked upright to a sitting position, as a hand flew to her chest. "Oh my goodness! How is she?"

"Dead."

Chantel had spoken in a whisper. Surely what Jett thought she heard wasn't correct. "What did you say?"

"She didn't survive the accident. She . . ." Jett heard her sister's sniffles at the other end of the line. "I left a message for you to get here as soon as possible. For a while the doctors were optimistic and thought they could save her. But last night . . . she . . . just stopped breathing."

Jett absorbed this news like a slow punch to the gut. She'd never experienced the close relationship with Anna that Chantel enjoyed. Theirs had been strained for many years, many reasons. But there'd been a moment, a specific situation when her love as a mother had saved Jett's life.

The tears that had hovered on the rims of her eyelids slid down her cheeks. "Mama?"

"Yes, Jett." Chantel's murmured reply was accompanied by a muffled sob. "She's gone and she's not coming back!"

A pain gripped Jett's heart. It threatened to cut off her breath. Ignoring Randall's outstretched arm and questioning expression, she slid off the bed and reached for a nearby robe while trying to compute the words *Mama* and *dead* being in the same sentence. She couldn't. It had been weeks since Jett had spoken to Anna by phone, almost a year since she'd seen her. And now the chances for phone calls were over? Her mother was gone forever? Guilt wrapped itself like a blanket around her. And something else—fear.

"I'm so sorry, Chantel, for not calling you back. What happened?"

"They're still investigating and don't know exactly how it occurred, though there were no obvious signs that either drugs or alcohol were involved. It'll be a while before a toxicology report can totally rule that out. One officer speculated the person could have fallen asleep or been checking a text. Like I said, they really don't know. I guess it really doesn't matter. They lived. Mama didn't."

Again, it became quiet on the other end of the line. Jett imagined Chantel either holding back tears or wiping them away.

"When's the funeral?"

"I'm still trying to process there having to be one." Jett heard Chantel sigh, then blow her nose. "Mama's friend Miss Blanche is going to help me plan the service, but we need you, too. Can you fly in tonight, or as soon as possible?"

As devastating as the news of her mother dying was, there was no way Jett could leave LA right now. Not with tons of other amazing singers and beautiful B-list actresses chomping at the bit and ready to take her spot on *Seeking Stardom*. No time would have been optimal to lose her only parent, but with the new life her career had been given and the high stakes betting on the show's success, this was the worst possible time.

"I can't, Chan. The show—"

"The show? Did I seriously hear you mention your job just now? I don't give a damn about that show, or your work. I don't know what happened that put such a strain on y'all's relationship, Jett, but she's your mother, too!"

"Yes! She's *my* mother!"

"She's our mother," Chantel yelled back. "Not just yours."

"You're right. I'm sorry. I'm just in shock."

"So am I. Which is why more than ever we need to be there for each other right now. I know we're not all that close, but—"

"I agree. You're right. I'll come home for the funeral."

"How soon can you get here? I don't want to do this alone."

Jett eased out of bed and stepped out of her master suite onto the balcony that ran the length of the room. From her perch in the Valley she could see the lights on the avenues near her home and the mountains framed in shadow beyond them. What she couldn't see was how she'd get through returning to Kansas City to bury her mother, or how she and Chantel, practically strangers, would navigate around each other without her.

"I'll pay for the funeral and attend the services that day, but that's all I can do. You may not want to hear it, but the timing of this couldn't be worse. I'm under contract and can't break it. Pre-taping for *Seeking Stardom* is happening right now, along with photo shoots and interviews. Filming the auditions begins next week. I beat out half of Hollywood to get this gig. Every artist over thirty auditioned, one almost sixty-five. Any of them would be more than happy to take my chair. Sorry, sister, but I just can't . . .

"Hello? Chantel?"

Jett looked at her phone. Chantel had hung up.

"Shit."

"Baby?"

Jett gasped as she spun around. She'd forgotten all about Randall, which, given how good he looked and how he could make her feel, was hard to do.

"Sorry to startle you, baby. Did I hear you say someone died?"

Jett nodded. "My . . ."

The word *mother* puddled like goo in her mouth, stuck to the back of her throat. She couldn't push it out. To do so would make it real and force Jett to consider long-held secrets the two of them shared and that she was nowhere near ready to face. On the other hand, not stating a fact didn't make it not so. She swallowed past the lump in her throat. "My mother."

Randall quickly closed the distance between them and pulled her into a tight embrace. "Jett, baby, I'm so sorry."

Jett clung to Randall, crying softly, finding solace in his strong arms.

"I thought I was your only family."

There he went again with that possessive bullshit. His comment helped Jett regain her composure. She stepped away from him, wiping her eyes.

"What I meant was that I can't remember ever hearing you talk about your mom."

The chill she felt had nothing to do with the weather. "Outside of your demanding instructions and magic wand mojo, I don't remember us talking much at all."

"You've got a point. I'm very sorry for your loss."

"Thank you. Me too."

He moved to embrace her again. She sidestepped him and walked back into the master suite. Randall followed behind her. He reached for his T-shirt to add to the briefs he'd hurriedly slid on. "I can't imagine how you're feeling right now. What can I do to help?"

Jett stepped toward him. "Stop dressing, for one thing." She placed a hand on his six-pack and the other on the rapidly hardening massive package mere inches below said abs.

"You can help me feel better. You can help me try and forget the call I just got, act like it didn't happen, for just a little while."

It wasn't the first time Jett had used sex as a way to cope with or run away from something she wasn't ready to face. Randall's skill made escape easy. On most days there could have been an argument as to who gave whom the best workout—Randall on the patio or Jett in the bed. Soon after the orgasms, however, Randall left and the pain returned, deeper than before. She called Chantel to apologize and got no response. Sent texts. Same thing. Jett understood. Anna was their mother, and just like that, she'd been forever taken out of their lives. Unfortunately, Chantel didn't and perhaps couldn't understand Jett's position. *Seeking Stardom* was her chance to appear on one of the nation's most popular shows, a rare opportunity for middle-aged Black women in Hollywood. The decision obviously felt wrong to her little sister, but Jett knew it was the right one for her. *Seeking Stardom* was her comeback. Breaking the contract wouldn't bring Anna back.

The next morning, as Jett weaved in and out of bumper-to-bumper traffic on her way to work, Chantel called. Jett apologized again and offered to cover any funeral expenses beyond the five-thousand-dollar burial plan Anna had purchased. A truce was reached.

Jett arrived at the studio. The guard waved her through. "Sorry, Chantel, but I have to go."

"Can you call me back later today? We need to finalize everything as soon as possible."

"I can't call, but text me. I'll try and respond quickly, okay?"

Over the next several hours, a flurry of texts hit her phone.

Here's the obituary. What do you think?

Beautiful, Chan. Couldn't have said it better.

Which of these pictures should I use?

Jett immediately skipped over the earlier versions of Anna, the ones taken during their fallout years, to one taken just a few Christmases ago when the family had celebrated in Las Vegas. Fond memories. *I like this one.*

Do you want to sing at the service?

No. The focus should be on Mama, not me. Jett could count on one hand the times she didn't jump to grab the spotlight. Now was one of those times, and not because it was a funeral. She'd happily joined a popular R&B artist during a televised homegoing for an iconic politician that came to prominence during the civil rights movement. But this was different. This was Mama. She'd barely been able to tell Randall she'd died, much less sing "Amazing Grace."

For the remainder of the week, Jett's waking hours were spent being primped, primed, shot, and recorded as she and three other judges listened to people audition, from talented songbirds whose gifts would never be heard on the radio to hilarious hopefuls who couldn't sing their way past the fifteen seconds of commercial shame that helped secure high ratings. In between takes and the short trips from her home in the San Fernando Valley to Hollywood's Dolby Theatre where the show was being filmed, she and her sister continued to finalize plans, recalling fond but separate memories of times with their mom. Jett took down her wall and shed more tears for the woman who'd given her life. For the fights that had kept them at such odds. For the conversations that should have happened and now never would. By the time she boarded the plane for the flight to Kansas City—under the less recognized legal name Jeanetta Williams and sans the near waist-length trademark curls—the sisters, along with the women from Anna's church and her best friend and neighbor Blanche, had put together a homegoing celebration worthy of the kind, giving woman Anna Scott had been. The kind that would make Chantel proud and relieve some of Jett's guilt. Randall went from personal trainer/lover to bodyguard, traveling with her to provide a different type of relief and be a buffer between Jett and any past not worth facing.

Later that day, Jett walked out of the lobby as Chantel pulled into the hotel's circular drive. "I almost didn't recognize you," Chantel said. "What happened to your hair?"

"Hello to you, too, sister," The sisters shared a hug. "You picked up Jeanetta. I left Jett in LA."

"It's good to see you."

"I'm glad I'm here."

"Wish you could stay longer."

"Me too." Though not really. She'd barely been there two hours and couldn't wait to leave. The city brought back too many memories, though for the sake of her sister and mother, she'd try to forget them.

She pulled off her ballcap and ran a hand along short, natural curls while eyeing her sister keenly. "How you holding up?"

"As well as anyone who's lost their mother, I guess."

Jett noticed the puffy skin and dark circles around Chantel's eyes. "Have you slept at all?"

"Not much. The pain is so real it's suffocating. When I lay down and begin thinking about it, I feel like I can't breathe."

Jett reached over to give Chantel's shoulder a comforting squeeze. "I'm sorry I couldn't get here earlier."

"You did what you could. If it weren't for Miss Blanche, I could have never gotten through it. The planning, shopping for caskets, picking out clothes. She's had my back the whole way." Chantel slowed down as she exited the highway. "Do you want to see her?"

"Miss Blanche?" Jett shook her head. "I don't really know her."

"I meant Mama." Chantel's voice was barely above a whisper.

"Oh." Jett took a deep breath and tried to reconcile her feelings, which now, even a week later, were still all over the place. She knew the correct answer was *yes, absolutely*, that in fact she should have been the one making the suggestion. But the truth of the matter was that Jett dreaded the finality of what that moment would mean, even as she was guiltily relieved that their mother's body wasn't the only thing that would be buried tomorrow. So would the secret Anna Scott had promised Jett she would take to her grave.

"It's all right," Chantel said, with a weary sigh. "I know you two weren't close."

"I loved her," Jett replied.

"I believe that. But you didn't like her much. There was always tension. You rarely came home."

They stopped at a light. Jett felt Chantel's intense gaze.

"Why?"

"Selfish is probably the most accurate answer. I didn't have the best time here."

"Is that why Mama moved to Marquette?"

Jett paused a long moment. "Probably." She reached over and grabbed Chantel's hand. "But I'm glad I'm here now. And I do want to see Mama, okay? Just you and me."

They made it through the service, indeed a celebration, held at the Baptist church where Anna had been a member for more than half of her seventy-two years. The choir sang her into heaven as members, friends, and of course, Blanche lauded Anna's time on earth. The funeral home had done a wonderful job. Their mother looked as Jett last remembered—smooth, mocha-colored skin, slight smile, as though only sleeping. Chantel held it together beautifully, even joined in with some of the singing, until they reached the graveside. When the casket was lowered into the earth, Chantel went down to the ground with it. The sight put another chink in the armor around Jett's heart. In that moment she felt closer to Chantel than ever before. As she reached down to help the younger sister she barely knew back to her feet, Chantel's pain overshadowed her own. She was glad the service was over. She'd seen several familiar faces, mostly older friends of her mother but also a few people she remembered from middle school, before she'd been plucked like an innocent flower and placed into Hollywood's garden. Randall allowed them to speak to her, but not more than that. His presence was appreciated. When it came to the people she'd hung around back in the day, she hadn't much more for them than "hi."

On the way back to the limousine, Randall saw an older woman struggling in the cemetery's ground, made muddy and slippery from March's cold, unseasonal rainstorms. "I need to help her."

"Sure, go ahead." Jett continued to the car.

Someone called out, "Jeanetta!"

Jett turned around. She squinted at the short, round woman coming toward her with auburn hair made redder by the rays of sun now peeking through clouds. Big square sunglasses hid almost all of her face, but considering that she used Jett's government name, it was a given to be someone she knew.

The moment she took off the glasses and Jett saw the eyes and the freckles beneath them, she wished she'd ignored the voice and kept on walking.

"Brenda Moreland."

"Jeanetta Scott. Oh, but no, it's Jett." Brenda's laugh was condescending. "The name fits you because your ass sure flew out of here! Surprised you came back."

Jett's hand shot out and connected with Brenda's face before she could think of a better reaction, and it felt so good she wanted to do it again.

"I'm here for my mother," she snarled.

"I'm sure you're going to miss her," Brenda sweetly replied, rubbing the skin reddened by Jett's slap. "She did a lot for you." Her eyes slid over to Chantel standing a few feet away. "And your . . . sister?"

"She did a lot for everybody, including Miss Margaret when she was alive."

"Your mama and my mama were good friends. We were, too, once." Brenda stepped closer, the cold tone of her voice not matching her smile. "Which is the only reason my hand isn't wrapped around your throat right now and I'm not dragging your no-good ho ass through these tombstones."

"Still the sore loser, I see. Goodbye, Brenda."

Jett turned to leave. Brenda grabbed her arm.

"Just remember. I knew you when—"

Randall's strong fingers wrapped around Brenda's arm surprised her into silence. He stepped in between them.

"Everything okay, ladies?"

Brenda looked at Randall appreciatively. "This your man?"

"You're not his type." Jett turned to Randall. "Let's go."

They began to walk away.

Brenda took a step and said, "Hey, you seen Preston lately?"

The comment caused Jett to freeze, but only for a second. The situation her old friend referred to happened in another lifetime. A response wasn't worth her breath.

Jett skipped the repast. The funeral goers had been respectful during the service and at the graveside but she'd seen the furtive looks, the whispers followed by moments of wide-eyed recognition, the staring. For those who didn't remember her from the early days, word of who she was must have spread during the funeral because at the graveside the gawking increased. She wanted to avoid the less formal crowd. More specifically, she didn't want another run-in with Brenda, or any other fake friends from her past. Back at the hotel she declined an invite to join Randall in bed or the gym. She needed time with herself, a chance to try and unpack the emotions she'd bottled up inside. Feelings about the mother she'd lost and the sister she barely knew. As she released the clasp from the past and allowed in memories shut out for decades, a plan formed. She gave voice to it the next morning when, after not taking no for an answer, Chantel arrived to take them to the airport.

Jett entered the front seat while Randall handled the luggage. She patted Chantel's shoulder. "How are you doing?"

Chantel shrugged. "Rough night."

Jett felt a pang of guilt, an emotion that lately happened all too often.

"I should have gone with you to the repast but . . ."

"I understand why you didn't. All the people looking at you like an exhibit. And who was that woman who spoke to you at the graveside?"

"An old friend."

"Really? Y'all didn't act too friendly."

"Okay, keeping it real, we went to school together but I couldn't stand the bitch."

"Damn!"

Chantel laughed. Jett joined her. Laughter felt good. Randall slid into the back seat. "What'd I miss?"

The sisters looked at each other. "Nothing," they replied in stereo, and laughed again.

For the next several minutes the car was quiet, until Chantel merged on to the highway. "I went by Mama's house. Thought it might help me feel close to her, like she was still here. Instead it made her absence more real. It'll probably be a while before I go back to the city. Too many memories of places we went and things we did. It'll be the same when I get back to Marquette. She's everywhere there, too."

"How would you like to get away for a minute, maybe you and Artani come to LA for a quick little getaway?"

Surprise showed all over Chantel's face. "Really?"

"I'll buy the tickets and you two can stay at my place. I'll be working most of the time. But you'll have my car to get around. A change of scenery might do you guys good."

"I just started this job not too long ago. Not sure I can get off work. But if I can, are you sure it's okay?"

"Positive. Now that Mama's gone, it's just you and me. I say it's high time we really get to know each other, don't you?"

"Yes."

Chantel's shoulders relaxed as she delivered the first real smile Jett had seen since being picked up at the hotel the day before. In time she'd question the wisdom of issuing her sister this invitation, but right now, in this moment, it felt good.

Chapter 3
California Love

It took some finagling and unpaid leave she couldn't afford, but Chantel made it happen. She and her son were going to LA. They'd be there a week. It took two to get ready. She could have used two more. Jett had purchased their tickets but Chantel wanted to arrive with a little money in her pocket. Then there was the matter of getting time off from her job. The *Marquette Monitor* was one of only a few remaining small-town newspapers. In the age of digital publishing, it was holding on only through the loyal patronage of Main Street and the community's subscribers. Her not being there meant extra work for the already overburdened staff. But after being reminded of her recent loss and with promises of making up the time with double shifts and Saturdays, her boss gave in and made an exception of granting a vacation before the year was up—this one time.

Next, she'd called the club and talked to Terrence about finding a singer to replace her during her weekend away. That was easy. Kansas City was filled with amazing singers all vying for the handful of steady work anywhere within a hundred-mile radius. Had her emotions and nerves not already been shot, hearing who would be filling in as the guest artist would have done the trick. Jasmine Alexander was everything Chantel wasn't—tall, slim, gorgeous, her own hair reaching midway down her back. Plus, sister-girl could blow. Chantel had to give her that, too. The only thing Chantel had going in her favor was that Diplomat, which had quickly been renamed the Dip by the locals, was almost an hour away from Kansas City. She didn't see Jasmine wanting to make that two-hour round trip two nights a week, more with rehearsal time, or Jasmine's husband, a former KC Chiefs football player with a reputation for insane jealousy, letting her spend that much time away from home. That King Richardson and the regular patrons seemed to like the club vibe she created gave Chantel the belief that her singing gig would be there waiting for her when she returned to Marquette. Lastly, King's wife Tamela would likely have a problem with someone more beautiful than her having an ongoing gig at her husband's club.

"Is it time yet?"

"No, Artani," Chantel replied the morning of departure, for what seemed like the hundredth time.

"Is the Uber picking us up?"

"It's too expensive to get an Uber from here all the way to Kansas City. Terrence is taking us to the airport."

"Why are we going to Kansas City?"

"Because the major airlines, the really big planes, have to fly out of big airports, not like the one over on Highway 16."

"Is Terrence going with us?"

"No."

"What time are we leaving?"

"In a little bit."

"What's a little bit?"

"Artani, please!" Chantel caught herself before going off. She couldn't blame her son for being excited. She was, too. "Sorry, baby. Didn't mean to yell at you. Did you remember to put the Switch in your backpack?"

Artani nodded.

"What about your books?"

"Everything is in there, Mom. I'm ready to go!"

Chantel chuckled. Her doorbell rang.

"Terrence!" Artani ran to the front door and jerked it open.

"What did I tell you about opening that door without knowing who's there?" Chantel batted Artani out of the way. "Could have been anybody."

Terrence stepped inside. "But it wasn't. It's me."

"Hey, Terrence."

"Hey, Chantel." Terrence turned to walk into the living room but saw the luggage and stopped short. "You decided to stay longer?"

"No. We're only staying for a week."

"Then what's all this luggage for? You planning to buy out a store or two?"

"I didn't know what to pack."

"So you emptied out your closet?"

Chantel gave him a look. "Just put the luggage in the trunk, please, so we can go."

Artani ran to open the door. "Yes! Let's go!"

One last check of the house—doors, windows, alarm—and the trio was on their way. Artani was a bundle of jabbering energy until they stopped at a drive-thru for his favorite fries which he ate while settling into his favorite handheld video game. Chantel continued running through mental lists in her head of what all she'd planned to pack and hoped made it into one of three regular-sized suitcases and one carry-on bag.

She felt Terrence's eyes on her.

"What?"

"You all right?"

"Fine, why?"

"You're pretty quiet."

"I was just checking off a mental list, making sure I packed everything."

"Everything but the kitchen sink, from the looks of things."

Terrence's eyes were back on the road but Chantel rolled hers anyway.

"This isn't your first trip to LA, is it?"

"Artani has never been there, but Mama and I went a few times when I was little and Jett was on TV. The last time was five years ago to attend a friend's wedding."

"You stayed with your sister?"

"My friend had arranged a hotel group discount. We all stayed there. What about you?"

"Never been and don't have a desire to go."

"Why not? California is beautiful."

"So is Missouri."

Said as they passed a series of strip malls and businesses dotting the otherwise nondescript landscape. Both of them laughed out loud.

"Naw, I'm just messing with you. If somebody gave me a ticket to the West Coast, I wouldn't turn it down. It just seems like a city full of fake people, selling the rest of the world smoke-and-mirror dreams."

"Maybe."

"Is your sister like that?"

"Like what, a dreamer?"

"No. Fake."

Chantel looked over to see if Terrence was teasing. From the look on his face he was dead serious.

"Why would you think that?"

"Because of how she acted at the funeral. Did she really think she needed a bodyguard to keep people from talking to her?"

Chantel thought about the exchange she'd witnessed but not heard with . . . what was the woman's name?

"Maybe she did. Plus, she introduced him to me as her personal trainer. I think they've got something personal going on, but what he's training is up for grabs."

"She didn't even come to the dinner afterward. It's probably not my place to say anything, but you needed her support."

"I guess that's part of what this trip is, her being supportive. Plus, you know she's a judge on that new reality show. They just started taping, and considering that we've never been close, her making the effort to make it down here at all, even for a day, was a good thing."

"I hear you. I'm glad you're getting a chance to get away. Hopefully this trip will help the two of you get closer."

"We're hoping for that, too."

"With both of y'all being singers, that shouldn't be too hard. Has she ever heard you sing?"

"Not really."

"Maybe she can get you on that show!"

"I don't think so."

"Why not? She's one of the judges."

"That's probably why not."

She hadn't voiced it whenever speaking with Jett, but the thought of being on the show had crossed Chantel's mind. Once insecurities about her age, weight, and true vocal ability crept into her thoughts, she was glad Jett's position as judge prevented her from making a fool of herself on national television.

"Well, if you can't get on the show, you should at least do a club. You can outsing almost everybody out there these days. Your voice needs to be on the radio."

"And you need to do my PR."

The conversation shifted to the club's replacement singer, Jasmine Alexander, and other casual chitchat, until Terrence pulled into Kansas City International Airport and pulled up curbside. He jumped out of the car and helped Chantel wheel the luggage to the outside check-in kiosk. They shared a brief hug.

"Take care of your mom, little man," he said to Artani, giving the wide-eyed tyke a fist bump as he headed to the car. Just before getting in, he yelled out to Chantel, "Don't go out there and get all bourgie on me."

"Boy, bye."

Terrence didn't have to worry about Chantel becoming pretentious. Jett had a lock on all their family's share. The thought made the down-to-earth Missourian wonder just what a week with her star sister would look like. As she pulled out her ID and ushered Artani into the security line, Chantel thought, with the slightest bit of apprehension, that she was about to find out.

Three and a half hours later a tired Chantel and roused-from-sleep Artani touched down at Los Angeles International Airport, commonly called LAX. At the thought of reconnecting with her sister, the excitement that had died down during the mundane flight began to build again. A twinge of disappointment happened when a driver and not Jett met her down in baggage claim, and after she read the text that reached her once her phone was off airplane mode: *House key under side door mat. Car keys on counter. Won't be home till late tonight. Let's do breakfast tomorrow. Lots of restaurants on Ventura Blvd. Welcome to Cali!*

Chantel thought Jett being home on their first night there would have been nice. When she followed the driver into the parking lot and saw the snazzy-looking town car her sister had arranged for their transport, all was forgiven.

"Mom, look! Palm trees!"

The California scenery, so different from what they'd left behind, reenergized Artani. He oohed and ahhed as they traveled down the 405 freeway, nearly coming out of his skin when he saw the Hollywood sign. His excitement was contagious. By the time they reached Jett's cozy three-bed, two-bath home nestled in a quiet Toluca Lake neighborhood, Chantel was as ready to go sightsee as her son. The burst of energy was short-lived. By the time she'd unpacked their luggage, navigated the crowded av-

enue to a pizza joint and made it back home with Jett's Lexus and
the cars around her unscathed, eaten, and gotten Artani ready for
bed, Chantel was exhausted all over again. After spending time
on the patio, Chantel went to "lie down for a bit." She didn't
know she'd fallen asleep until she heard Jett's voice the next day.

"Good morning!"

Chantel blinked away sleep and offered a froggy hello. She
held up her hand against the sun pouring in from the open
shades, surprised that she'd slept so soundly through the night.

"What time is it?"

"Just after seven." Jett sat on the edge of Chantel's bed and
gave her a brief hug. "Did you sleep okay?"

"Like a log."

"Good. Y'all need to be ready to leave in thirty minutes."

"Isn't this my vacation?" Chantel yawned as she emphasized
the last word. "Why so early?"

"I have to be on set at ten for another long day of taping. It's
casual dining. Throw on anything."

"Like you did, looking like America's Next Top Model?"

Jett waved away the comment. "It's what my public expects."

Chantel watched Jett walk over and gently shake Artani.
"Wake up, sleepyhead," she whispered, giving him a kiss on the
forehead. "Mickey Mouse is waiting. It's time to wake up!"

Artani didn't move.

Chantel eased out of bed. "He sleeps like a rock, even deeper
than I do."

Jett shook him harder. "Artani. Wake up!"

He grumbled and pulled the covers over his head. Jett headed
back toward the door and threw over her shoulder, "I'll meet you
downstairs."

After pulling out a short set for Artani and sending him down
to bond with his auntie, Chantel eyed her options. Even with
three suitcases, she struggled with what to wear. Jett had paired

white skinny jeans with a flowery midriff tank top, effectively showing off pert boobs, slender waist, navel ring and naturally ample behind. Compared to her, the skinny jeans Chantel had packed looked more like jeans-for-fat-people-trying-to-look-skinny. The color black had some slimming effect, but nothing short of surgery would get Chantel anywhere close to her sister's tight frame. Deciding to work with what the good Lord gave her, she shimmied into the fat girl's skinny jeans, threw on an over-sized pink tee with vertical black pinstripes—another supposedly slimming trick that according to the mirror was clearly not working—and the Michael Kors sandals she'd splurged on last year. She splashed on her favorite fruity cologne, shook the easy long braids she'd adopted for no-muss, no-fuss fun in the Cali sun, and went downstairs.

"I like your braids," Jett said, though Chantel felt her sister's head-to-toe perusal was a beat too long. "You must have just gotten them done."

"Right before coming here. Figured it was the best style for the beach and . . . other stuff." Disneyland, Chantel mouthed over Artani's head.

"Speaking of other stuff, let's go. I was too tired to eat when I got home last night, which means this morning I'm starved."

During the twenty-minute drive to a popular eatery known for its chicken and waffles, Jett and Chantel had little conversation but Artani and his aunt talked nonstop. He was full of questions about what it meant to be a star, a topic Jett knew very well. Chantel tried not to be jealous that he'd never asked questions about her showbiz career, such as it was. Her name wasn't in lights per se, but it was spelled out in plastic letters on the Diplomat marquis. She tried to feel better by guessing that in his eyes she was just mom. Listening, she had to admit that by far Jett's life was more exciting. The places she'd been. The people she'd met. Not to mention that she was now on a show billed as the best and most exciting talent search since *American Idol* flipped the United States' reality/talent contest script more than a decade ago. Through Artani, Chantel learned more about her older sister's career than Jett had ever shared with her. Then again, Chantel realized, Jett had never stuck around long enough for her to ask.

Jett pulled into a crowded parking lot and stopped the car in the drive. "Let's go, guys."

"I don't think we can park here, Aunt Jett," Artani said, his wide brown eyes taking in the cars around them.

Jett winked at Artani. "Don't worry. I've got connections."

Within seconds a young man Chantel hadn't noticed walking toward them was opening Jett's door.

"Good morning, beautiful! To what do we owe the honor of your presence?"

"Me being hungry and y'all having food," Jett replied, in a tone that wasn't quite nasty and not quite nice either. "Come on, guys," she instructed the fam before returning her attention to the now more subdued valet. "I'll be back in an hour and fifteen minutes."

"Yes, ma'am." And then to their retreating backs, "Enjoy your meal!"

Even hidden behind large Jackie O glasses, the host recognized Jett immediately, as did several of the front area full of customers waiting to be seated. Chantel noticed how Jett's demeanor had shifted from the casual air she'd displayed while driving over to the diva energy her slightly raised chin and confident stride produced. Some in the crowd acted nonchalant, while others appeared to not know who she was. A few, however, weren't shy about getting their fifteen seconds with a bona fide star.

"Is that Jett?" someone whispered.

"Jett! Congratulations on your new show!"

"Hey, Jett! I want to audition!"

Jett nodded and smiled but didn't stop to chat. They were quickly ushered into a partially hidden corner booth at the back of the room. A half partition boasting tall palm plants provided a modicum of privacy. A server arrived within seconds, and in probably less time than it took for the poor valet to find a parking spot for Jett's sporty Lexus, their orders had been placed and drinks were on the way.

"How do all these people know you, Aunt Jett?"

"She's famous," Chantel offered in a lowered voice. "Now stop asking so many questions."

"How else is he supposed to get to know me?" Jett countered. Her gaze was warm as she looked at Artani, a type of look Chantel had never experienced from the family's firstborn. "Ask me whatever you'd like."

"Okay." Artani looked around, thought for a moment. "How did you get famous?"

Chantel's ears perked up at that question. Anna had been reluctant to share many details around Jett's big break, so she was as eager as Artani to hear the whole story.

Jett reached for the glass of lemon water the server had placed before her, sat back, and looked at Chantel.

"Have you taken Artani to the Gates on Forty-seventh and Paseo?"

"Girl, Gates hasn't been at that location for years. Not that Artani would have wanted to eat there anyway. Like most kids, he prefers McDonald's."

Artani looked wide-eyed at Jett. "McDonald's made you famous?"

Jett laughed. "I did a commercial for them years ago, but I was already well-known then. You remember that, Chan?"

"How could I forget? I made the dance team because of that commercial. After the school found out that you were my sister, they voted me in."

"I didn't know you danced in high school."

"There are a lot of things about me you don't know."

"True." *And vice versa.* "Back in the day, me and some friends went there after a party. We finished eating, then ran into this guy I liked in the parking lot. Whitney came on the radio and basically, I blew her away."

Chantel crossed her arms. "Come on, now. I'll give it to you for a fabulous voice. But, Whitney?"

The server who'd placed down a basket of muffins had overheard them. "Both of you ladies can sing," she said. "But between you and Whitney? Jett, I think you got her."

The women high-fived.

"I'll be right back with your order."

Chantel watched her prance away. "She just wants a tip."

"That's how to get one."

Artani looked at Chantel. "Mom, who's Whitney?"

Jett frowned at Chantel. "You haven't introduced your son to one of the biggest divas of the 80s?"

"You forget I'm a 90s and 21st-century baby?"

"Mom didn't play their music? Whitney Houston was one of her favorites."

"Sometimes, but mostly she went back to her favorite musical era, the 70s—Natalie, Chaka, and the Emotions were on our household's soundtrack."

"Classic voices!"

"Without a doubt!"

"Mom sings!" Artani proudly announced, surprising Chantel and pleasing her immensely. "She's going to be famous, too."

Jett laughed. "Anything's possible. Talent usually runs in the family. Belt out a tune somewhere in public and you never know who might hear you."

This was the moment when Chantel should have told her about the Dip and how her weekend singing gig was fulfilling the tiniest bit of a dream. But compared to Jett's story, the news seemed like small change.

"So Whitney came on the radio . . ."

"And after hearing me, the other guy in the car who I didn't know said his cousin was a producer. I thought he was lying, but . . . I met him and it was true."

Jett became quiet. With all of the blessings that had come from that encounter, not all of the memories were good ones.

"So he got you on *The Next Big Thing*?"

"We worked on a demo that landed on the desk of a show developer. Two weeks later I was taking my first plane ride and doing an audition. I was one of twenty people chosen for the televised part of the competition from more than twenty thousand who applied for a spot."

"Did you win?" Artani asked.

"Is coffee black?"

"Yes," Artani replied, with a gap-toothed grin. "Unless you put milk in it."

They paused when the server delivered the food—spicy, crispy wings atop fluffy waffles, with a side order of hash browns at Artani's request. For several minutes the only comments were about how good the food was, delivered between clanking silverware and satisfied groans. Chantel turned the talk back to Jett's singing.

"Did you always want a singing career?"

Jett finished off a wing and unashamedly licked her fingers. "I always wanted to get out of Kansas City, the Midwest. Other than that, I was too young to know what I wanted."

"Weren't you scared to go so far by yourself?"

A shadow passed over Jett's face but left so quickly Chantel told herself it was imagined.

"By the time it happened, I wasn't afraid of anything."

The talk about singing and show business continued. Chantel

kept hoping Jett would ask about her singing aspirations. But she didn't. They were nothing compared to what Jett had, anyway. Couldn't even be called a career. Still, Chantel was proud of the side gig she'd carved out for herself, a way to nurture the dream she'd had since the first time she saw Jett on TV. Jett's stories were endless, sensational, most involving the baller life with well-known stars. Her sister sparkled and laughed as before, but something was different. The joy didn't quite reach her eyes. Chantel wondered what had happed to shift the atmosphere, albeit slightly. As much as she'd learned today about her sister, it was clear she barely knew Jett at all.

Chapter 4
Family Affair

Jett didn't expect to enjoy her family so much. Being around Artani made her feel younger, more alive. His curiosity and excitement about life were infectious and in many ways reminded her of her younger self. Having him in her home, laughing, playing, had her rethinking the decision to forgo family and focus solely on her career. Chantel's forthright opinions and wry humor were unexpected. Until this visit, Jett hadn't given serious attention to how little time she'd spent with her sister. It was the first time doing so without their mom. The scarcity of details she knew about the woman almost sixteen years her junior was downright embarrassing considering that they were related. Jett didn't prolong these thoughts or come down too hard on herself. She'd been busy and almost two thousand miles away, living another life in a completely different world.

From the moment Jett had taken that first plane ride to Hollywood, she'd never looked back. Almost a year passed before she saw Anna again, and then only briefly. With all that happened after snagging first place on the then hot new show *The Next Big Thing*, the forerunner of shows like *America's Got Talent* and *The Voice*, it was easy for Jett to put Kansas City behind her. The nonstop schedule of photo shoots, guest appearances, and national tours made all that had happened and what she'd left behind in the small Midwestern town easy to forget.

The merest stirring of those memories reminded her why she'd forgotten, and how hard it was to recall them even now. Especially now. She'd made the right decision inviting Chantel and Artani to LA. She'd missed them. But leaving Kansas City had been a godsend.

A soft knock brought her back to the present.

"Come in."

Chantel walked in wearing the oversized gold and purple Lakers tee she'd bought in the fashion district the day before. Jett turned from the window and walked over to the sitting area on the other side of the L-shaped room.

Pouring a glass of water, she motioned for Chantel to sit down. "Want a glass of lemon water?"

"I'm good." Chantel stopped to admire the colorful painting that hung above the velvety-textured mustard-colored love seat. "Your home is beautiful, Jett."

"It's a continual work in progress, but I've managed to create a sanctuary. You need one after being out in these dog-eat-dog streets."

"The city is big and busy, but I love it. The week went so fast. I wish we had more time."

"Life moves fast on the West Coast. But it looks like you guys have had fun."

"This week has been amazing."

"I hear Lucia cooked for you."

"She let me try some of the food she made for a family gathering, before her daughter picked it up. She's a sweetheart. Said Artani reminded her of her grandson, Rico. After tasting her tamales and a real taco? I'll never look at those fast food Mexican chains the same again."

"Lucia's a grandmother?"

"Five times over."

Jett's eyes widened as Chantel told her more about her house-keeper of three years than she'd ever known.

"Artani was really wound up tonight. I think he enjoyed him-self, too."

Chantel rolled her eyes as she sat in one of two art deco–styled chairs opposite the love seat where Jett lounged. "You think?" She used her fingers as counting tools. "Disneyland, Universal Studios, Magic Mountain, the beach, and those expensive athletic shoes that cost almost as much as my rent. It'll take me six months to undo the spoiling you've done to my child."

"That's what aunties are for."

"If you say so." Chantel looked speculatively at Jett. "Why didn't you ever have children?"

Jett finished her glass of water in one long drink. "I've had several children. Every single or album I've produced had a conception point and delivery date. When was there time to make another kind of baby?"

"You were married three times."

"And?"

"I'm sorry, that wasn't meant to offend you. It's just that . . . do you realize this is the most time we've ever spent together and one of the first times we've had more than the most cursory of conver-sations?"

"It's not so hard to understand why. There are a lot of years be-tween us. I left home just after you were born."

"And you rarely came back. Why?"

"You've spent a week in California and had to ask that ques-tion? Really?"

"Sure, it's beautiful. You had your career, and your relation-ships. But . . . I don't know. I don't think I could have ever stayed away from Mama without more frequent visits. Can I ask you something?"

"You can ask. Doesn't mean I'll answer."

"Did something happen between you and Mama?"

"Something like what?"

"An argument or disagreement of some kind that made leaving a good thing and staying away easy to do."

"We never had the warm and fuzzy friendship that you two enjoyed."

"That's what I'm saying. I never understood that."

Jett sighed, swung her legs off the love seat arms, and sat up.

"If you don't want to talk about it . . ."

Jett ran a hand over the long custom weave that had set the network back almost five figures. "Mom and I were like oil and water, almost from the womb. She was a stickler for tradition. I was a rebel. She lived for Jesus. I was full of the devil. Dancing, boys, partying, sneaking out. Whatever she told me not to do was usually the very thing I most wanted."

"Mama was fairly conservative, but I don't remember her being that strict."

"Parents always go easier on . . . the second child. She didn't spare the rod, and I guess I gave her plenty of reasons. By the time you came along, I'd probably worn her out."

"You got spanked?"

"Jerome Bailey and Sarah Smith got spankings. I got whupped." Jett took in Chantel's frown. "I guess you didn't. Not even once."

"Maybe a spanking or two when I was little. Guess I turned out to be that good church girl she wanted."

"Bet she was glad it happened for one of us."

"Given her attitude, I can't believe she agreed for you to move here."

"She had no choice. Once I got the confirmation that my talent could get me out of that town, there was no stopping me. Plus, Mom believed the lies that Gerald told her."

"Who's Gerald?"

"My manager for the first few years of my career. Him and his wife Lisa flew to see Mama after I won the contest. You guys had moved to Marquette by then. They sold her a bill of goods about how religious they were and how much they cared. Promised her that they'd look after me as if I were their own."

"They didn't."

"Not unless Gerald fucked all his daughters."

Chantel was stunned. "Jett, no! He had sex with you while you were still underage?"

"We didn't have sex. He took sex. I didn't have a choice in the matter."

"He raped you." Jett didn't respond. "You couldn't tell his wife?"

Jett's laugh was hollow. "She had her own problems to deal with, which she mostly hid behind steady lines of coke."

"Geez. All that glitters isn't gold."

"Not even cubic zirconium in this fucked-up biz."

"How'd you get out of that situation?"

"Hot Linkz."

"Huh?"

This time, Jett's smile met her eyes. "The 74th Street Southsiders out of good ol' Inglewood. Hot Linkz was a twenty-five-year-old full of swag, who'd been with the gang since he was six years old. A wannabe rapper with street cred. Our paths crossed while we were recording at the same studio. I was there actually laying a hook down on another rapper's tracks."

"Would I know the other rapper's name?"

"You ever heard of Snoop Dogg?"

"Who hasn't. Wow. That had to be exciting."

"At that age, everything was, especially the bad boys. Arthur—Linkz's government name, as they'd say on the block—saw me, started flirting, and asked for my number."

"How old were you at this point?"

"Seventeen. He blew up my phone, came over to visit. Gerald tried to block the romance but there's no stopping a fool in love, and when it came to Hot Linkz I was all over that sausage! I ran away from the safe streets of Pasadena to the hood of Inglewood."

"I would have been terrified."

"It was dangerous at times, but that's what made it exciting. Plus, I knew Linkz would take care of me. And he did, along with his crew. He had a conversation with Gerald. I don't know what words were exchanged, and Gerald wouldn't let me out of my contract. But he stopped asking me to move back home and never tried to sleep with me again. That made Linkz my superhero. He was my first crush, my first boyfriend, my first true love. I loved everything about him. He loved me, too."

"What happened?"

"What happens to most gang members? He got a five-year bid on some trumped-up charges. Only did three but by then I was on *Glamagirls*, working fourteen-hour days. We tried to recreate what we'd had before, but both of us had changed. I'd met the man who'd become my first husband, a costar on the show."

"Vince Jones."

"You remember him?"

"The search engine did. I could only remember Ricky, his name on the show, which I not only watched while it aired but again in syndication and yes, I own the *Glamagirl* series on DVD. I was in love with little Ricky."

"Everyone was. Too bad the real thing wasn't as good as on TV."

"But you still chose him over Hot Linkz."

Jett shook her head. "I never denied Arthur. Went running whenever he called. He died a year after being released from prison. Some stupid beef from years before."

"I'm sorry."

"Life happens. But enough about my busines. Let's get into yours. Where is Artani's father? Sorry, but what's his name?"

"Art, and no worries. I'm trying to forget him, too." They shared a laugh. "We're divorced. He's moved on with one woman in a line of several who crawled in and crowded our marital bed."

"You left because he slept with another woman?"

"Not one, *several*. I left for many reasons, but yes, that was the main one."

"Girl, please, all men do that. I've had three husbands, and none were faithful. I think cheating is built into a man's DNA."

"Do you think you'll ever marry again?"

"I never say never but I'm good for now."

"With Randall?"

"He's one of them. But I'm about to move him out of rotation."

"One? Them? Rotation? Do tell!"

"Out my business, little sis."

Chantel's eyes sparkled. "I think that's the first time you called me that."

"Well, when it comes to describing me, don't let the word *older* slip out of your mouth."

"Why? You are older. Plus, no one would guess your age. You might be pushing fifty but it's not pushing back."

Jett threw a pillow. "I can't stand you."

"Fifty isn't old. It's the new thirty, or didn't you know?"

What Jett knew was that in show business, fifteen was preferred. Fifty was ancient. "You all packed and ready to go?"

"All packed but not ready to leave, definitely not ready to go back to work. Driving here on the regular would probably shave years off my life, but I could get used to a quaint little neighborhood like this."

"Trust me, nothing about this mortgage is little or quaint."

"How much is it, if I may ask?"

"Four thousand."

"Wow! That's twice as much as all my bills."

"The difference between the West and Midwest," Jett said with a shrug. "Was Mama's house paid for?"

"No, in fact, it's headed toward foreclosure. I hope while going through her finances, I don't find more surprises."

"Were you hoping to move into it?"

"I was hoping to sell it. Divorcing Art was costly, in more ways than one. Right now, though, I'm hoping to move here!"

"Oh, no. That won't work. This house is way too small for permanent company."

"Maybe not here, but to California. I've lived in the Midwest my whole life. A safe, predictable existence. But losing Mama so unexpectedly reminded me that life isn't promised. This trip has shown me there's so much more."

"It's easy to fall in love with LA after a weeklong visit. But trust me, being a tourist and being a resident are two very different things."

"It would be a huge adjustment, but you'd help me, right?"

"Um, that would be a negative." Jett stood and took a couple steps for more distance between them. "I've enjoyed you and Artani, don't get me wrong. But I'm on a roll and I've got to stay focused. It's a free world, so you can move where you want. But if you relocate here, don't expect me to be your tour guide, or assist in you getting settled."

"Not even financially?"

"Do I look like a bank?"

Given Chantel's expression, the words hurt. "Look, I'm making money now, but this is my first good gig in years. It takes a lot to maintain the celebrity lifestyle the public expects, one now necessary to succeed in this game. I might be able to send you something a little later, but I can't help you move."

"Or let me stay here just long enough to get a job?"

"Sorry, sistah. I need my space."

"Dang, Jett. You're serious."

"As an illness with no cure." She laughed to lighten the moment, but there was no way to bottle back that spilled milk. She walked over to where Chantel sat in shocked silence and pulled her to her feet. "I promise we'll spend more time together. But you've got an early flight and my call time is five a.m." She gave Chantel a hug. "Goodbye for now."

Chantel pulled back. "Oh no. I'll get up before you leave. Artani would hate not to have told you goodbye."

"I'll run in for a hug when the car arrives." Jett's phone pinged. "That's Randall. He's coming over to tuck me in."

Reaching for Chantel's hand, Jett walked her to the door. "How long have you been divorced?"

"Officially, about six months. But we were separated before then."

"And you don't have a man?"

"Don't need one."

"Every woman needs a tune-up every now and again."

"That's yet another reason for me to relocate. There's no good men left in Marquette."

"Try Kansas City," Jett said, opening the door and gently urging Chantel out. "It's only forty-five minutes away."

She blew Chantel a kiss. "Safe travels."

Jett closed the door and headed to the shower. But later, she was still thinking about Chantel's surprise declaration of wanting to move to LA. Even Randall's oral expertise, deep thrusting, and yoni-tingling loving wasn't enough to shake the dread at the mere idea of her and Chantel living in the same place. A one-week stint was one thing. Day in, day out was another. She'd felt bad about Chantel's reaction to her idea not being supported. Jett couldn't worry about that. Every ounce of her attention was focused on *Seeking Stardom* and securing any other bags she could during these fifteen additional seconds of fame. She'd lived just on the other side of broke for nearly ten years, and it didn't feel good to try and act all Dior on a Dollar Tree budget. Jett had been both rich and famous, and poor and obscure. She preferred the former lifestyle and was on her way back. She'd do whatever it took to get there, and this time, she was going to stay on top.

Chapter 5
Dilemma

Life in Marquette had always moved slowly. But after her whirl-wind week in LA, Chantel could have sworn that time in the town stood still. It felt like three weeks passed between the Monday she returned to work and now, Friday, her first night back at Diplomat. That was partly due to the long hours worked to make up for her unpaid vacation. She'd worked through lunch and took off an hour early, wanting plenty of time to get ready for her first set so that it could be perfect. With all the overtime, she hadn't talked much to Terrence, only enough for him to tell her about Jasmine, how well she'd performed and how she'd better bring it. Chantel tried not to feel too much about it one way or the other. She was looking for a singing gig when she found that one, and as much as she loved performing in her hometown, she wouldn't turn down one in the City.

A light tap sounded before the door to the office that doubled as her dressing room was nudged open.

"Are you dressed?"

Chantel eyed him from the mirror without turning around or stopping her makeup application. "Don't you think that's something you should have asked before opening the door?"

"Whatever." Terrence walked in and leaned against the wall. "You don't have anything I haven't seen before."

"You haven't seen this before." Chantel waved a hand along her body.

"Not for lack of trying."

"Boy, shut up."

Terrence wriggled his brows. "You can't blame a brother for keeping hope alive."

"You're almost like my brother."

"Almost ain't is."

Chantel laughed at the childhood throwback phrase. "Whatever."

"So tell me. How was it?"

"You mean besides the texts and pictures I sent from almost everywhere we went?"

"The pics of the theme parks and the ocean? That was the kid stuff you did with Artani. Where did you and your superstar sis hang out?"

"We didn't."

Terrence lowered his head and looked over his glasses. "What you talkin' 'bout, Willis?"

Chantel paused to straighten the long, dramatic lashes she'd just applied. "Jett didn't have much time to spend with us because the show was taping. She treated us to breakfast the day after we arrived. I made dinner one night. But she left home early and came back late. She thought we'd be able to come to the set and watch a taping, but the schedule changed so we got a tour instead. Mostly though, Artani and I were on our own. Traffic was crazy. I couldn't see driving in that madness every day. But I managed not to wreck Jett's car or kill anybody, so . . . it's all good."

"It looks like you had a good time, Chan. But all those clubs and her connections and you didn't get a chance to perform?"

Chantel reached for the bright red lipstick she'd purchased while going crazy at the Beverly Hills MAC store. Slowly applying a coat gave her a moment to shift the ache his question brought back. Something she'd tried not to think about since returning from LA.

"Jett isn't interested in my small-town singing career. She didn't even ask about it."

"And you didn't tell her?"

Chantel looked at her watch and now, finished with makeup, turned to look at him. "Honestly, Terrence, after hearing about her exciting life, it didn't seem important. A glimpse into her big world showed me how small and irrelevant all this"—she waved her hand around the room—"really is. I'm not saying I'm not grateful for being able to enjoy my passion, to share what talent I have with those who come to hear me. I'm just saying that being there put what I do here in proper perspective. Besides, that wasn't the main reason I was excited to go there. I wanted to connect with and really get to know my sister. We didn't grow up together and are near strangers as a result."

"Do you know her now?"

A knock interrupted Chantel's answer before her favorite server and best friend Rita stuck her head in the door. "Hey, girl!"

She entered the room. "I was going to ask if you were dressed but seeing knucklehead answered that question." She playfully punched Terrence's arm before crossing the small space and bending down to give Chantel a raucous hug. Chantel stood to complete the greeting before stepping into the snazzy, rhinestone-covered heels she'd gotten in LA.

"Welcome back!"

"Thanks, Rita."

"How was Cali, sistah-girl? Did you snag one of those fine East Side Latinos and bring him back in your suitcase?"

"Girl, please."

Terrence moved to the door. "This is clearly where I make my exit. We'll do a sound check as soon as the band finishes getting set up. I'll let you know."

"Thanks, Terrence."

Rita waited until Terrence closed the door. "You know he's feeling you, right?"

"He feels anything with a split and a clit." Chantel paced the small enclosure to get used to walking on the higher heels.

"Yeah, but I think when it comes to you, his feelings run a little deeper."

Chantel stopped and turned around. "Have y'all been talking about me while I was gone?"

"We didn't go ham behind your back, but if you came up in conversation, he'd get a certain puppy-eyed look on his face. I saw it just now, before he left."

"You're tripping."

"Maybe it's your new hair. The straight look is very pretty on you. It complements your face."

Chantel reached up to stroke the hair she was still getting used to seeing when she looked into the mirror. "Jett thought it might, which is why I let her hair stylist put it in."

"How much did it cost?"

"Jett paid for it, but from the looks of the salon and its high-priced location, I probably don't want to know. Have me taking it out, do a wash and a rinse, then resell to pay my bills!"

"And there's somebody in Marquette just ghetto enough to buy it, too."

"Don't give me ideas."

"Stop! You are not going to sell your sister's gift."

"My head, my hair, my prerogative."

They laughed but Chantel was serious. Everything Jett didn't pay for had been put on credit. On top of that she'd come home to a stack of bills, and a letter from the bank regarding her mother's house.

"I'm not going to let you go out like that. What else did you do in LA?"

Chantel spent the next few minutes giving a condensed recap of her whirlwind week on the West Coast. Terrence knocked again. Chantel joined the band for the sound check. At nine o'clock sharp the band jumped into a Motown classic to kick off the night. It had only been two weeks since her last performance, but the time felt longer as Chantel settled into a variety of grooves, joked with the audience, and felt tremendous gratitude for the chance to perform. It wasn't like *Seeking Stardom*'s fancy set, with a small army of production personnel catering to everyone's needs. It was far from the glitz and glam of Jett's world. The club was small but comfy. The people were welcoming and genuine, something in short supply among the few Angelenos she'd met. The band were mostly guys she'd grown up with, playing for the pleasure of it after working all week. But for Chantel, King's place was perfect. It wasn't Hollywood. It was home.

For the next couple weeks, Chantel continued adjusting to her new normal—life without Mom. The urge to speak with her was as strong as ever, but automatically reaching for the phone to call her happened less and less. Most of the time she could fool herself into thinking that Anna Michelle Scott had simply gone on a long vacation. But a phone call from Miss Blanche, Anna's longtime neighbor and friend, was a stark reminder that her mother had taken a one-way trip to paradise, and no matter how much Chantel wished it, she would not be coming back. After Saturday night's show, once the patrons had left and the club was near empty, Chantel asked Rita for a favor.

"I'm going to Mama's tomorrow. Can you watch Artani for a few hours?"

"I can, but are you sure you're ready for that?"

"I am sure that visiting that home without Mama in it is the very last thing I'm ready for or want to do. But even though the pain is as fresh as yesterday, it's been over a month since she . . . since it happened. Miss Blanche left a message while I was in Los

Angeles, and she called again this past week to remind me the yard needs mowing and about the mail stacking up that she's been retrieving from Mama's box. I need to take care of all that stuff and find the rest of her legal papers."

"Have you decided what you're going to do with the house?"

"Might not be my decision to make. Mama was in pre-foreclosure. I had no idea."

"Oh no, Chan."

"Yep. I had no idea, and it makes no sense. Mama made good money."

"That's crazy."

"It may be Divine Order. The bank taking it back will leave me with one less bill to deal with."

"I'll be glad to help in any way I can, including going with you if you don't want to tackle that alone. Sharon can keep the kids. Closing out a life is more than a notion. Trust me, I've been there. The motherless club is one you never want to join."

"Thanks, Rita. Right now, I'm feeling to do this alone, but I'll let you know if I change my mind."

"What time are you heading over?"

"In the morning, probably around ten or so."

Rita gave Chantel a heartfelt hug. "Don't be too proud to ask for help. I'm here if you need me."

The next morning, Chantel treated Artani to his favorite drive-thru breakfast before dropping him off at Rita's house. She had two boys around Artani's age, a house full of video games, and cabinets full of junk food. Chantel knew she could take as much time as needed in Kansas City. Her son would be just fine.

The hour-long drive from Marquette to Kansas City was uneventful. Her online playlist from the early 2000s kept her entertained. When she turned onto her mother's block, however, the carefree mood dissipated. Besides a yard that needed mowing, Anna's home, painted a cheery pale yellow with stark black trim, looked as it always had. Bright yellow and pink rose bushes,

Anna's pride and joy, were in full bloom. The home looked the same today as it had one, two, six months ago—as though nothing had happened. As if Anna was peeking out the window, food smelling up the kitchen, Aretha singing "Ain't No Way." For a moment, a second really, Chantel almost convinced herself that she'd see that scene when the door opened. But when she put the key in the lock, turned the knob, and opened the front door, Chantel stepped into the living room and into the loudest silence she'd ever heard.

It was almost too much.

Always remember who you are, Chantel. You stand on the shoulders of kings and queens. You can go anywhere, do anything.

Anna's voice floated around her like a warm shawl, drying the tears that threatened and enabling her legs to move. Chantel walked over and pressed play on the stereo's CD player. Marvin Gaye, Anna's virtual husband for as long as Chantel could remember, was the last CD her mother had played before leaving home that night. Before some fool fell asleep or read a text or did whatever that took his eyes off the road and eased his car into Anna's lane. Before Anna was hit nearly head-on. Before she left for paradise.

I used to go out to party and stand around . . .

She thought the sound would further sadden her, but something about Marvin's playful ditty about giving it up actually brightened Chantel's mood. She danced through rooms and walked through memories as Marvin used this live performance at the Palladium in London to recapture the magic he made at Motown before teasing Chantel about a distant lover and encouraging her to "come get to this." Pulling out her phone, Chantel made a list of all she saw that needed to be done, then went to the garage for boxes and started emptying the pantry.

"Chantel." The call accompanied a steady tapping on the aluminum outer door. "It's Blanche."

Chantel set down her phone on the kitchen counter and

walked over to turn down Marvin's crooning before answering the door.

"Hello, Miss Blanche," she said, as the two women embraced.

"I thought I saw your car pull up."

Chantel allowed a secret smile at the woman's casual remark. She knew from personal experience that nothing passed her corner, either driving or walking, that she didn't know about. She was the neighborhood snoop, sleuth, and busybody wrapped into a package that preferred muumuus to slacks and a colorful beauty store turban to a fancy hairstyle. A second mama to Chantel, who loved her as such.

"I'm working in the kitchen," Chantel threw over her shoulder as she walked back into the galley-style room that through the years had been a great source of Chantel's culinary happiness.

"When mentioning the yard, I wasn't trying to rush you into tackling this, baby. You could have just given the word and I would have had Dennis cut Anna's yard when he did mine. Should have done that anyway," she continued, more to herself than Chantel. "Let my nephew be good for something rather than bothering you at a time when you're still grieving."

"I'm glad you kept hounding me, and I'll be more than happy to pay your nephew for his work. Otherwise it would be this time next year without anything changing."

Blanche followed Chantel into the pantry. "What are you doing?"

"Boxing up these canned goods to take to the church. You still have the homeless program, right?"

"Yes, and after all that's happened from last year until now, we're handling twice as many people. If you'd told us what you wanted to donate, we'd have been more than happy to come over and do this, so you didn't have to."

"Really?" Chantel asked, while looking for a can of corn's expiration date.

"Girl, do you ever listen to your messages?"

"Not often, and that's such a bad habit."

"It sure is. No wonder when I tried to call you just now your message box was full."

"You called?"

"Yes, but you couldn't hear me over the noise." She tilted her head toward the much quieter sound of Teddy Pendergrass, who'd replaced Marvin and was now serenading them both. "I made that suggestion the week after the funeral."

"That week is a blur, all of last month really."

"Which is why I called and offered our help on behalf of the ladies' circle." Blanche pulled an armful of cans from the pantry, placed them on the counter, and began checking the dates. "We all know how hard it is to get through this kind of loss. It's the worst one, baby."

"You're right about that. Going to LA helped a bit, but at the end of the day . . . Mama's still gone."

"How was that, your trip to LA?"

"Busy, with enough distractions to make the world feel normal, temporarily at least. Artani loved it. He's ready to move there. By the end of the week, I was, too. But Jett wasn't keen on the idea at all."

"Hmmph. I bet she wasn't."

Blanche's comment brought a chill and stopped Chantel's packing. "Why did you say that?"

Blanche continued checking dates and placing cans in the now almost full box. "How was Jeanetta when you were out there?"

Chantel pulled two bottles of water out of the fridge, placed one on the counter by Blanche and leaned against the counter while opening the other. "You know, Miss Blanche, that's a good question. You know my sister and I were never close."

"I know."

"She wasn't that close to Mama either. I never understood it."

"Did you and Anna ever talk about it?"

"I tried. Mama blamed it on everything from Jett being busy to being selfish to not having a close relationship with her dad. I felt there was more because I never knew my dad either. But the last time I brought it up, Mama told me to ask Jett."

"Did you?"

"No."

Blanche eyed Chantel as she opened her bottle of water, then looked out the window beyond her as she took a long drink. "Maybe you should. Now where are more of these boxes, because I'm getting ready to call in the troops and really get this cleanup show on the road."

Chantel felt there was more that Blanche could tell her, but the neighbor's change of subject and expression sent a clear signal that anything else she learned would be what Jett told her. An hour later, she'd forgotten all about it. Five more of her mother's friends and church members joined her and Blanche at the house. The music changed yet again, this time Whitney wanting to dance with somebody and bringing in a party mood. Except for the more personal effects of Anna's that Chantel would handle, the task of clearing out the house was divided among the older women. Chantel placed all the jewelry, paperwork, mail, and a small, locked wooden chest she'd found at the back of the closet into a large suitcase and hugged the women who'd deemed themselves her new mamas. The ride back to Marquette was decidedly lighter than when she'd left earlier that day.

That happy mood lasted all week and into the weekend, through the well-received sets at the Diplomat on Friday and Saturday and on Sunday, while she and Artani enjoyed a lunch of pizza and wings with Rita and her sons. Except for the time in LA, it was one of her best weeks since Anna died. Chantel was grateful and felt strong enough to go through more of her mother's personal effects without breaking down crying. Sunday night, after saying good night to Artani, Chantel went to her bedroom, slid on a pair of comfy pj's, then rolled out the piece of luggage she'd brought from her mother's house. Her eyes were immediately drawn to the wooden chest she'd found in her mother's closet. It hadn't looked familiar when she first saw it and even now, a week later, Chantel didn't remember seeing the box before. Had Anna forgotten it was up there? She held the box against her ear and gently shook it. The silence that followed canceled Chantel's first thought of there possibly being some expensive jewelry, diamonds or gold coins inside. Maybe money? The folding kind that didn't make noise? This thought brought to Chantel a sense of excitement. She rummaged through the luggage contents to find the key, finally dumping everything onto the floral comforter covering her king-sized bed. Within a small bag tucked inside another bag—a small silk drawstring bag from years ago that Chantel did remember—was a ring of what appeared to be luggage keys with one just slightly bigger than the rest. She tried it first, placed it inside the wooden box's keyhole, and . . . voilà. It opened. She'd found it.

"Dang, Mama," Chantel mumbled under her breath. "The way you hid this key, there really must be money in here."

The lock opened easily. Her high hopes for a stash of Benjamins that could fund another trip to LA and a quick shopping spree, or more sensibly pay down debt, were quickly dashed. The box contained a thick stack of folded papers that Chantel reviewed one by one. Funeral programs, including the one for her aunt Janice, Anna's sister, who'd died from an undetected brain tumor before Chantel was old enough to remember much about her. Various clippings from the *Marquette Monitor*, the local newspaper where Chantel now worked, and magazines like *Ebony* and *Jet*. A black and white picture of a young girl wearing an oversized tee and baggy pants. Chantel squinted her eyes to identify the subject. Was it her aunt Janet, or a much younger

Anna? She set the picture to the side and moved on through church programs, expired credit, insurance, and business cards, and other items that had carried Anna's government name over the years, both her maiden name Scott and her married name, Jefferson, from her marriage and divorce that happened before Chantel was born. At the bottom of the box was a yellowed envelope with the address of a Texas hospital engraved across the front. Chantel's grandmother had lived in Texas. She too was deceased.

Is this from the hospital stay before Granny died?

More than a little curious, Chantel quickly pulled the contents from inside the envelope. Her surprise at finding a birth certificate turned to shock when she read her name on it.

"This isn't my birth certificate."

Chantel knew this for sure because she had the original certificate that Anna had given her to apply for a driver's license at the age of sixteen. The paper certifying that she'd been born at Trinity Medical in Kansas City. She checked the personal stats—time and date of birth, height, weight, race. They were all as she remembered from the birth certificate in her personal records file. She pushed back the cover and was just about to retrieve said certificate from the file cabinet on the other side of the room when her eyes fell on something that took her breath away. There was another name on the birth certificate where the name *Anna* should have been.

In the words of the millennials who worked in her department, Chantel's discovery had left her shook. Now, more than twelve hours after the discovery, she still had no answers. Of course, she'd called Jett and as usual got voicemail. She'd left a message and sent a text stating that the matter was urgent, a definite 911. It was radio silence from her celebrity sis. Chantel felt upset, confused, and more alone than she had since the night she learned her mother had died. Rita was her closest friend, but Anna was the only person with whom Chantel would have shared this. Except she wasn't there. After unsuccessful attempts to clear up the matter by phone, Chantel was about to burst from the turmoil swirling inside her.

She walked to her boss's open door and tapped before entering. "Hey, Phil, you got a minute?"

The sandy-haired man just a few years older than Chantel leaned against his swiveling leather chair. "No, you can't take another week of vacation."

Silence.

"That was a joke, Chantel."

"Sorry, but I'm not in the mood for laughing right now. I need the afternoon off."

Phil's expression turned serious. "What's wrong now?"

"That's why I need the time off. To find out."

"Is this regarding your mother's estate?"

Chantel nodded, allowing the assumption. A nonverbal answer meant she wouldn't have to lie.

"You know how short we are with Jackie now out on maternity leave. Are you sure this can't be handled over the phone, or after hours?"

"I had hoped so, but no. It's something I have to take care of in person."

Phil sighed. He sat forward and began gathering papers. "Okay, Chantel. But this is all the time you can have off. I can't imagine how hard it is to lose your mother. But we've got a business to run and a paper to print. Hopefully whatever business you have to handle can be finished this afternoon."

"Thanks, Phil."

Chantel left the office, pulling out her cell phone as she strode to her car.

"Hey, girl."

"Hey, Rita. You got a minute?"

"I will if you can hang on a sec."

"Sure." Chantel started the car, eased out of the parking lot, and headed for the freeway. A grumbling stomach reminded her that she hadn't put any food on top of the coffee she'd had earlier. The mere thought of putting anything edible on top of taut, jumbled nerves made her queasy.

"I know divorce ain't pretty, but sometimes I swear being married is overrated. Sean being around the house all day is about to get on my last nerve. Laid off and all of a sudden he's Freddie the fixer. In the past week he's started fifty-nine and eleven projects. Ask me how many he's finished. Chantel? Girl, I'm sorry. You didn't call to hear me fuss. What's going on?"

"I don't know."

A slight pause and then, "Are you okay? Is Artani all right?"

"Artani's fine, but I might need another favor. I'm headed to Kansas City and may need you to pick him up from daycare if I'm not back by five."

"Oh."

A lifetime of understanding went into the way she said that word. Chantel's smile was bittersweet.

"That's no problem. Going back to your mom's?"

"No, I'm going to Trinity Medical."

"Why? What's going on there?"

"I found a birth certificate in Mama's papers." She hesitated to say the rest out loud, as though once said the mistake would become a living thing. "My name was on it but hers wasn't."

"What do you mean her name wasn't on it? The spot was blank?"

"No. Instead of Anna, it said Simone."

"Who the hell is Simone?"

"I don't know."

"Was that your mother's middle name?"

"Her middle name was Michelle, same as mine."

"I can understand why you're confused. Obviously it's some type of administrative error. Don't trip."

"I wouldn't if that was the only difference from the certificate Mama gave me. But it's not. The hospital listed is different. And the state."

"What?"

"Exactly. This birth certificate is from a hospital in Texas."

"Do you know anybody who lives in Texas?"

"My grandmother lived there, but Mama left Texas decades before I was born."

"That's crazy, Chantel. Okay, I'd be tripping, too. What about Jett? Did you call her?"

"Yes, but they're still taping. I left a message. She hasn't called me back."

"I'm sure there's an explanation. There's a bunch of angels out there, but incompetence runs through the healthcare system. Did you call the hospital in Texas?"

"It closed twenty years ago."

"Damn."

"Then I called Trinity and got the runaround. That's why I'm going to Kansas City. To get answers."

"Don't worry, sis. Miss Anna is definitely your mama. I surely hope you don't have any doubt about that."

Chantel smiled. "No, I don't. It's just that this is weird."

"I'm sure Trinity Medical will clear everything up. Then you can stop at Saltwater and get me a catfish dinner."

Rita's confidence made Chantel feel better. The knot in her stomach uncoiled, bringing back her appetite. Some good old fried fish with greasy fries and tangy coleslaw would be the perfect accompaniment to her drive back home.

"Sounds like a plan. Thanks for listening. Needless to say, what we talked about stays just between us."

"Yes," Rita dryly replied. "That was needless to say. Don't worry about Artani. Call if you're running late and I'll pick him up."

"Will do."

For the rest of the drive, Chantel convinced herself that Rita was right, and she'd been foolish to make a mountain out of what was obviously a molehill. When she reached the records department at Trinity Medical, she was smiling.

"Hello! Yes, I was born here a few years ago." Chantel winked. The clerk smiled. "And I seem to have misplaced my birth certificate. Can you look me up and verify that information and also tell me how I go about obtaining a new birth certificate?"

"Sure. I need to see your ID."

Chantel handed over her Missouri driver's license, then pulled out her cell phone to check messages while the clerk looked her up.

"I'm not seeing this record on file," the woman behind the counter said upon returning, her brows scrunched and eyes narrowed as she continued to peruse the screen. "But I know these records were updated several years ago when the system was changed. It's quite possible that it simply didn't get transferred. Have you tried the Department of Vital Statistics in Jeff City?"

"This was my first stop." Chantel shook her head with a sigh. "It was really difficult trying to get any information over the phone. It's why I drove here from Marquette. Do you think there's any way you can help me by calling Vital Statistics? As a hospital employee, you might get better results."

"I'm sorry, but agencies are very strict when it comes to confidentiality." The woman looked at Chantel with kind gray eyes. "But I can call them, explain the issue, tell them I've checked your ID, and then put you on. No guarantees that they'll bend the rules, but . . ."

"It's worth a try. Thank you."

For the next several minutes, Chantel and the clerk worked with a supervisor in Jefferson City to locate the birth record that

Trinity couldn't find. The supervisor had no better luck. When Chantel left the hospital and headed for Saltwater, she was no closer to an answer than when she'd arrived in Kansas City. Jett still hadn't called back either. Chantel engaged her Bluetooth.

"Hey, Jett. I'm sorry to keep calling but I have a matter that's urgent. Nobody died," she hastily added, remembering the last such phone call she placed. "But I ran across something of Mama's that confused me. I'm here in Kansas City trying to figure it out. I just need five minutes for a few questions. Please call as soon as you can. Okay, sis. Bye."

Chantel was almost to Saltwater when she remembered something, or more precisely someone, who might help her find answers. Blanche and her mother worked together at Trinity Medical years ago. Her mother's neighbor snooped enough to know all the happenings on the block. If she was equally nosy while working at the hospital, Blanche might have the info Chantel needed.

Chapter 6
Too Close

"Jett! Over here!"

"Hey, Jett! Can I get your autograph?"

"Jett! A selfie . . . please!"

"I am a glamagirl," a young girl belted out from behind the rope, throwing waist-length braids while gyrating to the music inside her head.

"I'm gonna rock your world!" Jett joined the woman singing the theme song from the 90s TV show that sealed her celebrity status. Landing her that recording opportunity along with a starring role in *Glamarama* was Gerald's last negotiation as her manager. It didn't make up for him lying to Anna or the multiple sexual assaults, but it had made her a star.

She signed a few autographs, posed for a couple selfies, blew a kiss to the paparazzi, and waved to fans before slipping behind the human barrier Randall created. They hurried to the town car that awaited them both. The option of not having to wrestle LA's crowded freeways was a perk her agent had recently secured.

Randall opened the back door. Jett slid into the roomy seat. "I'll see you later, okay?"

"I don't think so, Randall. I'm beat."

"You don't look that tired."

"Do you think that I'm lying? I may not look tired but it's how I feel."

"Then I'll come over and give you a massage, let you fall asleep in my arms."

"I'll see you in the morning. Now, close the door."

Jett sighed. The man worked her nerves. Another month, she told herself. Another five pounds gone and she'd have to give up the peen. It was good, but not worth the extra. LA was full of good lovers. She just needed to find another one. That decided, she pulled out her phone and began checking texts and voice-mails. She saw Chantel's missed call along with a couple others, but read and replied to texts from her manager, publicist, stylist, and the designer creating her customized wigs before listening to the voicemails.

"I ran across something of Mama's that confused me. I'm here in Kansas City trying to figure it out."

"Something confusing at Mama's house?" Jett grumbled, be-fore disconnecting from voicemail and tossing the phone on the seat beside her. Fourteen-hour days at damn near fifty didn't feel like those at twenty. Jett rested her head against the seat and closed her eyes. Just a quick catnap . . .

Curiosity about what Chantel found made sleep elusive. She'd confirmed no one had died. What else could be so urgent? Jett had spoken more to Chantel in the past six weeks than she prob-ably had in sixteen years. It felt good getting to know her. Hope-fully she wouldn't become a nuisance and make Jett live to regret it. Jett guarded her heart. It wasn't easy to get close. In the past, those she let in had either used her or died. She wasn't trusting, especially of females. They seemed to want to get close just to take your man or your money. Jett didn't necessarily think that Chantel was like that. But old habits died hard. She couldn't help but be cautious. Just because there was shared blood between them didn't give Chantel an all-access pass.

The phone buzzed on the seat beside her. She looked down expecting to see Chantel's name on the screen. Instead it was her manager, Myles. She answered the call and pressed speaker.

"I hope you're calling with good news."

"Hmm, I don't know. How good of news would you call recording the show's theme song?"

"*Seeking Stardom?*"

"No, *Glamagirls*," Myles dryly replied. "Of course, *Seeking Stardom.*"

Every ounce of weariness fled in that moment. "They want me to do the theme song?"

"Someone gave them the bright idea to tie in your past stardom with this present success. They listened to "Glamagirl World." The whole song, not just the ditty played at the show's intro, and they liked what they heard."

"You're bullshitting."

"I told you that since you're filming at Zenith Studios, I'd see if one of my boys at Zenith Records would be interested in doing something with you. I did and he is. We approached the show's producers with my idea about a theme song and they gave the green light."

"Zenith is huge! But they're hip-hop."

"That's what made the label. But they want to expand into pop and R&B by pairing a classy, mature singer with some of the guys on the roster."

"Mature? You're full of manure."

"What's wrong with mature? Would you prefer childish?"

"Basically, you're saying they want someone old."

"They want someone classy, a throwback to the glamour days—pun intended—along the lines of a Diana Ross or Whitney. They're coming up with a song to promote *Stardom*, one they'll use in the commercials and other PR, and feel your voice will match well with someone spitting rhymes."

Jett's phone beeped. Chantel again. "Myles, hang on a sec. Hey, Chantel. What's up?"

"I've been trying to reach you for two days! Why don't you return calls?"

"You know why. I have a career back on track for the first time in ten years and a manager with more good news holding on the other line. You had a question for me?"

"Yes, but I don't want to feel rushed about it. I can hold until you wrap up your other call."

Jett, exasperated, took the call off speaker. "After that call, there will be another. I don't have time to chitchat, Chantel. If you have something to ask me, spit it out."

"Am I adopted?"

The question was like somebody slapping her square in the face. She recovered quickly. "You're kidding, right?"

"I found a birth certificate showing me born in Texas, not Missouri, and instead of Anna listing someone named Simone."

Damn.

"Jett?"

"I'm here."

"Do you know who that is?"

"I have no idea, but what does it matter? You were born in Kansas City, at Trinity."

"That's what I thought, but they have no record of it."

"I can't explain that but I know one thing for sure. Your mama's name is Anna, same as mine."

"The Office of Vital Statistics couldn't find anything either. The hospital in Texas on that second certificate closed years ago. I asked Miss Blanche. She remembered Mama needing to redo a certificate. I think she knows more than she's telling me."

She's involving people outside the family? Jett had to shut down the madness. "Look, hold on a minute. On second thought, let me call you after I get home."

"As soon as possible, okay? It's almost ten o'clock here and to-morrow I'm going in early to work."

"As soon as I get home. Okay?"

Jett switched over and finished talking with Myles. It didn't take long. The joy from the news he shared had been dimmed by Chantel's revelation. Why had Anna kept the original birth certificate, leaving the possibility of explaining age-old secrets to fall in Jett's lap? How was Jett supposed to speak on matters from decades ago? Anna had been adamant. What Chantel didn't know wouldn't hurt her. Yet Chantel had made a discovery that could lead to all sorts of pain. It felt like a super-sized mess in the making. Jett's show contestants were seeking stardom. Her sister was seeking the truth.

Chapter 7
Confessions, Part 1

She wasn't adopted. Anna Scott was her mother. That's what Rita believed and Jett had confirmed. So why did Chantel still feel so unsure about it? Why couldn't she get that old, yellowed birth certificate out of her head? The one in a chest she'd never seen before at the back of Anna's closet? Because nobody was supposed to have two birth certificates, that's why. Not unless they were involved in some type of high crime or were a government spy. Even then it wasn't legal. Chantel was neither. Nor Anna, as far as she knew. Why had one been issued in Texas? And the million-dollar question, who in the heck was Simone? Blanche Johnson had known her mother for at least as long as Chantel had lived. What did she know that she wasn't telling? That she felt she couldn't say? Had Chantel perhaps been abandoned and then adopted by Anna, details she could imagine someone as kind and loving as her mother not wanting her to know? She thought back to the conversation in Blanche's living room, the uncomfortable expression and tense body language that happened when Chantel had shown Blanche what she'd found. That there was more to the story than an administrative error was written on Blanche head to toe.

*   *   *

Chantel knocked twice and was about to knock a third time when the door opened.

"I thought I heard somebody out here," Blanche said, pulling off gardening gloves. "What are you doing back this way so soon?"

"Hi, Miss Blanche. I had to go by Trinity."

"The hospital?"

Chantel nodded. The subtle shift in expression she'd recognize later.

"What for?"

"May I come in?"

"Of course." Chantel entered the living room, at once familiar even though the furniture had been updated and the walls painted. Being transported back to the comfort of a home she'd visited many times helped her relax a little bit. But her mouth was dry, and she felt the beginnings of a headache. If Blanche did have answers, were they ones she wanted to hear? She had a problem even pushing the big ball of questions out of her mouth.

Blanche bypassed the living room and continued into the kitchen. "What can I get you to drink?"

Liquid. Yes. Then I can do this. "Whatever you're having."

Blanche gave Chantel a look before reaching into a cabinet and pulling down a fifth of brown liquor. "You sure about that?"

Chantel surprised herself by laughing. "Good one, Miss Blanche. Maybe a soda."

"I'm glad you haven't lost your humor, darlin'." She placed the bottle back on the shelf. "Had to take that strain off your face to focus on what's on your mind."

After pouring glasses of soda, Miss Blanche gave one to Chantel and continued into the living room. She sat on the sofa and patted the space next to her. "Now, what were you doing at Trinity?"

"Trying to get a copy of my birth certificate."

Chantel noticed a slight catch in Blanche's breathing, the merest stiffening of her neck before she sat back and relaxed. Other than that she was old-school cool.

"You need a copy of your birth certificate?"

"I needed to see one, yes, ma'am."

"Did they provide one?"

"For some strange reason, they had no record of my birth."

Miss Blanche's expression didn't change, but Chantel swore something shifted in the room.

"You can never be sure about those medical records departments."

"Are you saying it not being found could be due to an administrative or human error?"

"Anything is possible," was her noncommittal reply.

"Miss Blanche, do you know something that I don't know?"

"Child, I'm seventy-five years old. I know a lot of stuff that you don't."

Chantel smiled. "About me, I mean. You and Mama were both at Trinity when I was born, right?"

Blanche nodded. "I was working there, then, but wasn't around for your birth."

"Did you . . . see my birth certificate?"

"I wasn't working in medical records. I was on another floor, in another ward."

Chantel paused, considered Blanche's words. It seemed the older woman was answering every question without telling her a thing.

"And even if I had been working there and seen anything," Blanche continued, "it's not something I would share with you. Patient confidentiality."

"We're talking about me. I'm the patient!"

"No, honey. In a maternity ward, the mother is the patient,

there to deliver a child. But like I said, I didn't work in medical records or on the maternity ward either. However, I do know that about ten or fifteen years after you were born, they completely changed the system. Anna had long since moved to Marquette by then."

She shifted so that she could see Blanche directly. "Do you know anybody named Simone who could have possibly been friends with my mother?"

"Your mother and I were friends for more than fifty years. I can't possibly remember all the people we met across those five decades."

Chantel grew irritated with what she perceived as Blanche's word games. She asked what she wanted to know straight out.

"Miss Blanche, am I adopted?"

"Why in the world would you ask that?"

"Because I want an answer, and as the best friend of my mother, for fifty years as you just pointed out, I think you might know."

Blanche's eyes narrowed. "You got every right to ask a question, but don't get snippy with me, child."

"I'm sorry, Miss Blanche. I didn't mean to sound sarcastic. It's just that . . ." Chantel reached into her purse and pulled out the certificate from Texas. "When cleaning out Mama's house, I found this."

She held it out to Blanche, watching the older woman's reaction closer than a blockbuster movie. Blanche slowly reached for the paper. She studied the front for a long moment before turning it over to read the back.

"This was in Anna's house?"

"In a small wooden chest at the back of her closet."

"Hmm." Blanche handed the paper back to Chantel without another word.

"Miss Blanche, if I'm adopted and you know that, please tell me. Mama may have asked you not to, but she's not here."

Miss Blanche eyed her a long moment before her expression softened, her eyes grew warm, and she reached for Chantel's hand.

"I don't have an answer for that question, baby, but what I can tell you is this. You were the sun in Anna Scott's life. No one could love you more or better. Her world revolved around you. That I know for sure."

Miss Blanche crossed her arms in a way that signaled she was done talking. Still, her eyes were kind. Chantel finished her soda, thanked Blanche for the visit, and left to get the fish dinners from Saltwater she'd promised Rita, but that Chantel had no appetite to eat.

While replaying the conversation with Blanche in her head, Chantel had cleaned the kitchen, taken a shower, and crawled into bed. She picked up her Kindle and tried to lose herself in a novel but the storyline most intriguing to her was the one in her own life. Television wasn't much better. How could one have over two hundred channels and find nothing on TV? She almost called Jett again, if for no other reason than to curse her out. But knowing tomorrow would be another long day, she shut everything off and snuggled up to her body pillow. Nonstop thoughts made sleep elusive. She finally fell off, only to be awakened by her cell phone vibrating on the nightstand. Jett. It was almost midnight.

"Is this you calling back ASAP? We talked hours ago."

"I didn't have to call you back at all."

Smart ass. That Jett was almost impossible to get ahold of, and that Chantel wanted answers more than sleep was the only reason the call wasn't disconnected. She flipped on her back and took a breath to calm down.

"Earlier, you asked me a question."

Yes, heffah, much earlier. "Yes, Jett. I asked if I was adopted. You said no."

A beat and then, "I lied."

"You . . ." Chantel slowly sat up. Her heart plunged to her stomach. "Am I?"

A second passed. And then another. Finally, Jett responded. "Yes."

Chapter 8
Confessions, Part II

Jett held her breath and awaited Chantel's response. The longer the silence, the more she considered delivering that kind of news over the phone may not have been the best idea.

"Chantel? Hello? Chan, say something!" She pressed the phone against her ear and could detect the sound of faint breathing. "Chantel, I'm sorry I told you."

"No."

Jett felt every ounce of strength it took to say that one word.

"I just . . . I can't . . ."

"I know. I'm sorry." Jett truly was, more than the woman on the other end of the line could ever know.

"How? Why?"

Spoken through tears. Jett was sure of that.

"It's a long, complicated story, and like you said, it's already late." Jett eyed the clock on the wall. "After midnight there. My call probably woke you up. I'm sorry. I should have waited until morning."

Chantel sniffled. Jett heard muffled sounds, then Chantel blew her nose. "I'll be okay. Just tell me . . . what happened."

Jett took a deep breath. This part was going to be tough.

After she'd gotten home, Myles had called with more information. He'd talked with the producer again, who'd had a conversation with the VP of Zenith Records. If the single based on the show was a hit, they wanted Jett to do a whole album. Like everything else in the world, the record industry had changed. The suits felt they could create a brand with Jett that would target professional Black women over thirty with disposable incomes and college degrees. A segment of society that could boost the industry's fledgling sales and align them on the right side of the burgeoning women's movement that had helped America elect its first female Vice President.

Smart. Grown. Sexy. Sophisticated.

An image and character that the culture, and the country, could proudly embrace. Jett could represent the hell out of a brand like that. Which is why she knew she had to speak with Chantel and answer her question. It was difficult, but necessary. Putting this situation to bed would be best for everyone.

"Jett?"

"I'm here." Jett cleared her throat. "Mama didn't want you to know. She didn't want you to feel different than the other kids."

"The woman, Simone. Who is she?"

"I think she was Mama's brother's niece."

"I don't remember Mama ever mentioning a brother."

"Or maybe it was her uncle, I'm not sure. I was a teenager when all of this happened, and . . . everything was kept hush-hush."

"I don't understand."

"The girl was young, from what I remember. Her getting pregnant was . . . complicated. The brother or uncle or whoever was religious, didn't want her to have an abortion. You know Texas, the Bible Belt and all. They didn't want you given away to a stranger either."

"So they called Mama?"

"She was there when you were born, brought you home right after."

"Is Simone still in Texas?"

Jett bitt her lip. This was so painful. She could only imagine how Chantel felt right now. "I think she's . . . gone."

Knowing the next question, Jett continued. "I don't think Mama ever knew the man."

"My father?"

"Yes. I don't remember him ever being mentioned. I barely remember my biological father. We both turned out okay, though, right?"

"I can't believe this."

"For sure, it's a lot to digest. I think that's why Mama wanted to keep it a secret, because she thought knowing would be more hurtful than leaving life as it was."

"What hurts is that I was lied to about who I am."

"Nothing changes. Anna Scott is still your mama."

"Right."

"I'm still your sister."

"Uh-huh."

"Mama loved you the most, Chantel." Unexpected emotion pushed against Jett's chest. "I love you, too."

For a while there was only silence. Understandable, given the bomb that had just been dropped.

"Talk to me, Chan. What are you thinking? How do you feel?"

"I don't know what to think, or how to feel. I need to go."

"Are you going to be okay? I mean, is there someone you can call, maybe a guy friend who can come over?"

Chantel sucked air through her teeth. Clearly, she and Jett used different coping mechanisms.

"I need to go."

"Call me tomorrow? I'm worried about you."

"I'm in shock, okay, but I'm not suicidal. Having just lost my mother, I wouldn't do that to Artani."

"Okay. Give my nephew a hug from Aunt Jett."

The call ended. Jett slowly placed the phone down on the

table. She sat motionless, staring at nothing, feeling empty and numb. Jett's life had been far from easy, yet having that talk with Chantel was one of the hardest things she'd ever done. Hopefully, once Chantel processed and accepted what Jett had told her, she could put that part of her past behind her and live a wonderful life. To a skeptic like Jett this was a fairy-tale ending, but she knew firsthand that sometimes what began as a dream could turn into a nightmare.

That Chantel made it through the workday was a miracle; the breakneck pace of getting a paper ready for print, a Godsend. She'd worked on autopilot. Except for work-related questions and comments co-workers had kept their distance, could probably sense the tsunami of mixed emotions emanating from the core of her being. Artani served as a temporary distraction, going on and on about a mobile petting zoo that came to his preschool. For Chantel, his conversation was a bunch of "wah wah wah," but being focused on feeding chickens and petting rabbits made him oblivious to her sad mood. She put him to bed almost an hour early. Then, after taking a shower, she stood staring at herself in the bathroom mirror as though viewing a stranger for the very first time. She scrutinized the shape of her face, the slant of her eyes, the way her nose flared, and how she always thought the well-defined lips that some women paid money for and endured injections to obtain had been passed down from her mom.

Maybe they had come from the girl named Simone. Not Anna, the only mother she'd ever known, but the biological mom who'd given her away. Jett had described her getting pregnant as *complicated*. What did that even mean?

What about the relationship between Simone and the man who impregnated her? Had they been dating, casual hookups? Was she the product of a booty call or a one-night stand? Why had Simone put Chantel up for adoption? Why had Anna felt it necessary to keep all of this on the low, so much so that she crafted a fake birth certificate? Had Chantel been formally adopted and if so, where were those papers? Or was hers an off-the-record exchange in a Walmart parking lot? Chantel had been too shocked at Jett's revelation to ask more questions. Yet it seemed the more she knew, the more she needed to find out. The one person who could tell her the whole story was Anna, which made Chantel miss her even more.

After finishing up in the bathroom Chantel donned a robe and walked into the kitchen. Retrieving a bottle of Cabernet purchased at least two months ago, she pulled out the cork and sniffed the contents. Once the bottle was opened, could wine go bad? Not being much of a drinker, Chantel didn't know. The strong smell that greeted her gave her pause, but only for a second. It didn't matter how the contents tasted. She wasn't drinking it for the woodsy depth and citrusy notes the label advertised. She was drinking to feel better, would have swigged a jar of moonshine if she thought it would ease the pain in her chest. After swapping the small wineglass she'd first retrieved for one that would impress *Scandal*'s Olivia Pope, Chantel filled it up and took a huge gulp before heading back into the bedroom. She pulled the photo album she'd retrieved from Anna's house off the table, crawled into her king-sized retreat, and settled against the headboard. She opened the album. Nostalgia assailed her as she gazed at photos that captured birthdays, Sunday dinners, vacations, and more. Peeling back the plastic covering, she removed one of Anna taken when she was younger, apparently before Chantel was born.

Before you were adopted, she self-corrected.

Chantel took another drink.

Chantel ran a finger over the photo's once shiny surface. It was a waist-up shot of a smiling Anna, dressed for a special occasion. Maybe church, Chantel thought. She studied a picture she'd seen many times, wondering whether the resemblance she always thought they'd shared was instead a product of her innocent imagination. Tonight, armed with new info and looking at this young, slender version of her mom, differences that she'd never before realized seemed to jump off the page. Her face wasn't as round as Chantel remembered, the cheekbones more prominent than she'd realized. Or was it her mother's severe hairstyle that made them look that way? As far back as Chantel remembered, her mom had mostly worn wigs—short, asymmetrical bobs or shoulder-length curls that complemented her face. For a while, when Chantel was a teenager and braids were high fashion, both she and her mother had worn the look. Her hair appeared natural in this picture, pulled away from her face and secured with a band. Her eyes beamed in a way that suggested she was happy to be photographed and knew she looked good. Anna Michelle Scott was an attractive woman. Chantel rarely felt that about herself, yet she'd managed to snag a husband, such as Art could be described. Why had her mother never remarried and had more kids of her own?

For the umpteenth time Chantel thought about Rita and wanted to call her. She looked at her cell phone but didn't reach for it, even though it was silly to be scared of Rita's reaction. Chantel couldn't imagine the news changing their friendship. The two women had known each other since grade school, when Rita's family had moved to Marquette from Chicago. Her grandmother had been born in Marquette, raised in Kansas City, and knew Chantel's grandmother through a husband who'd been raised and had family in the same small Texas town. It seemed in one way or another everyone in Marquette was connected; at least among the small yet vibrant Black population. The grandfather had passed some years back, but Chantel wondered if Rita's grandmother knew Simone.

Chantel looked through the entire photo album and finished

her glass of wine. The cabernet was much stronger than her white wine favorite. Drinking the big, full glass on an empty stomach hadn't helped. Inebriated, she was no longer able to keep it together, to continue absorbing the adoption revelation with a steely spine and dry eyes. She missed one mother and didn't know the other, and had a famous sister who was virtually a stranger as well. Basically, Chantel deduced, she had no family. She was an outcast, unwanted and alone in the world. Chantel took full advantage of the shameless and abject pity the wine allowed her. Rita called near the end of her meltdown.

"Chan? Girl, you've been on my mind all evening. Are you okay?"

"No." A one-syllable word was drawn out into three.

"Are you crying? What's the matter?"

"I'm adopted."

"I'm on my way over."

"Stop and get another bottle of wine."

When Rita arrived a short time later, Chantel had changed into a pair of sweats and lay curled on the couch. She'd left the door unlocked on purpose so she wouldn't have to raise her head and cause the room to spin.

"Oh my God, Chantel!"

"It looks worse than it is."

"What have you eaten?"

"I'm not hungry. Did you get my Moscato?"

"You don't need alcohol. You need this greasy burger and fries. Go splash your face with cold water. You look a hot mess!"

Rita's scolding helped Chantel get it together. She didn't need someone feeling sorrier for her than she did for herself. Along with washing her face, she gargled with mouthwash to remove the sour wine taste and pulled her wild mane into a short top pony.

Barely a foot back into the living room and Rita assailed her. "Drink this."

"What is it?" Chantel reached for the glass.

"Water, fool. Drink all of it." Rita watched Chantel down the contents, then abruptly pulled her into a hug. "Don't worry, girl. We got you. Ain't nothing changed."

Halfway through the hamburger and spicy fries, Chantel began to feel better. She relayed to Rita what Jett had told her, ending the commentary with, "Ain't that some shit?"

"Sounds like something you see on reality TV."

"Yeah, the reality that isn't real at all?"

"Well, now, at least you know."

"Yeah."

"It can't be easy to process."

"Not at all. Before, even without knowing my father, I felt like a whole human being. Now I feel parts of me are missing, an alien in my own life with a history I don't know about."

"Dang, I wish Pawpaw were alive."

"I thought the same thing. Do you think your grandmother might know something?"

"If she did, she doesn't now. That curse called dementia is the devil for real." Rita reached for the wine bottle and poured some into a glass she'd brought from the kitchen. "You don't know anybody in Texas who might be able to help you find out more information?"

Chantel shook her head. "As far as I knew Grandma was our only relative in Beaumont. I never met anyone else."

"Dang, sis." Both became quiet as Chantel finished eating and Rita sipped wine, absorbed in their thoughts.

"I have an idea. One of those DNA websites. People find relatives there all the time."

"Name somebody." Chantel finished the last bite of burger, crumpled the paper it came in and placed it in the bag, along with a few uneaten fries.

"I don't know anyone personally, but it happens all the time on *Long Lost Family*."

"Just because my story sounds like a television show doesn't mean I want to be on one." Chantel got up, cleaned their items off the table and continued into the kitchen to throw them away.

Rita followed her. "You don't have to go on the show. Just do what they do, which is usually to register the person's DNA with a company like Ancestry.com. Often other family members have done the same thing, in hopes of finding relatives they may not know."

"The last time I went digging for information, I found out I was adopted. Maybe I should just leave well enough alone."

"It's your decision," Rita countered. "But if you want to try it, I'll be there to help."

It took a couple weeks for Chantel to make a decision and decide how best to proceed. The more popular companies took months to process their samples. Not wanting the feeling of limbo to drag on that long, she and Rita decided to do their own sleuthing. The first step was finding a company, preferably local, to process her and Anna's DNA. It was Rita's idea to include Chantel's mother, believing that since she was more closely related to Simone, her sample might lead to relatives not detected in Chantel's bloodline. The good news was that they found a company in Kansas City. The bad news was the price to get tested.

"Three hundred and fifty dollars! I can't afford that."

It was late on a Monday night at Chantel's house, where Rita had taken to hanging out once or twice a week.

"What about the check you'll get from the Dip this weekend?"

"Both that check and the next one I get are already spent."

"What about Jett? Will she loan you the money?"

"She turned me down the last two times I asked her. You know I'm not one to beg."

"You sure about not doing a TV show? Those housewives make hella cash."

"Yeah, acting hella fools."

"You could always try one of those at-home kits."

"And wait six to eight weeks for results? Time is money and when it comes to getting answers I don't have that much."

Two days later, Chantel received a Ca$hApp of exactly three hundred and fifty dollars from an account that simply said Blessed. Of course she asked Rita, who denied sending the money but offered to go with her when she had the test done.

Mere weeks after Chantel found out she was adopted, the DNA test results brought more unsettling news. Anna wasn't the distant relative of Simone that Jett's story had suggested. The test showed that she was more than likely a "close relative," which the center identified as either a sibling, uncle, aunt, grandparent, or cousin. This news left Chantel more confused than ever and made her determined to solve one more mystery. Who in the hell was Simone Scott, and how was she related to Mama?

Chapter 9
Live Your Life

Normally, Jett could separate and compartmentalize her professional and personal lives. But as the limousine carrying her to the Burbank airport reached the airstrip for private planes, her mind was in turmoil. Chantel was never far from her thoughts. Over the past few weeks she'd all but stopped calling. Lots of overtime and working on Saturdays was the reason she'd given in response to a text. Jett hoped it was work that had her turn quieter than a church mouse, and not what she'd shared about her being adopted and what happened in Texas. Jett should have been relieved at not being pestered. Instead, she missed the phone calls. Go figure.

Chantel's infrequent calling wasn't the only recent change. Jett had fired Randall, both from her patio and from her bed. When he asked who else she was seeing and then went through her phone, she knew it was curtains. That and the fact that they'd wrapped up the audition tapings for the first season of *Seeking Stardom* and she'd successfully shed the extra ten pounds the television lens put on her. Taping the competition rounds would begin after the holiday. When that happened, Jett would be focused on judging new talent and if all of the planets aligned correctly, checking out a new man as well. For the next week, however, it would be all about her.

She'd eyed Randall's potential replacement the same week she'd changed the locks and demanded her key. Oliver Canyon was a Blaxican chef who'd recently catered a party on the *Seeking Stardom* set. Coal-black hair—long, curly, thick—dark eyes, tanned skin, plush lips and toned muscles. Jett had quickly made an assessment. He was straight up *caliente*! That women swarmed around him like bees made it hard for him to appear modest. He was cordial with everyone but maintained a professional demeanor. No overt flirting. Points for that. Jett had kept her distance to see how he handled himself, and got noticed, as planned. He'd discreetly slipped her his card before leaving. She agreed to call him when she got back from New York.

"Here we are, miss!"

Jett looked up to see the slight, older driver hop out of the car and turn to open her door. Jett gingerly placed her brand-new red bottoms on the pavement and eased out of the back seat. Having considered a possible tryst with Myles, she'd donned a sexy mini with a thong underneath. Didn't want to embarrass the kindly driver, a dark-skinned Black man, probably older than his smooth skin suggested, by giving him a show of her bare booty. He was probably old enough to be her father, if that man was still alive.

The driver removed her luggage from the trunk and began wheeling them toward the plane's open luggage compartment.

"It's a beautiful morning, isn't it, miss? Not a cloud in the sky. You'll get up there and be able to see for miles."

Jett didn't intend to ignore the gentleman. She'd gotten distracted by her manager, Myles Colbert, who'd sauntered down the stairs to meet her.

"You obviously look better than you feel," Myles murmured, pulling out a fifty and tipping the driver. "You're exactly correct, sir. It's a beautiful day. Hopefully you'll make the best of it."

The driver bowed slightly. "I appreciate that, sir. Will do."

Jett turned and blessed the driver with one of her signature star smiles. "Thank you."

"Miss, you're very welcome."

Once the driver was out of earshot she told her manager, "Fuck you, Myles."

"Later perhaps, once the deal is done."

Jett smiled coyly as she turned and glided up the steps. Her hips swayed from side to side, adding extra sexy to the show she provided. Once she reached the door she turned and leaned against it, fully aware of the image she presented.

Myles, smiling broadly, reached for his cell phone and snapped off several pics. "All right, Ms. Scott, I see you."

I see you, too, Jett thought while taking a seat in the luxurious executive jet the record company had generously sent over. Myles was chocolate, sweet, ready to lick and as smooth as the kid leather covering the recliner. Later, after work was done and business had been taken care of, she'd consider contributing to her mile-high club account by doing just that.

The attendant offered a smile as he approached her. "Good afternoon, Ms. Jett. May I get you something to drink?"

"I'm fine for now."

"Not even sparkling water, or perhaps a glass of cool alkaline aqua with lime slices?"

"The alkaline sounds good."

The attendant looked up. "What about you, sir?"

Myles took the seat next to Jett. "Two fingers of your best bourbon and a splash of club soda."

"Coming right up!"

Jett raised a brow. "Hard morning?"

"After seeing that luscious ass of yours, the only thing that's hard is my dick."

The two relaxed into the cross-country trip, enjoying five uninterrupted hours of extravagance, courtesy of Zenith Records. Salads dotted with Russian caviar and thin slices of European white truffle that the attendant explained had been sold at auction for $4k per pound. Medium rare slices of succulent Kobe beef over seasoned risotto, served alongside organic root veggies grown in mushroom soil. All of this deliciousness was washed down with one-thousand-dollar bottles of French champagne and topped off with decadent chocolate lava cakes sprinkled with edible gold. Needless to say, when they reached the two-bedroom suite of their five-star hotel with views of the bay, two beds weren't needed, much less two rooms. Their late-night snack was each other, both satiated before falling into a peaceful sleep.

The next day, the star treatment continued. Jett met Zenith's top brass, the producer tapped for her project, and the latest, hottest songwriting duo with multiple recent number one hits. Lunch was served on a yacht as they sailed around the harbor. They reiterated to Jett and Myles the importance of this single's success not only for the television show but for her chance to record a full album backed by an aggressive marketing and branding plan. With the right positioning, Jett could bring luxury and glamour back to the music scene, along with class and sophistication. They'd hire the best designers to style her. Everything, including movie-themed videos, would be top-notch. This wasn't an opportunity for a young starlet bound to create scandal before the first release dropped. They chose her specifically because she was just the type of diva to show those starlets how it was done.

That night, Jett left New York and Zenith Records more than impressed—she was flabbergasted. She didn't know how the stars had aligned to make this happen but was beyond thankful that they had. She'd called her attorney on the way to the airport. A contract would be drafted and sent to him before the end of the week. It was all really happening. She couldn't believe it. Jett was starring in what was slated to be the number one fall show on a top television network. She'd dated wealthy men and attended A-list parties. But this experience was on a whole other level, one she'd dreamed of and aimed for her entire life. Now, inches away from grabbing not a brass ring but a platinum one, Jett knew Chantel's situation had been handled correctly. All that happened in the past would stay there, far away from the bright future ahead.

Chapter 10
One More Try

Chantel doubted Blanche would help her. Jett had already shared what she knew. Rita had gone above and beyond to assist in her search for answers. For this one, uncovering Simone's whereabouts, Chantel worked alone.

She started with the easiest, most accessible place to get information—online. She signed up for the two-week trial period on popular DNA websites and looked for her. Simone Scott was a common name with hundreds of entries. Chantel narrowed the search by age, race, and location. She didn't find a match. Figuring it was worth the investment, she paid thirty dollars for a background check. The one she selected searched names against criminal cases, birth, death, and marriage certificates and property filings. Nothing.

A week passed. Chantel was discouraged. But she didn't give up. She treated the search like a hobby, a game, and began to almost enjoy her new role as private eye, the super sleuth of Marquette.

Jett said Simone became pregnant as a teenager, which would put her current age around fifty, same as Jett's. Armed with that info she searched for schools in Beaumont, Texas, during the years Simone would have attended. She created a spreadsheet listing the various schools, then searched their online yearbooks. A couple times she found listings that held promise but didn't pan out. During this time she and her sister hardly spoke. Jett was no doubt knee-deep in taping, and Chantel had read an online article about Jett recording the theme song. That announcement made Chantel smile. For her sister it was back to the future. Chantel texted her congratulations but didn't call. Nor did she expect Jett to reach out. Opportunities in Hollywood wouldn't always come knocking. Her sis had to secure the bag—several, if possible. At the end of the day, it didn't really matter. Now it was her with the busy schedule and unwavering focus. But this project wasn't about fame and fortune. What Chantel sought was much more personal—her true identity.

Summer came early in the Midwest. Triple digit temps announced themselves in mid-May. Chantel finished cleaning out her mother's house and surrendered it back to the bank. She thought doing so would make her melancholy but removing the keys from her ring was somehow liberating. Perhaps that was why her first weekend off since the trip to LA, when Diplomat had the rare opportunity to feature a 90s talent from St. Louis who'd toured with Nelly back in the day, Chantel decided to finally tackle the last major project from her mother's transition, the dozen or so boxes in her garage containing Anna's personal belongings. Clothes, shoes, purses, and the like. Blanche had volunteered the church ladies to do it the week her mom died, but Chantel wanted to be the one to decide where the items should be donated and what, if anything, she would keep. Shortly after Art had picked up Artani for the weekend, she went downstairs, turned on Pandora to her favorite 90s station, and opened each box. Her plan was to ascertain the contents, sort them by type, and then make piles of what would be donated where and what she'd keep. As she used a cutter to open the last top, she turned up the stereo and sang about scrubs with TLC.

She'd just busted a dance move to the popular refrain when she felt something hard and tickly slide down her back. She yelped, running across the garage before turning around. Terrence was doubled over, laughing.

"Terrence!"

She rushed toward him. He retreated, placing his hands in a defensive position to block her blows.

"That's not funny! You scared the crap out of me."

"Now I understand why you didn't hear the doorbell." He started dancing to the song, mimicking the lyrics with a girly voice.

"Ooh, you get on my nerves. Don't do that again."

"I'm sorry. Come here."

He pulled her into a hug.

She resisted. "No!"

"Ah, don't be like that." They wrestled until finally Chantel acquiesced and allowed Terrence to briefly embrace her, then stepped back and bopped him on the head.

"Ow!"

"That's what you get." She walked over to where the cutter lay on top of a box, picked it up, and slit the tape holding the cardboard.

Terrence examined the boxes. "What's all this?"

"Mama's stuff."

"What are you going to do, sell it?"

"No. After going through everything to see what's here, I'm going to give most of it to the church Mama attended. They're opening a gratitude store where people who can't afford to buy the items can get them for free."

"That's a good cause. Want me to help?"

Chantel stopped sorting the clothes she'd dumped from one of the boxes and gave him a look. "You don't have anything better to do on a Saturday morning than help me sort old clothes and shoes?"

"I have a lot of better things to do. But I've offered to help. Are you going to accept or not?"

"I don't know," Chantel teased, surprising herself by flirting back. "What's it going to cost me?"

"Ooh, girl. I'm glad you asked. Hey!" Terrence began swiveling his hips as the song changed and 2Pac and crew began asking a most appropriate question to which Terrence sang along. "How do you want it?"

Chantel laughed. "Does Sharon know you're over here asking that question?"

"Sharon? She doesn't care. That was just a friends with benefits situation."

"Uh-huh." Chantel began checking the boxes. "You've got a lot of situations. Okay, if you want you can go through this box of purses, make sure Mama didn't leave a hundred-dollar bill tucked away. How was the show last night?"

"It was cool." Terrence rummaged through a purse, found nothing in it, and tossed it to the side. "Looked like all the tickets were purchased by King's supporters. There were several familiar faces from KC in the crowd. One of the anchors from Channel Four. Even one of the Chiefs came down. King's campaign is starting to really take off. The crowd was feeling it. Everybody had a good time."

"I bet it was packed."

"Sold out."

"Even without King's friends, it should have been a sellout. That group helped put St. Louis on the music map."

"For sure. It'll be even better tonight. You should come!"

"I might. You want something to drink, a bottle of water or soda?"

"You got any beer?" Chantel shook her head. "I'm good."

The chitchat continued as organization began to form out of chaos. The music flowed from the 90s into the 2000s. Terrence reached the bottom of the box filled with purses, totes, organizer bags, etc.

"Whoa." Terrence laughed while looking inside what was once a bright pink wallet.

"What?"

"Isn't this your sister?" Chantel began walking over. "Yeah, it's her. Jeanetta Simone Scott."

Chantel froze. "What did you say? Let me see that."

She snatched the wallet. There, on the left side beneath clear plastic, was a faded middle school ID card with the picture of a young, smiling girl whose press and curl had been combed over to one side. To the right of the picture was the name, both typed and written in a loopy cursive signature, of the girl pictured. It was a revelation, the solving of a mystery, the truth of which Chantel felt all the way to her toes. Jeanetta Simone Scott was the Simone Scott for whom Chantel had been searching. Jeanetta was the teenager who'd had a baby in Texas amid "complicated" circumstances. Jeanetta was the part of the story Anna had wanted to keep secret. Or perhaps it was Jett who wanted the truth to stay hidden. Either way, the revelation hit her like a punch in the gut.

Jett, the superstar singer she'd idolized her whole life, wasn't Chantel's sister, but her mother.

Chantel felt the room spin and her legs buckle. Fade. To. Black.

"Chantel! Come on, now. Chantel. Wake up."

Chantel groaned. Her eyes fluttered before popping open. She tried to sit up quickly but Terrence stopped her.

"Not so fast, baby girl. Just lay there for a minute. Take deep breaths. Let me get you some water."

She obeyed without argument, lay there not remembering how she got from the garage to the living room couch. Terrence returned with a glass of ice water. He helped her to a sitting position, then handed her the glass.

"Just a few sips, then drink the rest."

Again, she did as instructed. She heard water running again, this time from the hallway bathroom. When she looked up, Terrence was coming toward her with a wet cloth. The coolness felt good on her forehead. She sat up and swung her feet to the floor.

"What happened?"

Before he could answer, she remembered. Jett.

Terrence sat beside her. "I think you fainted, passed out or something. One minute we were looking at an old picture of your sister, the next you were tumbling to the floor. What happened?"

Tears unexpectedly sprang to Chantel's eyes.

"What's going on, Chan?"

She couldn't think of a cover story. The only thought filling her head was the truth. "Promise you won't tell anyone?"

"Not if you don't want me to."

"I don't. No one."

"All right."

Chantel took a deep breath before looking Terrence in the eye. "I think Jett is my mother."

Eyes narrowed. Jaw dropped. A gaze conveyed the shock he couldn't express.

"Yes, you heard correctly. That ID just confirmed that the woman I've thought of and called sister all of my life is actually my birth mom."

"Damn, Chantel. How did that happen?"

"It's a long story."

"I've got time."

"I'm still trying to figure it out."

"Maybe I can help."

Over the next hour, Chantel shared her journey from finding the second birth certificate to Terrence finding Jett's ID.

"I don't recall feeling light-headed or anything, but I must have fainted."

"Makes sense. That's some heavy news to get unexpectedly."

"Thanks for being here."

"I'm glad I was. So, what are you going to do, given the fact Jett lied to you?"

"I don't know."

One thing she wasn't going to do was tell Jett what she'd uncovered. At least not right away, until she had proof. Anyone who lied as blatantly as she had before would do it again.

"I don't understand why she didn't just tell me, especially after I asked her about Simone"—Chantel used air quotes—"point blank. She's no longer a teenager. I'm almost thirty-four years old. Why does she feel like she has to hide it? Is she embarrassed, or ashamed of me?" She looked over at Terrence, tears once again welling up in her eyes.

Terrence slid over and folded Chantel into his arms. "I don't know, baby, but don't cry about it. You'll be all right. On second thought, cry as long as you need to. This news is fucked up."

Somehow, for the first time since losing her mama and despite finding out that Jett had lied, within the safety of Terrence's strong arms, Chantel believed that just maybe she would.

By the end of the following week, Chantel had come up with a plan to get Jett to admit on her own that she'd lied and was the mother Chantel had asked about more than a month ago. But first she had to have proof beyond a decades-old ID. To do so she'd have to max out her credit cards and risk losing her singing gig at the Dip by having Terrence call in Jasmine Alexander again, and during a holiday weekend at that, but this project was more important. Nothing underscored this more than her final preparation—making nice with Artani's father, who agreed to drive down from Kansas City so Artani could spend the long holiday weekend with his dad. When Saturday arrived and Art rang the doorbell just before seven, Chantel had already been up for two hours.

"Come on, Artani. Hurry up! Your dad's here."

Chantel moved away from the window where she'd watched Art pull up in his new BMW. She immediately noticed that the sistah who'd replaced the cocaine-snorting, gambling straw that broke her marriage's back and to whom he was now engaged was not in the car. She walked over and opened the door just as he stepped on the porch.

"Hello." Chantel managed a smile.

"Good morning."

"Artani's almost ready. Do you want to come in?"

Art showed surprise. "You sure?"

She nodded, completely understanding her ex-husband's hesitation. There was a time when to do so would have put his health at risk. Not this morning. Too much going on. It was no longer their troubled past but her own muddled history that held her focus. She didn't have the emotional energy for anything else.

"Thanks for driving down to get Artani. I appreciate it."

"No problem, though I wondered why you weren't flying out of Kansas City. Where are you going?"

Chantel glanced over her shoulder. She hadn't told Artani about her trip to LA, only that he was going to spend the weekend with his father.

She lowered her voice. "Los Angeles, but don't tell Artani. He'd have a fit knowing I went without him."

"Weren't y'all just there?"

"Yes."

"What, you going back to try and grab some of that fame and money your sister's pulling down?"

"No, that's her lane. I'm going to stay in mine."

"Singing is your lane, too, Chan. Your styles are different, but you can sing as good as her. She should try and get you on her show next season."

"That would probably be against the rules."

"Since you're not going out there to audition, it must be a man."

"I'm going out there to take care of some business, but if pleasure comes knocking, I won't turn it away."

Art's eyes telegraphed his desire to know more. He was the last person she'd tell about what she'd found out. He'd assume being Jett's daughter would somehow change the balance in Chantel's bank account and would run back to court begging the judge to lower his already minimal child support payments.

She turned toward the hallway. "Come on, Artani!"

Artani ran in with his Black Panther carry-on luggage rolling behind him. "Hi, Daddy!"

"Hello, son."

"Here, hold my bag, Daddy. Mommy, I have to use the bathroom!"

"Why are you making an announcement about it? Hurry up!"

Art watched his mini-me run down the hallway before turning to his attention to Chantel. "You're asking Artani if he's ready. What about you?"

"My luggage is already in the car." She shifted her weight, the next subject matter uncomfortable though the words had not yet left her mouth. "How's your fiancée?"

"Vickie's fine." Now, instead of feeling hers she noticed Art's discomfort. "She's, um, we're expecting."

"She's pregnant?"

"Well, it damn sure ain't me carrying the child!"

Art's reaction lightened what could have been a heavy moment between them. A part of Chantel wanted to feel some type of way about the announcement but the other, bigger side of herself prevailed. She and Art were no longer married. Except for how it affected Artani, what he did was not her business.

"Congratulations," she replied, with only a teaspoon of sarcasm when there could have been a whole bowl. "Is Artani going to have a little brother or a sister?"

Art shrugged. "We only found out we were pregnant a couple weeks ago."

She wanted to ask whether or not a wedding was in the works, but the chance passed when Artani turned the corner and ran back into the room at breakneck speed.

"Slow down, son. Grab your bag, let's go." Art looked at Chantel. "It can't be easy for you since . . ."

Finishing the sentence wasn't necessary. Art's expressive eyes were one of the things Chantel had loved about him.

"I miss her every minute of every day. How's your mother?"

"She's good; can't wait to see her grandson. She asked about you."

"Tell her I said hi."

"Oh, yeah, both Vickie and I are working from home now, so if you need us to keep him longer, or take him more often, let me know."

Five hours later, Chantel touched down at the Burbank airport. She rented a car, drove straight to her sister's house, and immediately ran into a problem she hadn't anticipated—not being able to get inside. The key wasn't in its usual spot. She'd never believed in the angels her mother swore by but they must have been hovering, because just when she'd started the car and was about to drive off, Lucia's blue Honda pulled into the driveway. Chantel got out of the car, walked up to the housekeeper, and hugged her as though she were a long-lost relative.

"What are you doing here?" Lucia asked as she walked around to the open trunk and began pulling out bags. "Your sister's not here. She's in New York."

"I know. We talked. Here, let me help you." Chantel prayed forgiveness for that little white lie. Jett's phone call and text messages were how Chantel had known the LA coast was clear. When

Jett texted about spending Memorial Day weekend in KC, Chantel panicked. But only for a second. She texted back that she wasn't in KC but would call her next week.

There were a few lies that Chantel needed grace to cover.

She reached for one of the bags Lucia carried without waiting for a yes. "How's your grandson? Rico, right?"

And just like that, she was in the house. Less than ten minutes later, she was out and on her way to the hotel. While waiting on irrefutable proof that Jett was Simone, her biological mother, Chantel methodically plotted her next move.

Chapter 11
Mo Money Mo Problems

Mocha, the award-winning producer tasked with making hits, opened the mic that fed into the booth where Jett had just sung her heart out. "Come on out, ma. That's a wrap."

A slight frown flitted across Jett's brow as she exited the booth and sidled over to the man whose toned body and smooth skin lived up to his nickname.

"I told you about calling me that. I'm not your mother."

She could have been, but that was beside the point.

"Sorry, ma, I mean Jett. It's habit."

"Keep on and I'll seduce you to help break it."

Said even though word on the street was that Mocha preferred the hard-bodied rappers he hung with over softer body types.

Myles chose that moment to walk into the studio. "Cut that out. No fraternizing in the workplace." He walked over and squeezed Jett's butt. "None of this," he continued, wrapping his arms around her and nuzzling her neck. "Or this," as a finger slid down the deep vee in her blouse.

"Get a room, guys," Mocha drawled, unimpressed. "Let me play this back for you. Once Rodeo adds his spit, it's going to be fire."

Jett slid her hand along Myles's crotch before perching on the edge of Mocha's mixing board. She and Myles had been spotted by and speculated on in several trash mags, *Celebrity Gossip* being the biggest and most influential. When questioned, neither had confirmed nor denied anything romantic happening between them. Both enjoyed the speculation, as it fueled more stories of them in the press. Her publicist couldn't have been more pleased. Everyone knew that any pub was good pub, especially in Hollywood. Privately, their priorities were clear. The business relationship was most important. If either wanted to scratch the other's itch that was fine, but there were no expectations, no strings attached. Each was free to follow their own hearts and desires. Jett knew that Myles did this quite frequently and like Mocha, was rumored to swing both ways. For now Jett was content keeping company with Myles and cooking with the chef. The arrangement kept her satisfied. Those two and the occasional ride on Randall's big dick, which was better and more thrilling than any amusement park horsey, especially since it was infrequent. After hearing why she'd given him the heave-ho, he'd promised to be good. So far, he toed the line by not blowing up her phone with incessant calling or acting too much like a bitch when she refused his coming by. Though not assigned to her anymore on *Seeking Stardom*, he'd hung around the set a bit more than she'd like. Not quite obsessed but showing mild stalker tendencies. For now they were cool, but she'd be watching.

By far the best lover right now was her career. It was stroking her in all the right places. She was excited about the theme song that had been specifically written for her, designed to capture not only the hip-hop, R&B and pop markets but to make a dent into country music, too. Ever since Lil Nas had taken a stroll down Old Town Road, the company had been determined to cash in. The song had a contagious beat and a catchy hook that would work across genres. Rodeo would rope in the country fans. The rapper Fundamental would draw in the younger, hipper crowd. Jett would hold it down for the grown folk.

Life was good! She'd shocked Mocha and the sound engineer by not needing her rich, second-soprano voice auto-tuned and nailing her part in two takes. Rodeo's hook would be recorded in Nashville. Fundamental was laying tracks in Detroit. Not even mixed and the suits were excited about using the song, *Star Searchin'*, in all promotions and dropping it as a single in August as a teaser to the show's fall debut. They were also talking to Myles about songs for her full-length album. Two decades had passed since her career saw this kind of momentum. Television guest roles, commercials, a jingle here or there, and stage plays when they paid well had kept her from being homeless. In fact, more comfortable than many actors who worked steady nine-to-fives. But it had been a minute since she'd been able to experience what happened the other day on Fifth Avenue—placing something on the counter without knowing the price and being confident that whatever the total her card could cover it. All of this added up to an exciting, revitalized career that most people didn't get to see, whatever their calling.

Recording wrapped up late Friday night. The next morning, Myles left for Atlanta to spend the Memorial Day holiday with family. He invited her to join him but she declined. It had been years since she'd done the whole family gathering-BBQ-picnic sort of thing. Her family had never participated in the tradition of visiting gravesites and placing flowers. Aside from her grandmother in Texas, the small Scott family had never lost anyone close. Until now. Jett's mood changed as she went back to that awful day in March when she watched her mother's body being lowered into the ground. For all of their battles, an unshakable love had been there, too. Jett thought about Chantel. Maybe she'd fly to Kansas City so they could go together and visit the grave. A true bonding moment, albeit a sad one.

Jett called and got voicemail again. Anger replaced sadness, and a little worry, too. Where in the heck was her sister and why wasn't she calling back? She sent a text about coming to Kansas

City. Finally, a response. Chantel was out of town but would call her next week. Jett wondered where her sister was, and with whom? Funny how she never thought about Chantel having a life, a circle of friends and a lifetime of experiences Jett knew nothing about.

For the first time in years, Jett didn't have plans. In the past she spent the weekend performing at a Las Vegas or California casino or on the Queen Mary docked in Long Beach. A few years had been enjoyed in the Caribbean with whichever island cutie was her flavor of the moment. After several long moments scrolling through her contact list, Jett called one of her longtime East Coast tune-up friends. Gary was one of the few men Jett hooked up with who was around the same age. They'd met decades ago when Gary was in Hollywood chasing champagne wishes and caviar dreams. He made a decent living as a studio musician but after years of trying and not grabbing the brass ring of superstardom, he moved back east, got married, got a "real" job, had kids, lived like regular folk. Not at all the life for Jett, but the two kept in touch and after Gary's divorce would hook up if Jett was between men and they were on the same coast.

After spending a quiet weekend holed up with Gary in her plush hotel suite, and Monday on a yacht in the harbor, Jett headed home. Instead of a private jet she flew first-class commercial, but wasn't about to act like a spoiled celeb and complain about the downgrade. Being back in the studio had been nothing short of amazing. Surprisingly, Gary had provided a comfort she hadn't known was needed. He was a great listener, an adequate lover and had been genuinely sympathetic about Anna's death. Too bad she didn't feel anything for him beyond a friendly affection, and that his laid back, suburban lifestyle held little appeal. She'd never be a Helena Homemaker or Stay-At-Home Susie. With Chantel taking so long to respond, she also no longer felt like a Generous Jett.

An advance from the record company had added a few zeroes to Jett's bank account balance. Her call on Wednesday to Chantel had been to get her banking information or ask which cash transfer app she used. Jett knew Chantel struggled, and that Anna had left an estate in financial disarray. A few short months ago, Jett had been struggling, too. *Seeking Stardom* had changed all that. Having money brought an instant uplift to her attitude. She wanted to spread the feel good around.

Jett hadn't left those intentions in the message, had just said to call back. Chantel hadn't responded by phone or text. That wasn't like her. Once again it occurred to Jett how little she knew about Chantel's life. How in case of an emergency she didn't have the number of one soul she could call for information. Who were her friends? Where in Marquette did she live? Thankfully it was a small enough town that finding her wouldn't be too difficult. Now that Jett was in a better place all around—mentally, physically, financially—maybe she could make a little more time for the only family she had. She was open to it, unless something amazing like a movie deal or concert tour came along. When you had the kind of blind ambition Jett was born with, money, men and materializing dreams would always come first.

Jett preferred showers, but tonight as the limo ferried her from the airport home, she looked forward to a long, hot bath and Chinese from her favorite delivery hub. Randall would be over later. While in New York, he'd worn down her resistance with his sexting messages and tempting dick pics. After entering the home and having her luggage deposited, she poured sparkling water into a crystal goblet and headed to the master suite. She reached the top of the stairs, turned the corner, and almost gave the housekeeper a heart attack.

"Dios mío!" Lucia steadied herself against the wall, clutching her heart. "You're home a day early. The water was running. I didn't hear you come in."

"Sorry, Lucia. I should have called."

"No worries, ma'am. Last week, your sister. Today, you." Lucia chuckled as she shook her head. "You are definitely sisters. Both full of surprises."

Jett had continued down the hall toward the master suite's doors. This news had her all but moonwalking in her hurry to retrace the steps she'd just taken.

"You said my sister?"

"Yes, ma'am. Chantel."

"She called?"

Lucia slowly shook her head. "No. She was here."

"Here as in California?"

"Yes, here. At your house. She came here to—"

"Wait. Chantel was here? What did she want?"

"To look for the jewelry she thought had been dropped in the bedroom."

"She was in my house?"

Lucia, seeing the storm gathering in Jett's eyes, took a step backward. "She said it belonged to your mother, and that she'd spoken to you about it."

"She hasn't talked to me about shit! You let somebody in my house without my permission? While I was out of town?"

Chantel hasn't been returning my calls but took a flight to find a ring or a bracelet or some shit?

Somewhere it registered that her anger was misplaced, but Jett didn't care about that right now. Instead, she yelled louder.

"What was it she said belonged to Mama?"

Lucia half shrugged, half cowered, wringing her hands. "I didn't ask. She's your sister and said you two had talked. It didn't seem wrong for her to be here."

Jett took the step that allowed her to jab a manicured finger in Lucia's face. "Well, guess what. It seems wrong for you to be here. Get your shit and get out."

"Jett. Ma'am, please. I didn't know."

"Which is why you should have contacted me." Jett held out her hands. "Keys."

"Please, I'm so sorry. I really need the job."

"You should have thought about that before letting folk in my house without my permission. Give me the keys and get out!"

Tears shimmered in Lucia's eyes as she reached into her pocket and handed Jett the house key. She opened her mouth to say something. The scowl on Jett's face communicated the futility of that move. Hurriedly gathering the supplies she'd left in the hall bath, Lucia headed down the stairs and toward the side door she normally entered through.

Jett followed behind her. "Wait a minute."

Lucia turned, her expression hopeful. "Ma'am?"

"Tell me what happened."

Lucia recounted the previous week's events. "She seemed the same as before when she was here on vacation. Not like she shouldn't be here or that anything was wrong."

"And you say she was only here for a few minutes?"

"Yes. She went upstairs. I was cleaning the kitchen. It was quick, maybe five or ten minutes and she came back down, said she'd found what she was looking for and that she was going to visit friends. If I thought for even a minute that she shouldn't be here I would have never . . ." Lucia's shoulders heaved with the weight of despair. "Again, I apologize."

Jett's eyes narrowed. "Wait here."

She was up the stairs and in her master suite in a heartbeat. Hands on hips, she looked around for anything that would tip her off to Chantel's motives, anything out of place or that might have been left. Nothing. She strode into her massive dressing room, into the bathroom and the sitting area where she and her sister had shared conversation. There was no way Chantel could have known about the safe hidden behind the abstract picture she'd so admired. Jett removed the picture and opened the safe anyway. Inside was her $20k stash of emergency cash, along with her precious stones jewelry, important papers, and the handgun given to her by a police officer ex—fully loaded but never fired. Satisfied that nothing was missing following a final turn of the room, she repeated the same in the guest room that hadn't been used since Chantel and Artani. The room was organized, spotless, just like the master. Something else was going on. Jett was determined to put together the puzzle. Her life was too good right now. Almost perfect. She didn't need any scandals or shenanigans to mess up her groove.

She retrieved her phone, dialing Chantel's number as she headed downstairs. The call went to voicemail.

"Chantel, what the fuck is going on? What were you doing back here and why in the hell were you in my house? Lying to Lucia and saying we talked. I know your mother raised you better than to think any of that shit was okay. I hope you found whatever you left here because it's the last time you get through these doors unless I'm home. And maybe not even then."

Her voice lowered to a near growl. "Don't you *ever* come to my house again without permission as long as you're Black, understand? And trust me, any chance of my granting that is going to take a minute."

Jett punched the button to end the call, mumbling, "What in the hell was that about?"

"You know, Jett, I might have the answer. When your sister was here on vacation, she showed me a bracelet that came from your mom. Chantel said it meant a lot to her. Maybe that is what she left here."

"You clean that room every week. Did you see it?"

"No, but if it fell under the bed or behind a piece of furniture, I wouldn't have seen it. She had to know what she was looking for because she wasn't here long."

Lucia offered a nervous smile after sharing this theory. The more she talked, the more Lucia's explanation began to make sense. It didn't explain why Chantel hadn't returned her call or texted a response, but the housekeeper was right about how much Chantel loved Anna. Jett's relationship with their mother had been different. She'd never felt that deep maternal connection from Anna, the feeling of being not only loved but cherished. Had never been made to feel that in her mother's orbit she'd drawn the sun and hung the moon. Chantel and Anna had that. She'd witnessed it every time the three of them were together. A light came on in Anna's eyes when she spoke with Chantel that was never there when they conversed. Jett had resented Chantel in those moments, and pushed the jealousy so far down in her soul that she'd forgotten about it, and somewhere along the way it had turned into a resentment that widened the emotional distance between them. As Lucia relayed stories about the mother/daughter relationship that Chantel had shared, Jett could believe the unbelievable—that her sister would fly all the way out to California from Missouri, spend hundreds of dollars in airfare and, since she hadn't spent the night in her home, a hotel room, too, to look for a cherished piece of jewelry that had belonged to Anna and that she thought she'd lost.

Jett didn't fire Lucia. Given that Chantel was Jett's sister and Lucia had met her before, it was reasonable that she allowed her into the house. Randall called. She'd calmed down considerably, but the conversation had worn her out.

"Hey, Randall."

"I'm on my way over."

"Sorry, change of plans. I can't see you tonight."

"Why?" Said with way too much attitude for a canceled booty call.

Jett immediately ridged up. "I told you why. Change of plans."

"Is somebody else over there?"

"That's none of your business."

"Is it that Romeo-looking Mexican motherfucker? I know he's been over there."

"You know too much."

"I'm five minutes away. Let me hollah at you."

"You're going to make me start hollering in a second, and I don't think you'll like the words coming out of my mouth!"

"Dammit, Jett—"

She ended the call, then silenced her phone before the calm she'd just retrieved went scurrying away.

On Wednesday, *Seeking Stardom* tapings resumed. The competition rounds were serious fun. Jett didn't hear from Chantel, but Myles called with more good news. *Melanin Magic*, the newest magazine for women of color, wanted to feature her on the cover of their December edition, which would coincide with the release of the second single from her yet-to-be-recorded album. Jett hadn't been on a cover since appearing on a teen magazine during her TV sitcom's heyday. A December cover was the perfect choice. She'd wear one of her favorite designers for the shoot, which would involve the top stylist, hair, and makeup team. Chantel bringing her sneaky ass into the house was forgotten. Jett's life was back to being good. Until that evening in the limo, when she got around to opening the mail that her new personal assistant Zola had retrieved from her box on Ventura. Right up until she opened an envelope with a greeting card inside. A large sunflower with a smaller one beside it, the petals touching almost as if holding hands.

It had been a while since Jett had received fan mail, which almost never happened in this age of electronic transmission. She admired the card's warm, simple presentation, and made a mental note to add live, cut flowers to her home's décor. The dining room table would be perfect, as the patio doors beyond it let in bright, natural light.

Life was good, perfect, right up until the time she opened the card and read its brief inscription.

Mom, I get it now.

Jett's brow creased. She turned over the card, looked again at the envelope. There was no return address. Reexamining the card's interior, she realized none was needed. A simple cursive *C* was scrawled at the bottom of the card. Her stomach tightened and her insides flip-flopped as she re-read the first word of the simple inscription.

Mom.

Chantel knew the truth. But how?

She tossed the card onto the bar counter, got up, and began to pace. Chantel had only guessed the truth, Jett decided. She didn't, couldn't know for sure. Because if she knew, the public could find out. Jett wouldn't allow that to happen. She was presenting her rebranded self to the world. Had gotten sexy, classy back and wasn't ready to replace that with maternal elder. Hadn't she told Mocha not to call her ma?

If she were honest with herself, Jett would have to admit that she never expected this day to come. Never thought she'd have to reconcile with the choices she'd made as a teen, or admit the truth. She hadn't raised Chantel, but she'd given her life. She was a mother, even though for all intents and purposes, Anna had been Chantel's real mom. Jett was and intended to remain her big sister. It wasn't true, but the lie had been repeated so often and lived out so well that Jett believed it, too.

Hers had been an easy pregnancy with a quick delivery. Barely two months after having Chantel, Jett was in Los Angeles being prepped for stardom. Six months later she'd won a televised talent competition and was thrust into the public eye as the latest sensation. By then Jett hardly even remembered what being pregnant felt like. It was as though it had never happened.

And if she had anything to say about it, life would remain that way. She had to convince Chantel that the phantom girl in Texas—Simone, not Jett—was the one who'd had her and then given her up for adoption. Walking over to where she'd tossed her purse on the couch, she retrieved her phone, then went back over to the bar and picked up the envelope and the card. Only then did she realize that the envelope wasn't empty. She put down her phone and pulled out a single folded piece of paper. She read the company letterhead. Her stomach plunged all the way down to her toes.

Midwest Health & Diagnostics

In an instant the true motives behind Chantel's recent actions became clear. The casual questioning in their last phone call. The clandestine visit conveniently planned when Chantel knew Jett would be in New York. The subsequent silence until she'd proven what she believed, then mailed said proof inside the cute, cryptic card.

Jett's anger increased with every thought. She snatched up her phone, angrily tapped the buttons on its face, and placed the call on speaker. She marched up the stairs. The rings seemed to reverberate along the narrowed walls. The phone rang and rang.

Coward.

Just when Jett was about to disconnect the call to dial again, Chantel answered.

"Hello, Mother," was the greeting, in a tone tinged with sarcasm and sadness.

Jett had no time for compassion or pity. Her dreams were on the line.

"Bitch, you've got some kind of nerve!"

Chantel said nothing. The call disconnected.

Did that conniving heffah just hang up on me?

She looked at the now blank face and got the answer. Yes, Chantel had hung up. Jett called again. It went straight to voicemail. Jett hurled out a string of expletives, her anger now through the roof. She threw the phone against the wall, shattering the face. Cracking the body. She paced the length of her master suite much as she had the open concept space below, her mind racing. What was Chantel trying to pull? What did she want? How could Jett keep her quiet about the truth she'd discovered, and keep her secret hidden?

Hours later, after receiving a strange phone call, Jett's eyes narrowed as she considered her options regarding Chantel and the truth she'd uncovered and obviously spread. One possibility brought back memories of her days with Hot Linkz and his crew, and how well they could take care of business. Little sister didn't want to make her go there, engage a little use of force to make her newly minted daughter keep her mouth shut. Nothing was going to get in the way of the success of *Seeking Stardom* or the drop of her album. It had been a while since she rode gangster, but Jett could still find her way to the hood.

Chapter 12
Ready or Not

Since the moment she'd mailed the card with the DNA results enclosed, Chantel had expected Jett's phone call. She knew her sister—mother?—would be upset and angry about how she'd gone about getting the truth. Had imagined several reactions. Being called a bitch wasn't one of them. She hadn't been prepared for that level of attitude, as though Jett was the victim. Seriously? Chantel refused to be disrespected, but desperately wanted a conversation with Jett. There were so many questions. She took a deep breath and hoped for the best.

"Good morning."

"Bitch, you'd better not hang up on—"

Click.

Obviously, having a night to sleep on their new paradigm hadn't dimmed Jett's anger one bit. Chantel understood her sister's shock. How did Jett think she felt? But what her sister/mother wasn't going to do was make her feel worse than she already had by disrespectfully cursing her out first thing in the morning.

A few minutes later, the phone rang again.

"Jett, I know you—"

"You don't know a got damn—"

Click.

Chantel sent a text.

I know you're angry. I'm feeling all kinds of ways myself. We need to have a conversation. I want to talk. Not argue.

The phone rang again.

After a brief hesitation, Chantel tapped the call button. She didn't speak.

"Chantel?"

Chantel heaved a sigh of relief. "That's my name."

"Bitch! You'd better not—"

Click.

Over the next couple days, Chantel refused to take Jett's calls or continue those that began with a variety of curse words. She knew it was a gamble, but she also requested another weekend off from the club. When Terrence asked what he should tell King if asked, Chantel suggested the truth. She wasn't in a partying mood. She was drained. Confused. Hurt. Angry. Depressed. This week she'd seen a different side of her sister. Angry, threatening, unforgiving, mean. She shouldn't have been surprised. Wasn't Jett giving away her daughter, basically abandoning her mother, leaving the city, and not looking back proof enough that she thought only of herself? Obviously, and for Chantel that was a shame. Had she not once thought about what her daughter was experiencing? What it was like for Chantel to discover the truth behind not only the lie that Anna told but the one Jett created? Did Chantel want to speak with Jett? Absolutely! Did she think they could have a civil conversation? Possibly. But Jett was going to have to get over herself. In Chantel's mind she owed Jett nothing. It was the other way around.

There were other reasons Chantel avoided this version of Jett. She feared being rejected twice, even cut off altogether. She wondered if she truly wanted to know how Jett felt. Jett left the Midwest shortly after Chantel was born. The two were never close. Still, Chantel had always been in awe of Jett, the high-profile sister on television, with hit songs on the radio, listened to by Chantel and her friends. The one who on those rare home visits always brought excitement and fun. Chantel now felt an emotion from Jett that bordered on hate. She felt she could handle being ignored by Jett more than she could being hated by her.

Since finding out that Jett was her mother, a million thoughts and emotions had continuously vied for attention in Chantel's head. Mental videos of the past several months' events played on a loop in her head. Anna's death. The funeral. LA and spending time with Jett. The discovery. That scene of finding the birth certificate at the bottom of the wooden chest replayed a lot.

And words. A million of them—churning, haunting, reverberating—in her mind. Conversations with Anna, especially the mother/daughter kind. Tight-lipped Blanche, her mother's best friend. Snatches of talks with Jett in LA. How her four-year-old son had absorbed his aunt's fantastical stories with adoring eyes. Encouragement from Rita. Hard questions Terrence asked. And the words that had upended life as she knew it.

Your mom was in an accident.

I'm sorry to inform you that . . .

Chantel shook the doctor's final declaration from her memory. It was immediately replaced by even more transformative words. Those that had jumped out from the piece of faded paper she'd found listing Texas, not Missouri, as her birthplace and Jett, not Anna, as her mom.

She tiptoed into Artani's room, smiling as she observed her sleeping son. She envied how he could be deep asleep in minutes and sleep the whole night through. Being careful to avoid a myriad of toys and books scattered across the floor, she reached the closet and pulled out the hamper of dirty clothes. After sorting them and beginning the first load she went into the living room and turned on the television. She flipped to an entertainment news show, wondering if she'd see her sister. Even with the DNA results as proof, Chantel couldn't relate to Jett in any other way. Anna would always be her mother. As for what type of relationship she and Jett would develop, only time would tell.

She turned on the television and scrolled through over one hundred channels. Nothing exciting, interesting, or distracting enough to catch her eye. She switched to her streaming platforms. Tried to get into a good movie starring Common, one of her fantasy husbands. Didn't work. The video on constant replay in her mind trumped all other images. Her trip to Los Angeles and all that had happened since gaining the proof she needed to verify that Jett—not Anna, not a fake distant relative named Simone—was her biological mom. After watching a third of the movie and not having a clue what it was about, Chantel shut off the television and pushed off the couch to get her cell phone. She called Rita and got voicemail.

"Hey, sis, it's me. Are you still out of town? Give me a call when you get this. Want to run a few thoughts by you. Okay, bye."

Still feeling restless, and a bit hungry, Chantel went into the kitchen in search of a tasty distraction. Popcorn? No. Frozen dinner? Hell, no. Chicken hadn't sounded good when she stopped at their favorite drive-thru for Artani's nuggets and fries, but now Chantel wished she'd ordered something heartier than the shake she'd called dinner. After opening a few more cabinet doors and the refrigerator door—twice—and taking a long peek into the freezer, she decided on a pizza. She checked the laundry, placed the first load in the dryer, a second one in the washer, and then decided to take a shower before the pizza arrived.

She'd just finished drying off and was picking out her curls when the doorbell rang. It was too soon for the pizza. Had to be Rita. Chantel slipped into flip-flops and reached for the mini muumuu hooked to the bathroom door, threw it over her head, and adjusted it around her body as she walked down the hall. She caught a glimpse of herself in the mirror hanging not far from the front door. Wild hair. Bare face. Bags under her eyes from fitful sleeping. She looked a hot mess.

Glancing through the peephole was more from habit than anything, especially since she knew who was on the other side. Or so she thought, before realizing the strong shoulders above the broad back blocking her vision couldn't belong to her petite friend. The person stepped back, revealing the man's face. Chantel's hand flew to her unruly hair. The other tugged on the dress bodice to make sure her girls were covered and secure. The doorbell rang again.

Chantel jerked open the door. "Boy! What are you doing coming by my house without calling?"

She froze as the words she spoke reverberated back to her, remembering how her sister had asked a similar question in one of the as yet unreturned voicemails.

"You in the middle of something illegal or got a man in the house? No, it's not my business, but you look guilty as hell."

Chantel sighed. "Shut up, Terrence. Why aren't you at the club?"

"Came here to check on your ass, literally."

She turned and walked down the hall into the living room, hearing Terrence's footsteps behind her. Feeling the satiny caftan fabric move across her bare skin, she became self-conscious of her big, jiggling booty, sure that if she investigated, she'd find Terrence's eyes fixated on it.

"Damn, it's juicy."

Chantel whipped around. "I knew it!" She said, with as close to a laugh as she'd produced in days. "You are so uncouth."

"I'm a booty man, what can I say."

"You're a drool-over-any-woman's-body-parts man, almost a pervert. You need to watch that shit."

Terrence grabbed her from behind. Chantel squealed.

"Come on, girl, let me get some of this brown sugar." His exaggerated dry humping made Chantel laugh out loud. The action relaxed her. Only then did she realize how tense her shoulders were, that they'd been carrying the stress not found in her neck. Sure, when Terrence rescued her from an unexpected meeting with concrete after almost fainting behind the Jett-was-her-mother revelation, she'd appreciated the feel of his arms around her. His strength had become her own. That was then. This was now. In this moment of clear thinking, Terrence was still the playa-play play on she'd known for most of her life. Reaching up, she gave the muscles a squeeze and swiveled her head around.

"Here, let me do that."

"Terrence, quit." Chantel swatted his hand. "You're always trying to get some, and I already told you, I want no part of that public peen."

"Public? Girl, what are you talking about?"

Chantel retrieved a band from the bathroom and tamed her curls. Terrence had followed her down that hall, too.

"Where are you going?"

"Wherever you are."

"Terrence, go sit your butt down in the living room. I'll be right back. And don't be nosy," she added over her shoulder, aimed at his retreating back.

After throwing on a pair of sweats and the oversized Lakers tee she'd bought in LA, Chantel returned to the living room.

"I don't know why you come over here acting all innocent. You've screwed half the women that come in the club, or go to the gym, or live in Marquette. Try and deny it."

"I don't have to try because that's not true."

Chantel rolled her eyes. She grabbed her phone from the table. "When did you call me?"

"When I was on my way over."

"Why aren't you working?'

"The band just went on. I asked Walter's brother to hold it

down until I got back. He's been trying to get a job over there anyway. I'm thinking of bringing him on part time." He watched her face change when she saw his missed call. "Glad you can see that I was brought up with manners. It's not my fault you didn't answer the phone."

"I was . . . never mind."

Terrence's eyes swept her body. "I know what you were doing. Sorry I wasn't there to scrub your back. I could still massage your feet, though."

The sexy in his voice caused muscles to clench in spaces growing dusty from lack of use. The reaction wasn't totally unexpected. Still, Chantel dismissed it outright.

"What was so important that it warranted a visit instead of a phone call?"

"You're about to lose your job."

This got Chantel's attention. She sat across from where Terrence had sat on the couch. "What are you talking about?"

"King's at the club. I had a feeling he'd be there."

"Didn't Jasmine agree to work this weekend?"

"That's exactly my point. She killed it last weekend. Holiday crowd, the place was packed. Her pro-baller husband and their bougie, semi-celebrity friends giving the place status, probably donating to his mayoral campaign. Snoozin' is losin', that's all I'm saying."

"Did Nate say something specific about replacing me?"

"No but he definitely asked about you and wanted more details on why you weren't there."

"Did he forget I lost my mom?"

"That's the first thing I mentioned. He hadn't forgotten. I told him you were handling her affairs and let him assume that you not being at the club had to do with that."

"Did it work?"

"That explanation seemed to satisfy him, at least for now. It's only been what, barely two months?"

Chantel nodded. "He was probably comparing my show to Jasmine's undoubtedly flawless performance."

Terrence thought for a long moment, rubbing his chin. "No, he seemed genuinely concerned. I am, too."

"Why?"

"Because you've been back from LA for almost a week and still haven't told me what happened. Did you confront your sister? Is that why you're over here looking tore up from the floor up?"

"I hate you." Chantel laughed even as she shook her head. "Jett was in New York."

"Didn't she know you were coming? Oh. Probably not." He thought on that for a second. "Why did you go out there knowing she was somewhere else?"

"To get proof that she is really my birth mother."

"A birth certificate with her name on it wasn't enough?"

That comment drew a side-eye. "I have one that says Anna is my mother. That wasn't true."

"That's a good point."

"What's so good about it?"

"You know what I mean." Terrence turned to face her more fully. "Did you get the proof you were looking for?" Chantel nodded. "What?"

"DNA."

"Word?" Terrence's look was a mix of surprise and respect. "Damn, shorty. I thought you said you didn't watch *CSI*."

"I don't. I watch *Maury*."

"Did you get it?" Chantel nodded. "How?"

"By retrieving some of her personal items."

"You just got back from LA, though. I thought those tests took a long time to process."

"Sometimes they do."

"How did you get yours results back so fast?"

"As soon as I returned, I drove directly to Midwest Health and Diagnostics, paid an additional two hundred and fifty dollars to have the test expedited and gave the technician what I'd brought back."

"Oh, so it was you who needed the money."

"Huh?"

"Don't act like you don't know what I'm talking about. The money Rita borrowed from me a while back. It was for you."

"You're Blessed?"

Terrence deepened his voice. "Definitely."

"I'm not playing. A month or so ago I received a Cashapp payment from an account called Blessed. That's you?"

Terrence nodded.

"So much for asking a friend to keep a confidence."

"Rita didn't tell me anything, if that's what you're thinking. She asked to borrow the money for herself. That didn't make sense. Sean's a damn good engineer who's been on the job for twenty years. They don't need money. He also keeps those purse strings pulled tight, which is why they don't ever need it. I thought she might have borrowed it for you, that you'd gone overboard in LA and needed to pay bills or something. Feels good to know that it went for something even better—helping you get answers about where you came from. Stop being so proud and independent, Chantel. I'm happy to help you. You don't even have to pay that back."

"I'll pay it back."

Chantel meant these words but had no idea how it would happen, especially since a payday loan had paid for this second DNA test. A drug dealer would have given her better interest rates.

Terrence shrugged. "Suit yourself. So you got something with your sister's DNA on it. Like . . ."

"A Kleenex from her bedroom—thank goodness her thorough housekeeper hadn't yet cleaned her room—and a floss pick from the trash."

"Damn girl, that's gangster! I'm impressed."

"You impress easy. Want something to drink?"

"Got any beer?"

"Why do you keep asking me that?" Chantel asked, her hand resting on a sizeable hip. "I don't drink beer."

"Doesn't mean you shouldn't stock some for the occasional visitor who does."

"How about a glass of wine?"

"Wine is for sissies . . . if you're a dude."

"Whatever."

Chantel went into the kitchen and returned with a glass of wine for her and a cola for Terrence. Instead of returning to the chair, she joined him on the couch.

"So, Chantel. If Jett was pregnant, who was her baby daddy?" Terrence spoke rapid fire, running the words together.

Chantel laughed in spite of herself. "Has anyone ever told you that you are a fool?"

"Never hurts to be reminded."

"Anyway, you asked a good question. I haven't gotten that far. Still reeling from finding out that Jett is my mom." She set down her wineglass and rubbed her temples. All this thinking was about to make her head explode. The doorbell rang. Chantel got up to answer it.

"Who's that?" Terrence asked.

"Pizza."

Terrence's voice boomed down the hall as she walked. "Hope you bought a large. I'm hungry!"

Chantel didn't bother with the peephole. She was sure a man holding her favorite meat-filled pie was standing outside. Opening the door, her expression changed. Her boss was at the door.

"Phil?"

"No, you're not fired. I ran by the office to handle a few things and saw this in the mailbox. Not sure why it came to the paper instead of your house but thought it might be something important, so . . ." He held out a small manila envelope.

"You didn't have to come all the way over here."

"Well, coming halfway would have thwarted the effort so . . ."

"You know what I mean." She took the envelope. "Thanks."

"No problem. It looks like someone just placed it in the box. There was no postage. So I thought it might be important, maybe a lead to a juicy story."

Chantel chuckled. "I doubt it. Thanks again."

After checking to see if there was a delivery car close by, Chantel closed the door. She walked down the hall and reentered the living room, examining the envelope with a frown on her face.

"What's that?"

Chantel shrugged, ripping off the end of the catalog envelope, only slightly larger than the business envelopes companies regularly used to send out threatening notices to the debtors from whom they were trying to collect. She reached in and pulled out a single white sheet of paper, folded in half.

She tossed the envelope toward the coffee table, her eyes glued to the paper. It missed the mark and fell to the floor. A few seconds later, Chantel wanted to do the same thing. Instead, she plopped into a chair.

"What. The. Hell?"

Terrence was on his feet in an instant, and standing beside her. "What is it, Chan?"

" 'Now you know the truth,' " she read in a low voice full of pissed-all-the-way-off. " 'How much is it worth to keep the secret?' "

She snatched the envelope off the floor, examining it more closely this time.

"Let me see that." Terrence pulled the paper out of her hand and stared at the short, simple sentences typed in a large, bold font. He peered over Chantel's shoulder to see the envelope.

"It's not addressed."

"No shit, Sherlock." Said with mild sarcasm as Chantel's eyes stared straight ahead before slowly sliding over to bore into him.

"What?"

"No address means it wasn't mailed."

"Who was at the door?"

"My boss."

"Somebody brought that shit to your job?"

"Evidently."

"That's crazy, Chantel. Sounds like blackmail. But how can someone threaten you with information that you just found out?"

"That's a very good question." She gave Terrence another look. Her eyes narrowed slightly. "Only two people here knew."

Terrence looked at Chantel. "And?"

"Rita's out of town."

"I'm in your house." Terrence's gaze turned intense. Chantel looked away. "What are you insinuating?"

She didn't answer. He took a step back. "That I had something to do with it?"

Chantel couldn't voice the thought that was obviously written all over her face.

Terrence strode toward the door. "I'm outta here."

"Terrence, wait!" Chantel hurried after him, but anger had added another foot to the six-foot brother's strides. "I'm not saying you did it, but . . . Terrence!"

He didn't stop or turn around, and nimbly sidestepped the pizza delivery man coming up the sidewalk. Both she and the pizza man watched as Terrence hopped in his gold-rimmed black Jeep, started it up, and rolled down the block.

"Here you go, ma'am, large meat and veggie with extra cheese."

She watched as Terrence reached the end of the block, and saw the taillights disappear. "Let me get my purse," she said, walking toward the porch. "Wait here."

Chantel paid for the pizza, walked back inside, and placed it on the kitchen counter. Her appetite had fled faster than Terrence had. Her suspicions about him? Not so much. On one hand, she couldn't imagine Terrence threatening her, or anybody else for that matter. On the other, who else could it be? If he was innocent, why get so angry and leave so quickly?

Because you just accused him of blackmail, a man who's been nothing but kind to you, who you've known for more than twenty-five years.

She reached for her phone to call and apologize, and saw she'd missed a call. As she tapped the screen, the name jumped out. Chantel immediately slid her thumb and hit redial. The conversation with Terrence would have to wait.

It was time to return the call she'd missed. It was time to talk with her mother.

Chapter 13
Not Gon' Cry

Chantel tapped the number before she could change her mind. She paced the room, holding her breath as tightly as she did the phone, her mind blank. That was probably a good thing.

"You don't answer the phone when I call and now you've got jokes?"

Jokes?

"Jett, can we have a civil conversation without accusations and name calling? I don't know about any jokes, but we really need to talk."

"We sure as hell do."

"I want to talk, not argue or get cursed out."

"I've calmed down enough to not want to jack you up. Though you have to admit, little sister"—with emphasis on that word—"that you sneaking in my house and going through my things while I was out of town was not only wrong, but criminal."

That's what you're focused on? That I was in your house, not once in your womb?

Chantel wanted to point out that Lucia readily invited her in and that the last time she checked no one had been arrested for stealing a sibling's trash. But since they were indeed having what amounted to a conversation, and there was much more Chantel needed to know and wanted to say, she swallowed a mouth full of sarcasm and went for a more acceptable response.

"You're right." She didn't have to work to make the words sound contrite. "I'm sorry for how I handled proving you are the woman who gave birth to me. After the way you lied, that story you made up about some girl in Texas, I felt it was my only choice."

"That I wasn't forthcoming should have told you something."

"I came up with many reasons why you lied, none of them good. But I had to know. More than that, I felt that as a thirty-three-year-old grown-ass woman, sorry for cursing, I deserved to know the truth."

"Is that why after finding out, your actions as a grown-ass woman, no apology, was to send the results in the mail with a card? Try and threaten me with this 'you're my mom' bullshit?"

"You believe my calling you mom in that card was a threat?"

"Don't play stupid, Chantel. Not the card, the voicemail."

"I never threatened you in a voicemail."

"Girl, please. Obviously you've watched too many movies, using one of those devices to disguise your voice. You forget I know how badly you need money, if as often as you try and hit me up is any indication. Had you returned the call I made while in New York, instead of flying out here and playing detective, you would have known I had planned to send you some money. Had called to get your routing number or CashApp name. But after this last stunt you pulled, I'm not going to send you shit."

"I swear to you, Jett. I haven't left any kind of voicemail, not recently. In fact, I received a similar threat and thought you might know something about it."

"Someone called you?"

Chantel could tell by the change in Jett's tone that she'd finally touched an inquisitive nerve.

"Someone dropped off an envelope at my job. Hold on." Chantel retrieved the single paper and read it out loud.

"That was it?"

"Yep."

"And it was dropped off, not mailed?"

"I found that interesting, too."

"It's also very telling. Either you or someone you've talked to about this is trying to cash in." A short pause and then Jett asked, "Who all have you told that I'm . . . that I had a baby?"

"Only two people, both close friends for a very long time."

"Why'd you have to tell anybody?"

The attitude was back.

Chantel recognized another emotion bubbling up inside her, one she'd felt since finding out but hadn't consciously identified. Hurt. The revelation that Jett and not Anna was her mother hurt deeply. It cut to the core of her very identity, because the woman on the other end of the line had yet to acknowledge the truth, or her. Had yet to act as if she gave a good gotdamn about how Chantel felt, or how this secret, now exposed, had changed everything she thought she knew about life. In the next second a thought entered that slowed Chantel's rising ire. How had her unexpected arrival impacted her sister? How much of Jeanetta was left behind to become Jett, and why were those parts no longer connected?

"The two people I told are like family. I'd trust them with my life, with Artani. Finding out that you, not Anna, are my biological mother rocked my world, made me question everything about myself that I thought I knew. The day I found out, I actually fainted. Rita and Terrence helped me start breathing again."

"Rita and Terrence, huh. Which one of them is in financial trouble?"

"I can understand you thinking it's one of them behind this, Jett. My mind went there, too. I even confronted Terrence about it."

"And?"

"The look on his face told me all I needed to know. He was hurt I'd even had the nerve to ask him that. We've been friends over twenty-five years."

"Friends with you, not me."

"He's not behind this, Jett. Rita isn't either."

"You've spoken with her?"

"Not yet, but I know her. She'd never do anything like what's going on here. Maybe it's someone you know."

"You said that note came to your job, right?"

"Yes, someone slipped it into the mailbox."

"When?"

"I don't know. Didn't think to ask."

"Someone else found the envelope?" Jett tsked. "Whoever brought it to you is probably the culprit."

"It was my boss, so I doubt it. If Phil uncovered something like this, he wouldn't bring it to me. He'd put a reporter on it, track down the facts, and run it as a leading story."

"You work for a magazine?"

"Newspaper. The *Marquette Monitor*, and before you ask, no. There's no way anyone at my job knows about something I only recently discovered. Most of them know you're my sister. Anyone who grew up in Marquette knows that."

The two were quiet for a moment.

"What about you, Jett? Who were you friends with when you got pregnant?"

"No one who'd have my cell phone number, which is getting changed tomorrow, just so you know. I'll text you from it so you can lock it in. Don't give it to anybody. As far as my current friends and associates, they are completely unaware of my past, especially my personal life. When I arrived on the West Coast, Gerald felt that the less people knew about my Midwestern roots, the better. My bio says I grew up in LA, and in a way, I did."

The past. Midwestern roots. That part of her life she didn't want to be reminded of or have anyone else know about was at the crux of the matter. Perhaps understanding Jett's past could help Chantel navigate the present.

"Can we talk about that past, Jett? The part of it that involves me?"

There was a long pause before she answered. "What good would that do? People should let what happened in the past stay there."

"I didn't go searching for yesterday. The past jumped out of a chest Mama owned and slapped me in the face. Try to imagine how it would feel to discover Anna wasn't your mother. That it was someone you'd known in a whole other way; someone who because of circumstances and distance was practically a stranger. I have so many questions, Jett, about . . . everything."

"Like what?"

"Why you gave me away. Why you stayed away. Why you ran away. Who is my father?"

"I didn't run. I was discovered and brought to Hollywood."

Chantel thought the timing convenient but, okay.

"Why didn't Mama tell me the truth?"

"You know what, Chantel? There are worse things than not having all the information you think that you need. Sometimes not knowing is better than finding out."

Chantel plopped on the couch. She imagined trying to extract information from her sister was harder than pulling teeth with a pair of paper scissors.

"Jett, I don't even know what that means."

"It means that the part of my life when you were conceived and born was a very painful, lonely one for me. Having you believe my mother was also your mother was best for everybody."

"Except maybe for the baby who didn't have a voice. Don't you think that after all these years I have a right to understand how all of this happened? Why you gave me up and why all of the secrecy around it?"

"Just let it go, Chantel."

"No, I won't!" She jumped up from the couch, in that moment too frustrated to care that her voice was raised and Artani was sleeping. She stopped, took a breath, and began again in a calmer tone. "Sorry about hollering, Jett."

Chantel worked to calm down as she paced the room. "What I mean is, I won't let it go because I can't. Since learning the truth I've thought of little else. Maybe knowing a bit more about the circumstances surrounding your pregnancy will help me feel more like a participant in an unfortunate situation and less like someone thrown away like trash."

"That's how Mama made you feel?"

"Mama? No, Jett. You gave me to the only person I could ever imagine as my mother. But her love doesn't cover the fact that you had me and then left without a backward glance. Like having a baby meant nothing to you at all. Like I meant nothing. I know it's not true, but that's what plays in my mind since I learned the truth."

She stopped pacing to collect her thoughts. "If you don't tell me, I'm sure there's at least one person who can give me answers, and that's whoever left a message on your voicemail and a note in my box."

"You go looking for trouble and you just might find it."

"Now who's issuing threats?"

"I don't issue threats, baby girl. What happened a long time ago doesn't matter. Leave it alone."

"Why?"

"I don't need this right now! And neither do you."

"That's easy for you to say. You know the identities of both your parents. Who is my father?"

Silence.

"Do you know who it is?"

"What the fuck kind of question is that?"

"Jett, I'm not judging. But I remember that woman at the gravesite calling you out of your name."

"Brenda considered herself a church girl. Everybody with a boyfriend was a whore to her."

Brenda. Chantel made a mental note of the name.

"Then why don't you want to tell me my father's name? I'm too old for child support."

A sigh and then . . . nothing.

Chantel was once again losing her patience. "Why don't you want to talk about it?"

"Because I was raped, that's why!"

Chantel's ears started ringing. All the air left the room. She walked over to the couch and slowly sat down. That piece of the puzzle was completely unexpected. But with it, the picture started coming together enough for her to begin to understand what it was.

"You were . . . oh my God. So that's what you meant by saying Simone's pregnancy was complicated?"

The phone went silent, as though it had disconnected. Chantel looked down. The call was live. Jett must have muted herself. Was she upset? Crying and not wanting Chantel to know? Reliving that kind of trauma had to be upsetting. Even though she had a right to the answer, she now wished the question hadn't been asked. But it had been asked and it deserved an answer. The best way to handle pain was to deal with it.

"I'm sorry, Jett. I had no idea."

"Of course you didn't."

"Was this in Kansas City? How did it happen? Who was it?"

"Damn! Even after forcing me to relive a nightmare, the questions just keep on coming!"

"I'm just trying to understand where I come from, my roots.

We're both hurting. I think talking about it and working through it is the only way to heal."

Chantel could hear Jett take a deep breath.

"Maybe you're right. Here's the deal. I'm going to share this one time and then we're going to close the book on this mother-fucker, do you hear me?"

"I hear you."

"Okay, here's what happened. Me and a friend went out one night. We were hanging out with some boys, one a dude from out of town. Alcohol and weed were involved. I was flirting with the out-of-town guy. Things went further than I wanted them to go. Told him to stop. He didn't listen. The next month I missed my period, and the month after that. Took a test. It came back with two stripes. Took another one. Same thing. Finally had to tell Mama. She took me to the doctor for a third confirmation. By then, I was almost seven months. Two weeks later we were on the road to Texas. Mama left a few days later. I stayed until the baby came."

Jett stopped talking. She'd delivered the facts as though reading a clinical textbook. No feeling. No emotion. As though the story happened to someone else.

"What did Grandma say about it?"

"Not much."

"But she . . . did she treat you okay?"

"She didn't beat me. I didn't go hungry. But if you're asking if she was thrilled to learn that her fifteen-year-old grandchild was about to have a baby, the answer is no."

"Was Mom with you when you had me?"

"Mama was there. Any more questions?"

Asked sarcastically. Chantel understood. "A thousand more, but for now, just one. Who was the guy that . . . guess you couldn't call him a father . . . who assaulted you?"

"Ha!" The laugh sounded coarse and held no humor. "I tried

to forget everything I ever knew about that motherfucker, including his got damn name. Charlie. Billy. Larry. Henry. Hell, I don't remember."

"Seriously? Some guy raped you and you don't remember his name?"

"My mind went blank. I think it's the brain's way of protecting itself."

"I know it's crazy for me to feel guilty, but I'm so sorry that all of this happened to you. Since you don't remember him, there were never any charges. Someone did an act that horrible and was never even prosecuted. That's effed up."

"Everything happens for a reason. It's how you came to be."

"I'm really sorry, Jett. I totally get it now. Why you left and almost never come back here. All of the secrecy. Why you didn't want anyone to know that you had a child. Why you didn't want me."

Chantel pinched herself hard to stop the tears that threatened just above her eyelids. "I feel bad for dredging all of this up. On the other hand, I'm at least glad to know the truth. Thanks for that."

"You're welcome. Look, about this blackmail situation. You need to talk to your friends, find out which one of them has been running their mouth and to whom. Somebody put a note in your box, which means that somebody in that town knows what's up. I'm not coming off any money, nor am I going to have my career ruined on some bullshit. I don't have to tell you what a special time this is for me right now. *Seeking Stardom* is being test-marketed and getting great reviews. I've been offered a record deal."

"What? Jett, that's amazing!"

"It is pretty cool. They want to brand me as a Whitney Houston type, early in her career, before all the scandal. Sophisticated. Classy. I've been warned to not have any crazy news stories come out about me and have promised them I'll be on my best behavior."

Chantel didn't miss how seconds after revealing truths that had her ready to break down, Jett had switched back to her and that damned career without missing so much as a beat. Even in this moment, it was all about her.

"You think that news of you being a mother would ruin your career?"

"No, but a scandal would. And that is how the media would play this out . . . as something scandalous."

"I don't know who's behind that note, Jett, or the voicemail."

"You'd better find out. I have friends who aren't so nice. One way or another, I'm going to nip this problem in the bud before it has a chance to bloom."

"I don't want any trouble either. Gossip flows like water in this small town. I work for the local paper. The last thing I want to do is wind up on the front page."

"Tell your friends what I said. They need to back the hell up."

"I'll ask them again, Jett, but I promise you. This isn't the work of my friends."

"I've got to go."

"Are you going to be all right?"

"Are you?"

"We'll see. Bye—"

"Don't you dare."

Don't call you mama? Her angered tone broke Chantel's heart. "Bye, Jett."

Jett hung up with no goodbye. Chantel scrolled to Rita's number and was about to call her. Instead, she went into the kitchen and poured a glass of wine. Before learning the truth of her birth, Chantel rarely drank outside of the club or hanging out with friends. She wasn't heading down the road Papa traveled, but could now better empathize with the town drunk, could better understand how tragedy had driven him to that terrible place. There was Alcoholics Anonymous for problem drinkers. Was there a Find-Out-Your-Mama-Ain't-Your-Mama group she could attend? She grabbed the now empty bottle from the counter, threw it in the trash, and checked her cabinets for another bottle she might have forgotten. Because to fully process being the product, the unwanted result, of a sexual assault, Chantel was going to need more wine.

Chapter 14
Remember the Time

Jett held the silent phone in her hand. For a while she didn't move, hardly breathed. Finally she tapped her phone, went to a search engine, and typed in the name she told Chantel she'd forgotten. The name of a man she could never forget even if she tried. The man who, when told he had a child coming, denied even knowing her, let alone having sex. The man who'd threatened her to keep her mouth shut or else. Her first heartthrob. Her first heartbreak.

King Richardson.

The internet was full of news about him—the prolific litigator, the successful attorney. And running for mayor? Wow.

Jett smiled as bittersweet memories flowed into her mind. King always was a smooth talker. It didn't surprise Jett that he'd made a career out of running his mouth. She was almost certain that given his family tree he wasn't hurting for money. But life was full of surprises. Anything could happen. A part of her had hoped the family's fortunes had changed. That the mighty Richardsons had been knocked off their high, haughty horse. She put in the names of his mom and dad, King, Jr. and Millicent. It appeared they were still alive and thriving, still upstanding members of high society, though King had retired as a judge. There was a sister, too.

What was her name? Jett couldn't remember but was almost certain she'd be married with children by now. Along with his law firm and several professional memberships, including the Boule, King was on the board of his family's foundation, one created to reduce recidivism among teenage boys. He had a wife and three children—two sons and a daughter.

Two daughters, asshole. So make that four children.

Jett tossed down the phone and cursed Chantel for unlocking a door she'd bolted decades ago. The dam had been broken. Memories flooded in. Those years as a preteen and then teenager, when she thought she was the sun the earth revolved around and her mama was "old" and didn't know nothing. She and Anna fought almost every day. She rebelled often in a defiance that included the boys her mother tried to tell her were up to no good. Boys like King, who was twenty-six or seven when they had sex. Technically, he'd been guilty of statutory rape. Also, technically, she'd wanted to be with him. Whether or not she'd been an unwilling participant could have been hotly debated. Jett wasn't at all sure her story would have held up in court.

Jett hadn't thought about that night in decades. Still, it came back as vividly as though it had only happened yesterday. King, driving his brand-new black Camaro, showing his California cousin how Kansas City got down. She'd met him a couple months earlier, when she and another fast girl, Yvette, had used fake IDs to go clubbing. Jett was hooked from the moment she saw him—tall, toned, fine as all get-out. He smiled and she was under his spell. They danced, and she was hooked. Long, flirty phone calls followed, along with a few nude pics taken and developed instantly via the Polaroid Swinger camera that had been all the rage. It went that way for a couple months. Until they ran into each other and his cousin heard her sing. He'd said his uncle was a producer for a new show coming out. King invited them over to his apartment to hear some unreleased tracks. Yvette was digging the dude from Cali and asked if he'd ride with her. Jett rode in King's new Camaro. More flirting, and then they arrived at the house. The music was dope. So was the weed. Jett willingly went back to King's room and lost her mind when he performed oral sex. Ditto when after initially resisting, they had intercourse. She woke up in a strange bed at two in the morning. King was gone. Yvette had left, too. Knowing she was already in trouble, Jett was too afraid to go home. What was a few more hours added to being gone all night? She went back to sleep and attended school the next day. Anna tried to beat her, but Jett ran away. Stayed gone until Anna became so worried that she promised to only ground her if she just came home. Chantel arrived nine months later.

Could Yvette somehow be behind the voicemail she received and the mail Chantel got?

Jett went back to pick up the phone, her brows scrunched in concentration. What in the heck was Yvette's last name? Jett figured she was probably married and divorced several times, just like her. She went to the search engine again and pulled up her old high school, clicked on a link touting yearbook pics, then scrolled to the year Yvette would have graduated. After a brief search, she found her—Yvette Olivia Yancey.

Why would any mother give her child a name with initials sounding like a question? One that was most appropriate for Jett right about now: Why, oh why? She copied and pasted the name into the search engine. The only sites that came up were those pawns of Satan trying to get all up in everyone's business, letting potential employers know why you shouldn't be hired or finding people who didn't want to be found.

Damn.

She was just about to finish scrolling when she saw a word next to the name that she wasn't expecting. Obituary. *Yvette died?* No way. Must be someone else with the same name.

She clicked on the link, a website for a funeral home in North Carolina. The obituary was brief, only one paragraph:

Yvette Olivia (Yancey) Horne, 39, passed away on December 21 at WakeMed Hospital in Raleigh, North Carolina. She was born June 2, 1970 to Willa Davis and Joe Yancey in Kansas City, Missouri. She attended Liberty High School, graduating in 1988. She leaves behind to mourn her passing her husband Calvin Horne, her son, Calvin Horne II, two daughters, Willow (Horne) Jenkins and Shania Horne, her mother, Willa Davis, two brothers, Claude (Lillian) Yancey and Edward Yancey, several nieces and nephews, and a host of family and friends. Her father Joe Yancey preceded her in death. Visitation will be at . . .

Jett stopped reading. She didn't know quite how to feel. Given that she hadn't seen Yvette in over thirty years, she was surprised to feel anything at all. At one time, though, they had been as thick as thieves. Jett had been the one person who knew about Yvette getting pregnant by a popular teacher and coach while in high school, and the one by her side when she ended the pregnancy. The Yvette she'd known had no desire to get married and swore to never have children. Yet she'd left this earth both married and a mother. The girl who Jett remembered being so full of life was dead. Which answered one question. Yvette hadn't left the voicemail. She clicked off the site and turned off the computer. If only shutting off her past was that easy. It wasn't, but life went on.

The next day started on a high note. The designer for the *Melanin Magic* cover photo shoot had sent over several outfit choices and color combinations. Pictures from the shoot would be used both for the cover and the accompanying article, which the editor had promised wouldn't revolve around aging gracefully or topics relating to Jett being older. Considering the alternative and the news she'd just learned about Yvette, she wasn't ungrateful at getting older. The industry was getting better, but especially for women of color Hollywood and older age did not mix well. She'd continued doing the workout Randall designed for her and maintained a reasonably healthy diet. When her makeup was slayed and the lights were right, she didn't look a day over thirty-five. That meant if she were lucky and the gods were kind, she could have ten good working years left. Jett planned to make the most of it.

With that in mind, she headed to her walk-in pantry and the case of Cristal Rosé sent by Zenith Records once the ink on their contract dried. She placed a bottle in her quick chiller, took a shower, then headed out to the patio armed with the opened bottle and a flute. It was a perfect summer evening in the Valley. The sky was clear, the wind mild. Jett eased onto her eight-thousand-dollar Karim Rashid sunbed—called chaise lounges by regular folk—that had been shipped from Italy, poured her favorite champagne that went anywhere from five to fifteen hundred dollars a bottle into a seven-hundred-and-fifty-dollar Baccarat champagne flute, and smiled as the fruity bubbles tickled her nose. One glass later, the memory-induced melancholy began to lift. Two glasses and she retrieved her phone, put King's name in the search engine, and leisurely scrolled pages and pics detailing his private and professional lives. She saw an article that touted one of his latest ventures—a club called the Diplomat in . . . Marquette? Jett sat up and continued to read. She was surprised to learn of his connection to her mother's hometown and flabbergasted after reading that Chantel was the lounge's resident headliner.

My mom sings! Yes, Artani had said that, Jett vaguely recalled. *She's going to be famous, too!*

Jett hadn't asked Chantel about her singing; had assumed it happened in a church choir, a good friend's wedding, or maybe

doing karaoke on a Saturday night. If she was being hired professionally, and at a nightclub no less, her little sister—*daughter*—
couldn't just sing, she could sang. Jett always believed the world
was small. But that King would open a club in her mother's hometown, where Chantel lived, and that her little sister would end up
working for her biological father seemed like more than coincidence. It seemed like fate, a sign that maybe it was time to stop
running from the past. To stop and let it catch up to her present.
Jett drained the champagne in her glass, then looked for King's
contact information. Since he was into politics she figured there
would be some way to at least leave a message, if not reach him
outright. She picked up her phone.

The outgoing messages at both the law firm and campaign office were voiced by strangers. On the third call, however, a blast
from the past floated into her ear. King sounded even sexier than
when they were kids. He was a whole man, full grown, having undoubtedly added to his arsenal of good loving in the thirty years
since they'd met.

"Hello and thank you for calling. This is King Richardson III,
ready to be of service. Whether the need is of an individual nature
or that of a community, hopefully soon to be my constituents, I
and my team have more than fifty years' experience combined,
and the expertise needed to ensure that you come out on top.
Over here, we like winning. Leave your information and we'll get
started on a victory for you."

As he was finishing up, Jett cleared her throat. "Absolutely
impressive, King," she cooed, in a voice with equal parts of pol-
ish and purr. "This is Jeanetta, calling from Los Angeles. I have
a matter to discuss regarding the Diplomat in Marquette. It's
been a long time, King. I look forward to your returning my call
at 818 . . ."

She tapped the end button, set her phone on a nearby table,
and poured another glass. A slight chill had crept onto the patio.

She stood up, swayed, and sat back down. Cristal 2012 was from a stellar crop that showed up in the punch packed in each glass. She stood again, slower this time, gathered her things, and walked into the house. Before she reached the bar counter, the phone rang.

Her heart skipped. King calling her back? No. Too soon. But wait. 816? That was a Kansas City prefix. Could it be?

"Hello."

"Jeanetta Scott!"

It could.

Jeanetta felt her body relax. "King Richardson."

"Well, as I live and breathe! Jeanetta Scott. Or should I say Jett, as the world knows you. Part of the jet set! I couldn't believe it when I heard your message. Listened to it twice. How on earth do I have the pleasure of this phone call?"

As King talked, a mentally fuzzy Jett had pulled a charcuterie tray from the fridge and set it on the counter. "I was having a conversation with someone." She walked into the pantry. "Your name came up."

"Whoa! I can't imagine who you'd be talking to out there who knows my name."

"Also . . ." She paused as she reached for a box of crackers and walked back to the counter.

They hadn't spoken or seen each other for more than thirty years. It seemed only polite to do a bit of catching up before telling the man he had a baby who was thirty-three years old.

"I ran across an article about you running for mayor. Congratulations."

"The election is next week. I have a tough, conservative opponent. Don't congratulate me yet."

"A mere formality, I'm thinking. You've always run that town."

"Wow, it's great to hear your voice. One minute you were at Liberty High and the next minute I'm watching television with a group of dudes and you came on the screen. Everyone wondered why you'd up and left town so quickly. A glamour girl! What was your character's name?"

"Lyra."

"That's right. The singing star. Man, young bloods went crazy when they saw you on TV."

"What did you do?"

"Played it cool. Tried to act as though I wasn't about to jump through the screen like the rest of them."

Jett laughed at that. His comment and their ease of conversation took her right back to Kansas City and Liberty High.

"Speaking of young bloods, though he's now an old blood, guess who I heard from, out of the blue? Roy Simpson."

"That name sounds familiar."

"Quiet, light-skinned, wore those Clark Kent-type glasses."

"And a Jheri curl?"

"Yep, that's him! Man, he remembered you! Talked about seeing you on TV back in the day and hearing you on the radio. He brought up things I'd forgotten, going all the way back to high school."

"I think I remember meeting him through Yvette. Did you know she'd passed?"

"Yvette, what was her last name?"

"Yancey."

"Yancey, that's right! No, I hadn't heard. Sorry to hear that. Crazy how life happens and time passes. Talking to Roy had me thinking about people I haven't seen in what feels like a lifetime. He asked if I ever heard from you and at that time I hadn't. This happened not more than a couple weeks ago. And here you call. Crazy. How long has it been, Jeanetta?"

"Almost thirty-four years." No hesitation there. Because of Chantel, that length of time was easy for her to remember.

"Crazy how fast the time flies. It's a cliché, but it's true."

"You know what I've been up to all these years. What about you?"

Jett placed slices of jalapeño cheddar and sausage on a wheat cracker and began filling up her near-empty stomach and soaking up champagne.

"Nothing as exciting as your life. If I remember correctly, I'd not long moved back to Kansas City when we hung out."

"Where had you been?"

"DC. Howard University School of Law."

"I would have imagined you more of a Harvard or Princeton guy."

"Bison brother, born and bred, as were my mother, father, and grandfather."

"And then?"

"Interned for a couple years at a friend of my father's law firm, then opened up my own practice."

"So, you've been in business for . . ."

"Thirty years."

"Is that how long you've been married?"

"How do you know that I am?"

"Google can tell a person almost everything they want to know."

"My grandmother says Google is the devil."

"Ha! She's probably right."

"Tamela and I have been married for twenty-six years. We have three children . . ."

He talked. Jett ate. As he finished pontificating about his perfect children in the proper schools or with the appropriate mate, she poured the remainder of the Cristal into her glass.

"My youngest, Theodore, is enamored with the world of entertainment. He's specializing in entertainment law. I must admit he came by that honestly. My path was set from a young age, however, I always loved music. Even played in a band for about five minutes as an undergrad."

"Really? What did you play?"

"Bass guitar."

"What was the name of your band?"

"The Diplomats." Jett chuckled. "What can I say, we lived in DC! We were almost the Politics."

She laughed harder.

"Barely missed being the Constitution."

They were both laughing now.

"There were a lot of good times back then," he said, as his chuckles subsided. "Haven't thought about this stuff in forever. College, the band, those early days of my practice."

Jett reached for a cluster of glistening black grapes. "You have a club now?"

"Damn, woman! You know all about me. Google again?"

"No, this information was derived from a more personal source." Not entirely the truth but perfect as a segue. "My sister"—*your daughter*—"works there."

"You're kidding. Who?"

"Chantel."

"Chantel is your sister? Well, I'll be damned. No wonder she can sing the dust off the floors! They say there's only six degrees of separation between everyone in the world. I never would have guessed . . ."

"Small world, huh?"

"Wow, it sure is. Funny she didn't mention you during the audition. Guess she wanted to get the job on her own."

"I guess."

"Um, hang on, Jeanetta." The line went silent. He'd put her on hold but was back in seconds. "I have to take this call, Jeanetta. It was great hearing from you. If you're ever in the area, please let me know. I'd love to buy you a drink. Hey, maybe even have you and your sister sing together at the Diplomat."

"I don't get back there much."

"Didn't figure you did. Listen, take care of yourself, okay?"

"You too, King."

"Bye, now."

Jett ended the call and slowly placed the phone on the table before her. She'd fully intended to tell King about Chantel. Something had stopped her. The timing was off. Seconds later, her message indicator pinged. King sent his private cell phone number, saying again that if she came into town to give him a call. She saved the number in her contacts, now sure that not bringing up their daughter had been the right thing.

Who knew? Perhaps disclosing that Chantel was his daughter when the time was right wouldn't be the death knell Jett envisioned. What she felt had been a mistake all those years ago just might be the ticket into her life after entertainment. Tamela could keep her husband. She had no desire to live in Kansas City and be a mayor's wife. But King was no doubt well connected, especially in the nation's capital, where senators and congressmen and power brokers resided. Jett wouldn't mind snagging some rich, congressional dick, Supreme Court justice dick. An older man willing to put a ring on her finger and a monthly five-figure allowance into her bank account. And heck, if for no other reason than old times' sake, she'd wouldn't mind a few pumps of Diplomat dick, too.

Chapter 15
Twisted

Chantel woke up with a headache. One day, she imagined, she'd learn to pair wine with food. She'd just finished brushing her teeth and was about to step into the shower when her neighbor called, asking if Artani would like to attend church with her and her grandson, and afterward get treated to their favorite fast food. Chantel didn't have to wake her son to get the answer. She asked what time to have him ready, and thanked Wanda for the call. Instead of taking her shower, she went in to wake her son.

"Hey, little man. Wake up!" She gently shook his shoulder. Nothing. Chantel shook her head and thought of Art. Her son could sleep through a hurricane, just like his father. "Artani! Wake up."

Artani struggled to a sitting position, rubbing his eyes. "Dang, Mama. You're always yelling."

"I am not always yelling."

"Are, too. You were yelling last night. You woke me up."

"You heard me? I'm sorry, babe. Mama was talking to someone and got a little angry."

"You were talking to Aunt Jett."

Oh, snap. "You heard Jett talking?"

"No." Artani yawned. "I heard you say her name."

"What else did you hear?"

"Nothing. I went back to sleep."

There is a God. "All right then, listen. Miss Wanda wants to take you out for chicken nuggets, fries, and ice cream."

"Yes!"

"You gotta go to church first."

Artani crossed his bony arms. "Oh, man!"

Chantel laughed out loud. "Boy, you got that honest. Church was never much my thing either. But you won't be alone. Her grandson is here."

"Kaleb is going, too?"

"He sure is."

Artani hopped out of bed and ran into the bathroom for his shower. Chantel swayed her big hips behind him thinking that wonders never ceased. While Artani showered, Chantel made his bed, laid out clothes for him to wear, then went into the kitchen to whip up a quick, light breakfast that was also, hopefully, a hangover cure. She placed strips of turkey bacon on a sheet pan and placed it in the oven, heated oil in a skillet, and poured in half a bag of frozen shredded hash browns.

"Don't forget the lotion, Artani! And hurry up. You need to eat something before you leave."

She pulled out three eggs, then on second thought went back and grabbed a fourth one. As she'd watched Anna do so many times, she cracked each one on the side of the glass bowl and dumped the contents inside the bowl. She added shredded white cheddar and seasonings, placed another skillet from a bottom cabinet on a burner, cut off a third of a stick of butter, and turned on the heat. Finally, she pulled three slices of bread from the bag and placed one in the toaster, ready to push the button down when the eggs were almost done.

"Artani!"

"You're yelling again!" This message was delivered at the top of his lungs.

Chantel shook her head and chuckled to herself. What was she going to do? Tell him to speak quietly when she'd been hollering like a fool?

A short time later, Chantel placed a plate on the dining room table. "Come on, Artani! Breakfast is ready."

As her son strode into the room dressed in navy slacks, a light yellow-button down, and a clip-on tie, she was struck with how the older Artani got, the more he looked like his dad. The observation took her back to the convo with Jett, and the father she'd more than likely never know. She sighed and quickly dismissed the thought. Nobody said life was fair. It was what it was.

After pouring two glasses of apple juice and setting the smaller one on the table for Artani, she fixed her plate, added a generous amount of hot sauce to her eggs, and joined him at the table.

"How's your breakfast?"

"Good," he mumbled around a forkful of eggs. "Are you going to church, Mommy?"

"Don't talk with your mouth full. No, I'm not going."

"Why not?"

"Because I'm not. Don't get sidetracked. Finish your food."

Chantel had just taken her son's cleaned plate into the kitchen when Wanda knocked on the door. Breakfast had done the trick. Her headache had subsided. It felt good to feel like herself again.

"Hey, neighbor!"

"Good morning, Wanda. Time to go, Artani!" Chantel turned back and saw that Wanda's grandson had joined her. "Hey there, young man. How are y'all this morning?"

"Blessed and highly favored!"

"I know that's right. Pretty dress. It looks good on you. Ooh, and those earrings, too. Go 'head now, sis. What are you trying to do? Catch one of them deacons?"

"Girl, don't you know I'm married to Jesus? He's all the man I need."

Chantel's mind exploded with all types of sarcastic comebacks.

But Wanda was being kind enough to take her son to church. No need to start an argument. As it was, Artani made a timely appearance.

"Good morning, everybody!"

Chantel opened the door. "Be good, Artani. Don't give Miss Wanda any trouble."

The boys ran down the sidewalk.

"Sure you don't want to go with us?" Wanda asked.

"Maybe next time. Let me get my purse so I can pay for Artani's meal."

Wanda waved off the comment. "Don't block my blessing!"

Chantel waved, closed the door, and turned up the air on another day of Missouri's unrelenting heat and humidity. Hearing India Arie snapping her fingers, she raced to catch her phone.

Steady love!

"Hello?"

"Hey, sis."

"Hey, Rita. No, girl. I had just closed the door and heard the phone ringing. Ran to catch the call before it went to voicemail."

"Where've you been?"

"Nowhere. My neighbor came over with her grandson to take Artani to church and out to eat afterward."

"That's nice. What are you going to do with all this free time?"

"Probably take a nap."

"Another night drinking? You probably don't need me to tell you how that can become a problem."

"No, I don't need you to tell me."

"I'm not judging you, sis. You've dealt with quite a lot these past few weeks."

"You don't know the half."

"I don't?"

"Terrence didn't tell you the latest?"

"What does Terrence know that I haven't heard?"

"He didn't tell you about the mysterious envelope?"

"No. What are you talking about?"

"The one that was delivered to my job and Phil brought over."

"Your boss making house calls now?

"He ran by the office, saw it, and thought to bring it over. He fig-ured it was important and knew I wouldn't see it until tomorrow."

"Was he right? Were the contents important?"

"What are you doing right now?"

"On my way over to that new store that just opened."

"High Five?"

"Yeah, the one where everything is supposed to be five dollars. Want to come with me? We can shop and talk."

"Sounds like a plan."

"Okay. Be there in less than ten."

Chantel took a quick bird bath, threw her hair in a ponytail, and slipped on a pair of jean shorts and a sleeveless tee. She'd just put on her second sandal when she heard Rita's horn outside. She grabbed her purse, keys, phone, and sunglasses and headed out the door.

"Here," Rita said, handing Chantel a bottle of water as soon as she sat in the car. "You're dehydrated."

"How do you know?"

"All that alcohol. Do I need to worry about you?"

"You think I'm becoming like Papa?" Chantel unscrewed the cap and took a long drink. "Speaking of, I haven't seen him for a while, have you?"

"He hasn't been in the club."

"I hope he's okay."

"I hope you're okay."

"I appreciate your concern, sis, but I'm a long way from turn-ing into an alcoholic."

"Maybe, but I'm still worried about you." Rita turned up the air conditioner and turned down the radio. "Tell me about this envelope."

"I have a whole other story to tell you before I get to that."

Chantel quickly recapped what had happened the past week. Flying back to LA. Finagling her way into Jett's home. Submitting a second DNA test. Getting the results.

"And?"

"Jett's full name is Jeanetta Simone. I can't believe I didn't figure that out earlier."

"Jett is Simone?"

"Yes."

"Jett . . . is your . . . mother?"

"Jett birthed me. The only woman who can hold the title of mama is Anna Michelle Scott."

"Whoa." It was a rare instance when Rita was speechless.

Silence filled the car until they reached the strip mall's parking lot. She pulled into a stall but kept the car running.

Chantel took another swig of water, then relayed the aftermath. "Jett finally calmed down enough for me to find out what happened around the time she got pregnant, and help me understand why she gave me away."

"What did she say?"

"Basically, that I was, am, the product of a sexual assault."

Rita was quiet for several seconds. "Do you believe her?"

"Of course I believe her. What kind of question is that?"

"A legitimate one, considering how much she's lied."

"Yeah, but why would she lie about being raped? I don't think any woman would . . . well . . . then again."

"Exactly."

"I don't think she lied to me." Said softly, and with less conviction.

"One more thing before you turn off that air." *Steady love!* "Shoot, hold on. This might be Wanda. Hello?"

"Hello, Chantel." Her eyes widened at the sound of someone using a voice distorter. She tapped the speaker button, looked at Rita, and put a finger to her mouth. "Did Jett tell you I called her?"

"Who the hell is this?"

"One hundred thousand dollars."

"What?"

"That's what I want to keep your little mommy-daughter se-cret."

"I don't know what you're talking about."

The sound of the distorted laugh brought chills. "I'll give you girls one month to come up with the money, although with your rich bitch sister-mama, it probably won't take that long."

"Listen, I don't know—"

"Shut up! You do know. And if you don't give me what I'm asking, *Celebrity Gossip* will be glad to do it. Then the world will know, too. I'll be in touch."

The call went dead. For several seconds the whirring air condi-tioner fan was the only sound.

When Rita finally spoke, she had only three words. "What. The. Fuck."

"There's your answer to what was in the mysterious envelope Phil brought over."

"Somebody's trying to blackmail you?"

"I'm just a means to an end. Jett is their real target. They placed a similar call to her last night. She called convinced that I was behind that bullshit. It's how we were finally able to talk."

"I can't believe that just happened," Rita said. "Was that the same person who dropped off the note?"

"That's what I think."

"And they called Jett, too. Hmm." Rita's fingers tapped the steering wheel as mental wheels turned. "It's got to be someone from back in the day, who knows or thinks they know that Jett had a baby. Since the envelope was delivered and not mailed it's got to be someone who either lives here or has connections here. But your sister grew up in Kansas City, right?"

Chantel nodded. "Jett believes it's someone I know. Terrence got angry when I mentioned that I'd only told two people and that you were out of town. We haven't talked since."

"I would have gotten angry, too." Rita glanced over at Chantel, who remained silent, causing Rita to look her way again. "I know you don't think I'm involved."

"No, I don't. Terrence either."

"Whew! Thank God you haven't lost your whole mind."

"No, but if I can't figure out who's behind this madness, I might lose the sister who doesn't want the world to know that she's my birth mother. And that will be just as bad."

Chapter 16
You Remind Me

Chantel was forced to put her problems on the back burner. That week at the *Monitor* and everywhere else, it was all about the mayoral election. The fight had been nasty and filled with mudslinging that left both candidates needing a bath. The conservative candidate, George Bush—no relationship to either former president—had been backed by Donald Trump and accused by King and his supporters of using racist and divisive tactics to try and secure the vote. Bush had accused King of money laundering—with no tangible proof—and financial improprieties by his campaign office. Since the paper came out on the Wednesday following the election, Chantel designed mockups of either outcome while staff writers created headlines and stories to fit either narrative. Knowing this edition would receive wide circulation, there had been an uptick in ad placement. It took the small team of five working around the clock to get it all done. By the time the winner was announced, the paper was completed and hit the newsstands Wednesday morning, Chantel went home and fell into bed, feeling like she'd run a campaign her damn self.

India roused her out of sleep. The song stopped, and within seconds, began again. *Ooh ooh steady love.*

Chantel answered with a gravelly voice and scrunched-up face. "Hello?"

"You have a new mayor!" Jett sounded as though she'd been up for hours even though in California it was six a.m.

"Jett?" Chantel pushed the speaker button, then let her head fall back on the pillow. "What are you even doing up?"

"Haven't gone to bed yet. King won! Isn't that exciting?"

"You're in LA. What do you care?"

"He's an old friend, that's why. King and I go way back."

This revelation helped push some of the sleepiness away, but not enough to open her eyes. She turned on her side. "You do?"

"Yes, and the other night, on a whim fueled by too much good champagne, I called him."

That was an eye opener. Chantel sat up against the headboard. "You did? I don't believe you."

"I'm serious."

"How did you get his number?"

"Looked it up online. I'm sure the number listed is attached to one of those answering services. I left a message. He called back."

"You know that I know him, too, right?"

"I didn't until he told me that you were the weekend headliner at his club."

"Dang, I guess you really did talk to him." A now wide-awake Chantel got out of bed. "Did you tell him that I was your—"

"Sister? I sure did. On finding that out, he said it was obvious that talent ran in the family. Why didn't you didn't tell me you sang professionally?"

"I think I mentioned it when I was there." She stepped into her house slippers, put on a robe, and headed into the kitchen. Sleep had fled. Might as well have a cup of joe.

"Maybe so. I don't remember. How do the two of you get along?"

That's a strange question. "Okay, I guess. He doesn't come to the club that often. When he does I'm working, so it's basically hi, bye, enjoyed your performance, thank you . . . that's about it.

Were you guys in school together?" Chantel's message indicator dinged. She went to the icon.

"No. He's several years older than me."

"Well, it looks like I'm going to see him this weekend. I just got a text from the club manager. There's going to be a private victory party on Saturday night."

"That sounds fun! Maybe I should fly down and surprise him!"

"Really? You'd do that? Did you guys date or something?"

"Or something. Then again, my being there might not be such a great idea. This is King's moment. I wouldn't want to steal the spotlight."

"Your being in Podunk Marquette would certainly do that."

"I'll send something congratulatory to the club."

"Okay."

"Ooh, that's my trainer. Gotta run."

"Tell Randall I said hi."

"He got deleted. This guy's name is Ike."

"Whatever, girl. I can't keep up with you and your . . . trainers. Bye."

Once off the phone, two thoughts slammed simultaneously into Chantel's head. One, it was the first civil, even pleasant, conversation the two had had since truth came out. Two, the blackmail issue never came up. Did she dare hope that whoever was behind the letter and phone calls had tired of their sick game? Or learned that the sentence for attempted blackmail was a maximum of fifteen years?

Phil had given the crew Wednesday off. Good thing, because Chantel doubted she would have been any good at work anyway. Not long after getting Terrence's text, the band leader Walter called to schedule an impromptu rehearsal, that afternoon if possible. He also wanted the band members to switch up from their ensemble of all black and have all of them wear white, including Chantel. She didn't relish spending money she didn't have, especially when her car payment was a month behind. But she had one credit card paid down below the limit, and every woman knew it didn't take a lot of energy to go shopping.

She had several hours before rehearsal started, so after she got Artani up and dressed the two of them headed to Kansas City. It was a carefree morning. They grabbed breakfast at a drive-thru, then for the next forty-five minutes sang to one of Artani's listen-and-learn fun song audios. They talked about what Artani learned at church (that this guy fed a bunch of people with nothing but fish sandwiches!), what he liked (the singing), and what he didn't (lasted *forever*). Chantel realized it had been too long since she'd truly focused on her son and they'd enjoyed doing something special together. It was easy for most to remember that they loved their children. The ride to KC reminded Chantel that she really liked Artani, too.

Finding a white dress that was a) inexpensive, b) sexy, c) stage-worthy, and d) in her size was not easy. After searching the clearance racks of some of her favorite higher-priced stores, Chantel headed to the discount outlets. It wasn't long before she found a simple gown with a side thigh split that if it fit would tick all of the boxes. She dropped off Artani in the toy area, told him to stay there and pick out something he wanted (and if he didn't stay where he was told he would not get a toy), then headed to the dressing room. She was given a number and headed into a stall. After removing her loose-fitting maxi she slipped the dress over her head, held her breath, and prayed.

Ooh, I think this is going to fit. There is a God! It was snug around the waist and hips, and she'd definitely need a slimming undergarment, but the spandex-like material and sleek one-shoulder design was classy and flattered her figure. A spray of rhinestones across the top added showstopper appeal. If only she could get it zipped all the way, she'd know for sure it was a keeper. The toy area was across from the dressing room, but maybe the person manning the dressing room . . .

She stepped from behind the curtain and walked to the three-way mirror at the back of the room. Turning one way and then the other, she imagined a pair of silver or rhinestone stilettos, the right jewelry, an upswept hairdo, and the mic in her hand!

"That's nice," someone said from behind her.

"Thanks. Can you . . ." She turned around to see a middle-aged woman holding an armful of clothes to try on. "Oh, never mind."

"What do you need?"

"I was going to ask if you could zip this all the way up."

"That's no problem. Let me set down these clothes." It seemed to take her longer than necessary, but soon Chantel saw her coming in the mirror.

"I had to make sure my hands were clean," she explained, as Chantel turned around. "You are wearing that white, sistah. I didn't want to dirty it up."

"Thank you," Chantel said, and turned around. "I wanted to make sure it could zip all the way."

"Hold your breath," the woman instructed when the zipper stopped moving. "There we go."

Chantel stepped back and smiled at her reflection. She'd found her look for the mayor-elect's celebration!

"I know you're buying it. You don't even have to tell me."

"Yes," Chantel said with a chuckle. "I think I am."

"Because if you didn't I was going to, and it ain't even my size." They both laughed. "You want me to unzip it now?"

"Please, before I pass out from lack of oxygen."

They both laughed again.

"Going someplace special?" the woman asked, as she unzipped her.

"I'm singing at a club this weekend."

"Nice! Which one?"

"It's called the Diplomat. Not here, it's in Marquette."

"That's King's club, right? Or should I say, Mayor Richardson!"

The women high-fived.

"Do you know him?" Chantel asked.

"We went to school together, but that was a long time ago." The woman emphasized the word *long* and made a face. She seemed funny, kind, and down-to-earth. Chantel liked her.

"Did you go to school here? You look familiar."

Chantel shook her head. "I grew up in Marquette and went to school there."

"My bad, though my nana used to say that everybody looks like somebody."

"Your nana was probably right. Hey, if you're not doing anything on Saturday . . . oh, wait. I'm sorry. I was going to invite you to check out the party but just remembered it's a private affair."

"No problem. My clubbing days been over."

"Thanks for helping me with the dress."

"No worries. Hey, what's your name? So that when you get famous I can say that I knew you when."

"I doubt that'll happen, but my name is Chantel. Chantel Scott. What's yours?"

"Brenda."

"Nice meeting you, Brenda."

"You, too, Chantel. Good luck with your show."

Saturday night at the Diplomat. The place was packed! If the fire marshal dropped by, Chantel knew they'd be fined. Maximum capacity was 210. There were easily three hundred bodies squeezed into the room with more who hadn't received invitations hanging around outside just to hear the music and soak up the atmosphere. The only thing that kept Chantel from totally freaking was knowing that one of the exits was right behind the stage.

The crowd had come to party! Upon entering, guests were handed party hats and noisemakers. Food was free and the liquor flowed. It was a great thing the band had rehearsed. They were tight and ready, started jamming as soon as Walter counted off the McFadden & Whitehead classic that they'd customized to highlight King's win.

"Ain't no stopping him now. He's on the move!"

Chantel and Walter went back and forth on lead. King and Tamela soaked up the adulation until somebody started the Electric Slide and forced them to join in.

"He didn't let nothin', nothin', get in his way!" Walter crooned.

Chantel swooped in. "Now you'd better listen to every word he says!"

They played forty-five minutes before the band took a break. Chantel freshened up, then came out the side door. She wanted to be sure to personally congratulate King. As had happened all evening, there was a crowd around them. When he saw her, he whispered something to his wife and came to where she stood.

"I just wanted to say congratulations," she began, stepping farther away from the crowd. "All of Kansas City, even those who didn't vote for you, should be very glad you won."

"Very kind words," he replied, as Chantel shook King's outstretched hand, then accepted his kiss on her cheek. "In time, I believe they will."

"I must say I—"

"You know my—"

They both started speaking and stopped at the same time. King motioned to Chantel. "Ladies first."

"I just found out you grew up with my sister, Jett. The singer."

"That is exactly what I was going to mention. I had no idea the two of you were related! We didn't grow up together, but met through a friend and saw each other from time to time. What a class act. Did you know she had a congratulatory gift delivered to my office?"

"No."

"Two bottles of premium Cristal, one of those stellar crops. One each for me and my wife."

"That was very thoughtful."

"Indeed. Great gesture from an old friend. She was Jeanetta back then, and talented, no doubt. What are the odds that all these years later, I'd end up hiring her sister to sing here? It is a small world after all."

"The two of you dated?"

King offered an ambivalent smile. "I wouldn't go that far. Flirted, hung out a couple times. We were young. Headed in different directions. One day she was riding around town with her friends, the next day she was on television! I am incredibly proud of her. You must be, too."

"I am."

"Chantel Scott!" A woman wearing a red jumpsuit and brimmed hat with a large multicolored plume cocked ace-deuce came toward her with a big smile and arms outstretched. "Girl, you are bad!" She threw her arms around a somewhat shocked, somewhat reserved Chantel. "It's Brenda. The zipper lady!"

"Oh, hey!" Chantel gave her a for-real hug this time. "With the hat and everything, I didn't recognize you."

"Clean up pretty good, huh?"

"I see the two of you already know each other," King said. "Which allows me to take my leave, let this lovely lady get ready to wow us again with her beautiful voice. Ladies . . ."

Brenda watched King walk off. "That man is still fine!"

"He is rather handsome."

"Tamela knows she's lucky. Lord knows there were a ton of women after that man." Brenda leaned close. "But she got pregnant with King the Fourth and it was a wrap!"

She stepped back and snapped her fingers four times.

"You're a mess." Chantel shook her head.

"That's true, but hey! I remembered where I saw you before. At Miss Anna's funeral. You're Jeanetta's sister."

Just like that, Chantel's mind went back to the graveside service and the seemingly testy exchange that happened between the two women. Her face remained cordial but the smile left her eyes.

"You're *that* Brenda?"

"Yes, the one who traded words with Jeanetta. Out of respect for your mother, I hate that it happened. I know she's your sister, but I can't stand her. Never could. It's hard to believe the two of you are related."

"Well, we are. So on that note . . ."

Brenda took a step toward her. "I'm sorry, Chantel. I meant no offense. I'm sure you love Jeanetta. And knowing her better than I do, you *know* that girl can be a lot."

Chantel felt it best to walk away, but a part of her was curious to hear more from a woman who knew Jeanetta before she became Jett.

"Why do you dislike her?"

Brenda answered immediately. "She stole my man for spite, then dumped him a week later. It would have been one thing if she was a stranger, but, Chantel, we were friends. Good friends, I thought. On top of that it meant nothing to her trif—to her, but at the time Preston Evans was the love of my life."

"If what you just said is true, and there are always two sides, I can understand you being upset. Back then. But you're still mad and it's thirty years later. Sounds like something deeper to me."

"It goes much deeper. And I'll admit there's probably some jealousy there, too. Jeanetta was always cute. Boys flocked to her like flies to shit. Not saying she was, you know," Brenda hurriedly added. "Just using that phrase for comparison. She got everything easy. Could sing, dance, act. Hell, only talent I had was my cootchie, so when she took the man who was helping me practice *my* act . . ."

Chantel couldn't help but laugh, even as she saw Walter tap his watch.

"We're getting ready to go on," she said, turning toward the hallway that led backstage. "Glad you made it down."

"Here! Take my number." Brenda dug inside her purse.

Chantel pointed to Rita. "Give it to her. She'll make sure that I get it."

Backstage she quickly downed the rest of her wine, then sat on the stool, closed her eyes, and tried to focus on her next set. Total concentration was difficult, since her mind kept drifting to the convo with Brenda, the woman honest enough to admit her feelings, who thought that Jett was a bitch. If it weren't the truth, Chantel would have dismissed Brenda already. But she'd pegged her sister/mother right on the nose. A part of Chantel couldn't help but respect that.

Chapter 17
This Is How We Do It

Chantel had no idea that King Richardson becoming mayor of Kansas City, Missouri, would impact her life, but that's what happened. The newspaper's photographer and a freelance reporter had attended King's private party at the Diplomat on Saturday night. Their presence was expected. The new mayor being in Marquette was a newsworthy event—front page, above-the-fold stuff. She'd spotted Diego all over the club, snapping pictures of the guests at King's table that included his wife, Tamela, along with their refined children and their dates. She'd laughed when, after taking pictures of dancers working the Electric Slide, he'd joined in and got his groove on. She was glad when he turned his lens on the stage. Chantel needed professional pics for social media and a potential future website. She'd even posed a time or two when he took pics of her and the band. She'd edited the detailed and well-written article by Ulla Lindgren for the following week's paper, was pleased to see her name, and was thrilled and a bit terrified when Phil directed her to include a picture of her and the band on the continued page.

What she hadn't known was that Phil had requested a second article from Ulla, one about her, that would run in the next week's paper. When Ulla dropped by her office after the issue covering mayor-elect King's celebration party went to print, Chantel assumed the young writer who lived in the next town over was simply curious about her growing up in Marquette, being a singer with a day job, and having a famous sister. It wasn't until shortly before she was set to lay out the paper that she inquired about the feature for that week's front page.

"Ulla still hasn't sent that to you?" Phil had asked, perching the skinny bone that passed for a hip on the edge of her desk.

"No, and I've texted her several times. She was so prompt with everything regarding the mayor last week. I don't get it."

"What did she tell you when you asked?"

"You mean how many different excuses did she come up with? Let's see. Waiting on photos from Diego. Accidentally deleting part of the copy. Not being where she could send it right then. I was impressed by the article she wrote on King Richardson, but I'd be leery about using her on a regular basis."

"Why didn't you tell me about your side gig, Chantel?"

The abrupt pivot in topic caused Chantel to look up. "Most people already know I sing. If I didn't tell you it's because it never came up."

"And Jett is your sister?"

"You're familiar with her music?"

"Not anything recent but everybody over, what, twenty-five remembers Lyra the Glamagirl. As kids, my little brother and his friends were in love with her. With that new reality show coming out, her and the other judges' faces are all over the place. Holding out on me, Chantel? That's so not cool."

"That's not it at all, Phil. When I'm here, I read copy and design layouts. At five on Friday I take off my day job hat and channel my inner diva."

"I think that's pretty amazing. Ulla says you're really good."

"Ulla needs to get that cover story over. She's on my list."

"Is that what the impromptu vacation was about? I heard you

went to California. Hey, wait a minute." Phil slid off her desk and began pointing his finger. "Are you about to be on that show with your sister judging? That's it, huh? You're going to leave us small-town minions to go off and be a star!"

"Sounds good, but no. The trip was to California, but not to audition or sing or anything. It was because my mother had just died and my world imploded. Jett invited me and my son out there to try and find normal again."

Phil's expression changed, along with his tone. "Yeah, losing your mother. That's got to be rough." He slapped her desk. "I'll try and reach Ulla, see if I can get that article for you."

"I need it before noon, Phil. Or I'm running a national story in that spot."

Five minutes later, Phil called her on the phone. "The story should be in your in-box."

The article was there. She clicked on the attachment, began reading, and almost fell out of her chair. That's how Chantel found out that *she* was the featured story with the headline "Local Newspaper Editor Moonlights as a Singing Star!" Phil indicated that the national story should go above the fold as the bigger story, which was correct. But he was equally adamant that she put her story on the front page.

You're a good copy editor and layout artist, he said in the email. *But I hear you're even better onstage. Congratulations. And don't leave here without a replacement. We're already short-staffed!*

Chantel read that and thought she wasn't going anywhere, but it felt as though her life changed before the ink dried. Everyone in the office congratulated her, then teased her about wanting an autograph or came over to take selfies. For the first time ever, she was recognized on the street. Most smiled and spoke. Several commented. Some stared. A few sent hater vibes. It was new, and overwhelming. She could only imagine how real celebrities like her sister felt. Chantel was thankful to be recognized as a talent, but not sure that the world of notoriety was where she wanted to reside. The Kansas City *Call* ran the article as a front-page story. For Chantel, that was huge. From the time she was born, Anna had maintained a subscription to the popular weekly paper that had served the African-American community since 1919. In her mind's eye she could see her mom clearly—feet up on the coffee table, reading glasses perched on her nose and sections of *The Call* spread around her. Main stories, the society and sports sections, and the extensive obituary section, Anna read them all. Usually on Thursday evening, after *Jeopardy* and before the ten o'clock news. The day after the story ran, King's office phoned her. Even though she'd worked at his club for months, it felt special to get a call from the mayor-elect. Would she be interested in performing at his inaugural celebration? Was fat meat greasy? Did birds fly? Of course she would! The biggest surprise was from Brenda. She had a beautiful bouquet of flowers delivered to the office, along with a card that read, *I'm so proud of you.* Chantel could count on one hand the number of times she'd gotten flowers, which was the excuse she used for the tears that trickled when she walked in and saw the vase on her desk. Brenda's gesture also made Chantel feel guilty for not calling her, mainly because Jett didn't like her. She sent a text thanking her for the beautiful flowers and promising to give her a buzz the next time she was in town. When the *Kansas City Star* and the *St. Louis Post-Dispatch* also picked up the article, Chantel got worried. She feared the story might catch the would-be blackmailer's attention and have them demanding even more money. Or that the story would go national. How would Jett react? Not wanting her to see a paper and be caught off-guard, Chantel called her. To her surprise, Jett answered on the first attempt.

"Hi, Chantel."

"Jett! You actually picked up. That rarely happens."

"Today is your lucky day." Said as though there was nothing lucky about it.

"Is this a bad time? You can call me later, but I do want to share some news with you."

"I've got a minute. What's up?"

"You know about King's win."

"Didn't I call you the day after? By now I think everybody knows."

"Remember when I told you about the private party he held at his club, the Dip?"

"The Diplomat?"

"That's what those outside of Marquette call it. Anyway, it was quite the event, a great celebration. The band played, I sang, everyone was so excited that he won. After our first set, I went to congratulate him on becoming mayor, but he was much more in-terested in talking about you."

"Is that so?" A perkiness replaced Jett's blasé tone. "Do tell."

"He had no idea that we were sisters and was very excited about the gift you sent to his office."

"As he should have been. That bottle was one of the finer years, very high-end. Honey, nobody sent a better gift than mine."

"From his reaction, I believe it. That you included his wife was a nice touch."

"What else did he say?"

Chantel shared their brief conversation. "I asked if you dated," she finished.

"Sure you did. You're always putting your big nose where it doesn't belong."

"Jett! Come on, now. Given the dreamy look on his face during his walk down memory lane, the question was appropriate."

The self-satisfied, girly titter Jett emitted upon hearing that news justified Chantel's slight embellishment.

"He told you we dated?"

"He described it more casually—flirting, hanging out."

"Hmph. We flirted all right."

"Sounds like you did more than that."

"King is a fine-ass brother. Can you blame me?"

"Not really. There's something else I need to tell you. Another place your name got mentioned."

"The *Marquette Monitor*?"

"You saw the paper?"

"No, but King being in that Mayberry replica was probably the biggest news y'all have had in years, maybe decades. You sang at the party. People in town know we're sisters. They want to sell papers and I'm starring in a hugely anticipated show set to appear on a major network. Of course they'd mention me!"

Chantel was too relieved at Jett not being angry to belabor the none-too-subtle putdown.

"So you're not mad about an article saying we're sisters?"

"We are sisters. Why would I be mad about that?"

Every cell in Chantel's body screamed that they were more than sisters, but the conversation had been far too amicable for her to open up that ten-gallon can of worms.

"I wasn't sure how you'd feel, but I'm happy that you're okay with it. Because the week after King's feature, without the benefit of my consent or knowledge, the paper did run an article on me. The Marquette native, yada yada."

"I think that's great, Chantel. Send me a copy."

"I can do that. You can also read it online. The story ran in a few papers. I'll text the links."

"Congratulations!" Jett sounded sincere.

"Thanks, Jett. That means a lot."

"I'd better watch out for you," Jett teased. "Little sister giving big sis some competition."

"As you so aptly stated, you're starring in a soon-to-be hit show on a major network. I made it in a few regional papers. So . . . don't lose any sleep, okay?"

"Ha! Well, put that way . . ." They shared a companionable silence. "I'm really happy for you, Chantel. Obviously, you love to
sing, and being recognized for your talent is the best feeling ever.
Send me something. I want to hear you. Not to critique or anything like that—"

"You are a judge, after all."

"I know, but this isn't that. I want to share in what others have
enjoyed."

After talking a few more minutes, the call abruptly ended.
Chantel called back and got voicemail. A minute later she received a text that said Jett's battery had died and that they'd speak
that weekend. Chantel was almost happy for the interruption. It
saved her from having to dampen the mood by asking if there'd
been more anonymous calls or mentioning her encounters with
Brenda. The Jett she'd spoken with today was the fun, cool sister
Chantel remembered. But once the words Brenda and blackmail
were mentioned, that would have most definitely changed.

Chapter 18
Too Close

Jett shivered from the aftereffects of an early morning orgasm, then smiled as Oliver slowly rose from between her legs and beneath the sheet, kissed her deeply, and cuddled beside her.

"That was delicious, papi," she purred. "Now that you've had breakfast, what will you fix for me?"

"Hmm, let me see." He flopped on his back. "One similar to what I just had might be nice. How about a dick sandwich between two slices of nuts?"

Jett pulled the pillow from beneath her and bopped him upside the head. He ducked, reached for a pillow, and hit her back. They laughed and tussled and tickled each other. Once on top he lifted her leg, rubbed his hardening shaft against her folds, then nailed a perfect landing. He set up a rhythm Jett matched stroke for stroke. His passion was intense, his sex electrifying, filling Jett with energy that quickly erased the seventeen-year difference between them. After a third burst of pleasure, she feasted on his sandwich. It wasn't long before he too went into orbit, speaking rapid Spanish as his body bucked, then collapsed. This had been their dance off and on all night. A light kiss and lights out. They went back to sleep.

A short time later, Jett woke up to the sound of Afro-Latin

music and the smells of breakfast in the air. After relishing the feel of a long, hot shower, she slipped on a smocked tube top and a pair of boy shorts. With her face freshly scrubbed and her hair in a high pony, Jett could have easily gotten carded, and not just because it was the law.

She walked into the kitchen, reaching for a strawberry as she gave Oliver a kiss.

"Morning, mami."

"Buenos días, papi." She pulled a wineglass from the cabinet and fresh-squeezed juice from the fridge. After pouring a glass she asked Oliver, "You want some?"

He looked over his shoulder. "Sure."

"Need any help?"

"No, I'm good."

"Good, because you weren't going to get any."

She plunked down on a barstool and watched the chef work his magic. He was truly a talented and beautiful man. If Jett were twenty years younger, she'd marry him and have lots of babies. But she wasn't, so she wouldn't. She was too old for that fantasy. As much as she enjoyed a beau buffet, the lifestyle was getting old, too. Good workouts and even better genes kept her looking thirty-five. But the truth of the matter was that the forties were giving her a kick in the rear and the fifties were mocking her with a throwback chant—red rover, red rover, send Jett right on over. Setting her sights on a rich, successful older man to settle down with was much more realistic.

So far, the call she'd placed to the number King gave her had gone unreturned. Preparing to assume his new duties as mayor, she figured. Jett wasn't used to being ignored, no matter the reason. If another week went by without him calling, she'd have to change tactics. Meanwhile, she'd done a bit of online research regarding her old friend with whom she'd shared "casual flirtations," as he'd explained it to Chantel, and found a gem. King was apparently very good friends with Godfrey Steward, a man who hadn't crossed her mind since the night they met, and who was also an unassuming, genteel billionaire. His wasn't a name known to the general public. He eschewed avenues like *Forbes* magazine that put wealth on display.

Jett knew of him because of a dinner party in the Hamptons she'd attended almost fifteen years ago. It was held at Godfrey's home along with his wife, in honor of an even wealthier Nigerian king. Though almost bored to the point of petrification, Jett had taken note of how the 1 percent of the 1 percent lived and decided that it was a style to which she could become accustomed. Godfrey was mannered and gracious, and totally attentive to his wife. Yet several times throughout the night, she'd felt his eyes on her and even caught him staring when she'd unexpectantly looked his way. They left without speaking further. She never approached him or vice versa. Back on the West Coast, he was promptly forgotten. According to the internet, his wife passed five years ago. He'd not remarried. He was probably lonely and in need of a stimulating companion. Jett believed she could be just what he needed, whether he knew it or not. King was her key to Godfrey's secure and guarded world, the one that looked fitting to occupy once the stage lights had dimmed. She just had to continue studying her human chess pieces to know when to make the right moves. And in the meantime make sure that nothing dimmed her bright star. Like her adoring public finding out she had a daughter turning thirty-four next month.

The plate Oliver set in front of her brought her out of her musings. Fluffy light waffles topped with berries, pecans, and homemade whipped cream. Crispy bacon and just-right scrambled eggs. Their endless lovemaking had left her ravenous. She was halfway through her plate before noticing that Oliver hadn't joined her.

"Oliver! Baby, where are you?"

He came around the corner fully dressed, his chef kit slung over his shoulder.

"You're not eating?"

"I did already, while I was cooking."

"It looks like you're leaving."

He blessed her with a boyish grin. "I am."

"But I thought we were going spend time together," she pouted. "I have the whole day."

Oliver walked over and kissed her forehead. "I wish I could. But I'm catering a large dinner party in Malibu. Seven courses. Everything I ordered has been delivered, but the list included items from several different countries. I have to go to the airport and sign off on the shipment. Make sure everything is correct. Then I have to go home and try and recover from my strenuous workout because more than likely, I'll be up again for most of the night."

"Who's giving the party?"

"Some A-list asshole with way more money than they know how to spend. The liquor order alone totaled almost a hundred thousand dollars. But I'm getting paid very well for my services, so I guess I shouldn't complain."

"No, you shouldn't. Sounds like that asshole is more like an asset."

"That's why I like you, mamacita. You give great . . . perspective."

"Ha!" Jett slid off the barstool. "Thanks for an amazing breakfast. Now get out of here."

"Call you later?"

"It's a free country. Do what you want."

Jett closed the door behind him and leaned back against it with a satiated sigh. Oliver had thoroughly attended to every one of her needs. After more than an hour and a shower, her body still tingled with the memory of his expert tongue, torch, and touch. She stretched, yawned, and dreamed of an ideal situation. Godfrey as her husband. Oliver as their chef.

Okay, sistah. Enough of that. Jett pushed off the door and looked around her, as though in the home of a stranger. So rarely did she have nothing to do that she wasn't quite sure how to spend the time. Then she remembered the conversation with Chantel and retrieved her laptop. She pulled a bottle of sparkling water from the fridge, poured it into a crystal goblet, and sat on the ridiculously expensive Italian leather sofa that she rarely used. She thought about Chantel's financial challenges, which if totaled probably equaled less than she'd spent on a place to park her ass. For a fleeting second, a pang of guilt assailed her. She quickly dismissed it and locked it away, the way she'd done every other painful, uncomfortable, or nonproductive memory in her life. She also made a mental note to get Chantel's cash app.

She opened an email account that she hadn't visited in a while. Amid what appeared to be hundreds of unopened messages were several from Chantel. She clicked on the first one.

Hey sis, here's the article from the Kansas City *Call*, otherwise known as Mama's Black folks' business bible, remember? I think she would have gotten a kick out of seeing me on the front page.

Jett clicked the link, sipping her water as the page loaded. The picture of Chantel brought a genuine smile to her face. It was a great shot of her at the height of performing. Her head was thrown back, mouth opened in song, one arm stretched out toward the crowd. The angle of the shot and the cut of the chic white gown made Chantel look slenderer and shapelier than Jett remembered. She quickly read the first page of the article, then clicked to the page where it continued. Three smaller pictures were placed amid the words. Jett tapped on one and enlarged it. Whoever set the lighting had done a great job, too. Just the right amount of blues, yellows, and reds to bring out the rich tones of Chantel's brown skin, highlight her cheekbones and bring out her smile. While gazing at her sister's face, Jett was struck by how much she looked like their mother—her mother. It was one of the reasons that Chantel being claimed as Anna's daughter had been so easily believed. It was almost as if Anna had indeed given birth, and wiped out all traces of King. The third picture was a close-up of Chantel looking directly at the camera. Her eyes glowed as she smiled. Jett could feel her happiness. As she enlarged the picture as she had the others, something else struck her, too. When she looked at Chantel's eyes, she saw her own. A decades-old conversation drifted into her mind. Unexpected. Uninvited.

It happened on Jett's first visit home after moving to LA—a year after Chantel was born. Anna had moved to Marquette by then. Other than commenting on the plain-looking duplex, and the baby's fat cheeks and cheap-looking outfit, she hardly paid attention to her daughter. Anna had to force Chantel into Jett's awkward arms, only to have the inexperienced mother almost lose it a short time later when Chantel had a bowel movement both explosive and rank. During the rest of that visit over a long weekend, Jett didn't hold Chantel again. She mostly stayed in Kansas City clubbing with newfound friends. She also attended a Chiefs game. Anna knew this only because Jett sang the national anthem to an enthusiastic sold-out stadium and both the evening and nightly news. She arrived back in Marquette that Monday with a man Anna didn't know, with enough time to grab the items she'd left in the duplex and make it to the airport for her first-class flight.

"Don't you want to see the baby?" Anna had asked.

"I already saw her." Jett had answered with a look of genuine confusion as to why Anna seemed irritated. She looked at the obviously uncomfortable stranger. "I'll meet you in the car."

Anna had waited until the young man left, glad to speak freely. "I agreed to raise Chantel as your sister, Jeanetta, but the child still needs to know who you are. Between you and me, this is the truth. I didn't have her, you did. Chantel is your daughter. That girl is your child. Don't forget that."

Jett left without another word to Anna or a glance toward Chantel, who was barricaded behind a blanket in the crook of the sofa, happily trying to eat her right foot. It wasn't until Chantel began kindergarten that she began to feel like the little sister to Jett that everyone else believed.

Jett clicked off the email tab and closed the tablet without looking at the remaining emails Chantel had sent. Now she realized why she so rarely had downtime with nothing to do. She didn't like it. Too much time for uncomfortable, unfortunate, or negative thoughts. She hopped off the couch and headed toward the stairs, ready to change and get out of the house. Away from the quiet where memories dwelled.

Just as she reached for the cell phone left on the counter, it rang. It was Zola, her assistant. Perfect. They could go shopping.

She tapped the speaker button and hit the stairs. "Hey Zola. Where are you?"

"Heading to your place. I was at the studio having lunch with a friend when one of the producers saw me and brought over your mail."

"I had mail at the studio?" Jett reached her master and continued into the dressing room. She placed the phone on a table and began to undress.

"Yeah, fan mail I'd imagine. That's usually what comes there. I'm on Ventura, not far from your house. Should I bring it over?"

"Absolutely. Do you want to go shopping? I'm buying."

"Heck, yeah!"

Jett laughed. She was feeling better already. "That's why I like you. See you in a few."

She pulled on a pair of leggings designed to look like torn skinny jeans, a black sleeveless tee, and a pair of black Alexander Wang sandals outlined with crystals and sporting a three-inch heel. At the top of the stairs she rethought her choice and switched into the still stylish but more comfortable Valentino Garavanis with the cute block heels. She eyed herself in the mirror, pulled a few tendrils from her high pony, and felt a moment of gratitude. Man, it felt amazing to be A-list again.

As she neared the bottom stair, the doorbell rang.

"Perfect timing," she said, leaving the door open for Zola to come inside. "I just need to get my purse."

"Here's the mail."

Jett looked from Zola's outstretched hand to her face. "One letter? That's it?"

"That's all they gave me."

Jett was disappointed. Clearly, her publicist had work to do. "You didn't have to come all the way over here for that."

"I was already in the neighborhood." She shrugged. "Besides, fans these days reach out mostly through social media. Your Instagram got ten thousand new followers last week."

"I need to check those more often."

"Yes, and interact with those who comment. That's how to increase visibility and draw more fans."

"I knew there was a reason I hired you." Jett tossed the envelope on the counter, picked up her phone, and slid it into her purse. "Let's go."

"You're not going to open the letter?"

"Later. It's probably somebody requesting an autographed

headshot or telling me how great I am. I'll give you a stack of signed head shots so that you can respond to those from now on."

The two ladies went out and, thanks to Jett's recently delivered black card, had an amazing time. It was near dusk when she returned home carrying bags that represented almost a whole block of shops down Rodeo Drive. The house was dark except for the pendant lights over the bar counter, making the manila envelope on her ebony countertops really stand out. She dropped the bags on the floor at the base of the stairs, pulled a utility knife from the drawer, and slit open the top. Peering inside she saw what looked to be pieces of a magazine or newspaper stuck to a sheet of white paper.

"That's original," she murmured as she pulled it out and read the letter that, except for her name, which had been scrawled with a Sharpie, was entirely put together with words cut from magazines.

> Hello, Jeanetta. You changed your # but I did not change my mind. Now it's $150,000 in two weeks or I talk. First to King. Then the tabloids. You know what about. Get the $$. Instructions to follow.

Before Jett could catch her breath from the wind that had just been knocked out of her, she heard the phone in her purse ringing across the room. Her movements were mechanical as she walked over and pulled it out of her bag. She saw the name and sighed. This was a call she'd been waiting for, though she couldn't say much for his timing.

"Hello, King." Still stunned, she was pleased at the smile in her voice.

"Jett, I just got the strangest call."

Uh oh.

It took every ounce of acting experience to sound unperturbed. "Who from?"

"I don't know."

"What did they say?"

"That they had information about you that I should know. Do you know what that means?"

Jett's eyes slid to the paper now clutched in her hand. Crumpling it, she calmly replied. "I have no idea."

Chapter 19
Just Kickin' It

Chantel and Terrence were still laughing as they exited Jokes, the newest entertainment addition to Kansas City's historic area at Eighteenth and Vine. The comedy club was modern, intimate, and casual, with an atmosphere that encouraged the patrons to go on in and make themselves at home. Tickets to the club's opening weekend had sold out within hours. The lineup of nationally known stars as well as up-and-comers was a scalper's dream. Terrence knew how much Chantel liked to laugh, so managing to snag a pair of tickets put him in the position to drive a hard bargain. After weeks of teasing, hinting, and straight-out cajoling, however, Chantel's defenses were worn down, and so were her excuses. She was thrilled when he invited her to join him and, now, very glad that she did.

"That was amazing," Chantel said, as they soaked up the atmosphere while strolling down Vine. "I thought that fool was going to take off all his clothes!"

"When he dropped those jeans to reveal those holey-ass boxers? Man!" Terrence cracked up again.

"I loved the setup, didn't you?" Terrence nodded. "There's not a bad seat in the house."

"It's bigger than it looks, too."

"Thanks to getting there after the lights dimmed and those second-row tickets," Chantel wriggled her brows, "I wasn't really aware of that until we were walking out. How did you manage to cop those?"

Terrence popped an invisible collar. "I got skills."

They passed other couples and groups who'd taken advantage of the perfect summer weather and diverse entertainment to enjoy a night out. Laughter, conversation, and smooth jazz notes floated on a gentle breeze under a clear, star-filled sky. They passed the Gem Theater that housed the American Jazz and Negro Leagues Baseball museums before reaching the Blue Note, a jazz club featuring the legendary Ida McBeth that night. As Ida's silky alto and the band's tight and right notes drifted through the club's opened doors, it was a natural move for Terrence to reach for Chantel's hand. She surprised herself by not chasing away the romantic thoughts that sprang up in her head at his touch. They were in the city. Artani was spending the night with his dad. She probably had cobwebs in her cock sock. With Terrence looking good, smelling nice, and being such a gentleman, she just might take Ida's advice and have a wang dang doodle tonight.

"Man, it's beautiful out here," he said.

"No humidity," Chantel added. "Almost July in Missouri, that rarely happens."

"Yeah, somebody's got a birthday coming up."

"Don't remind me."

"Guess that means you don't want any gifts either."

"Hold up, now. I didn't say all that."

"Uh huh. Mention gifts and you probably want to have two birthdays."

"One every month from now till December, just in time for Santa."

Terrence looked at her slyly. "You probably need somebody to sweep out that chimney."

"I can't believe you said that." Chantel failed at trying to maintain a frown.

"You know I'm telling the truth. Is Art bringing Artani home tomorrow or are you coming back to pick him up?"

"I told Art I'd pick him up, but that was before you scored those awesome tickets. I was thinking about calling to see how he felt about me picking him up now."

"You're ready for our date to end already?"

"Who said this was a date?"

"The price of those tickets."

"Ha! I'm not really ready to head back to Marquette. Just thinking out loud."

"Are you hungry?"

"Not until the smell of barbecue smacked me upside the nose when we passed that restaurant back there."

"I didn't say anything, but my mouth watered."

"Okay, now that we're being honest, my stomach's been growling for the last hour."

"Girl, I'm so hungry I'm about to swallow this gum."

Chantel burst out laughing, causing those close by to look at them and smile. One man's blue eyes twinkled as he passed them, a pleasant-looking woman by his side.

"You two coming from that new comedy club?" he asked.

"Yes, sir," Terrence replied.

"Lucky you to get tickets. Looks like your wife enjoyed it."

Terrence didn't correct him. Chantel was too caught off guard to say anything. As they continued to stand on the corner, Terrence's gaze seemed to reach the depths of her soul. Her nipples pebbled. Muscles in her chimney clenched. It seemed a million thoughts raced around in her head. She was thinking too much but couldn't help it. Was she really ready to take their friendship to the next level?

"What?"

"I'm thinking about . . . eating. Do you want to go back to the barbecue spot or check that place out?" He nodded toward the building behind her.

She turned around. "Bayou on the Vine? Have you been there?"

"No."

"Sounds different. Works for me."

"Me, too. Let's go."

The place was packed. There was a fifteen-minute wait. Chantel and Terrence scanned the menu while they sat in the foyer.

He called off the entrees. "Gumbo, jambalaya, etouffee, shrimp and grits . . ."

"When you're hungry, everything sounds good." Chantel bobbed her head to the sound of a steel guitar, fiddle, and harmonica blending with an upright bass. "It's like we left KC and landed in New Orleans, without the plane ride!"

The music was so lively that had her phone not been set to vibrate, she wouldn't have noticed a call had come in. She reached into her purse.

"It's Jett," she told Terrence, before getting up. "Be right back." She stepped outside and away from the music. "Hi, Jett," she almost sang, still rocking to the Cajun beat.

"What the fuck is going on?"

Chantel looked at her phone. "What?"

"Whoever's down there with this blackmail bullshit sent a letter to the studio and just called King."

Music poured out as someone exited the restaurant. Chantel put a finger to her ear and walked farther away. "Sorry, Jett, I'm in the middle of Eighteenth and Vine. It's noisy. What thing?"

"Not thing. King!"

"What about him?"

"Someone is trying to get him caught up in this blackmail bullshit."

"Someone you know is trying to blackmail the mayor?"

"No, someone you know."

"What kind of threat do they have on him, and why did he call you?"

"Don't play stupid, Chantel. You know what they called threatening him about."

"No, I don't."

Jett didn't respond. Chantel looked at the phone. The call was still connected. "Jett, can you hear me? I don't know why anybody would threaten King."

"The same reason they threatened me and you, clueless. Money!"

"Did you tell him what happened, the notes and calls we've gotten?"

"Didn't you hear what I said? I didn't have to. Somebody called King. He called me."

"But why would they call him?" Chantel thought about the article splashed across the *Marquette Monitor* front page, the one touting her as the singing sensation at the mayor's victory party, and as Jett's sister. Her heart dropped.

"You tell me! Whoever it is mailed a letter to the studio giving me two weeks to send them a hundred and fifty grand. Have you gotten any more letters or calls?"

With everything surrounding the mayor's election, she'd managed to forget about that. Subconsciously her hopes had been that the blackmailer did, too.

"Sorry, Jett, but yes. I did."

"And you didn't tell me?" Jett shrieked. "When?"

"Last weekend, I think."

"You think? You don't know?"

"I just got caught up. King's election, the party and everything that followed."

"So much so that you'd forget a threat that could ruin my career?"

"No. I guess I was hoping . . ."

"Chantel!" Terrence motioned for her to come inside.

"Can I call you back, Jett? I'm outside but our table is ready. The music inside is loud. Let me get back to you as soon as I get somewhere quiet."

"Are you fucking kidding me? We need to talk now!"

She began walking toward the restaurant. "Give me an hour. I'll call you back." She ended the call.

Terrence took in Chantel's worried expression. "Is everything okay?"

"I don't think so." He opened the door. They went inside. "I don't think everything's okay at all."

Chapter 20
Ready or Not

They decided to spend the night in Kansas City. Chantel told Terrence what Jett had said. He suggested she try and put the conversation aside; that until she knew more, there was nothing to do. She tried to get back into the groove, take in the ambiance created by the people, smells, and lively music. The food had been tasty. Terrence enjoyed his po'boy with fries, red beans and rice. But Jett's phone call had taken Chantel's appetite. They were in his SUV on their way to the Intercontinental at the Country Club Plaza, the smell of her boxed jambalaya pasta hanging in the air. It was a quiet ride. Terrence didn't turn on the radio. Chantel was thankful. He sensed her troubled mood. She stood near the lobby's windows while Terrence checked them in and obtained the card keys, looking out at a night that had ranked as near per-fect until just over an hour ago.

She smelled Terrence's cologne before he eased up beside her. "Ready?"

She nodded. He took her hand and led them across the lobby. While they waited for the elevator and as it ascended, no words were spoken. They reached the eighth floor. The doors opened. Terrence held it back and ushered Chantel out before him. Before the call, Chantel would have been feeling all kinds of butterflies.

Now as they reached the door to their room and Terrence slid in the card, all she felt was dread.

He'd booked a deluxe with a view of the Plaza, which even in her muddled state of mind Chantel thought a very smart choice. The king-sized bed was definitely the focal point, but there was a living space as well. That's where Chantel headed. She set her purse on the table in front of the couch, then sat down heavily. Removed her shoes and stretched out her legs on the ottoman. Stared straight ahead and tried to get her brain working again. Jett's call had blown her mind.

Terrence joined her there, and put his feet up, too. "I didn't think to stop and get something to drink. You want me to order room service from the bar?"

Chantel shook her head. "I should probably be sober for this conversation."

He put his arm on the couch but not quite around her. Enough so that she still had her space, but close enough for a nonverbal *I've got you.*

"What are you thinking?" he asked after a minute had passed.

"That I don't want to make this phone call."

"Then don't."

"I was having such a great time. The evening was going so well."

"Why spoil it? This isn't the first note or phone call. It's happened before."

"But time's running out. And why they'd involve King is something I still don't get. I mean him and my sister knew each other back in the day but . . ." Words died on Chantel's tongue as snatches of conversation pierced her mind.

More like flirted, hung out a couple times.

Because I was raped, that's why!

Charlie. Billy. Larry. Henry. Hell, I don't remember.

Chantel relaxed. There was no way King could be her father.

She couldn't see him raping anybody and he wasn't a person that Jett would forget.

"What is it?"

"Nothing." She leaned her head against his arm. "This is crazy."

"I agree. But what will talking about it with your sister gain either of you tonight?"

Chantel's vibrating phone rattled on the table, causing her to jump. She leaned over and saw the name on the face.

"I guess we're about to find out." She picked up the phone and pressed the speaker icon. "Hey, Jett. I was just about to call you."

"Took you long enough."

Chantel looked at Terrence, who motioned for her continue and to stay calm.

"Okay, somebody called King. Why?"

Jett didn't answer.

"Did they demand money?"

Silence.

Everything happens for a reason. It's how you came to be.

"Jett, what did they say?"

"They told him that I had information about him that he should know."

Chantel's heart began pounding. "What type of information?

It took Jett a while to answer. Chantel felt Terrence's arm tighten around her as she stared at the phone. "That he has a daughter other than the one he raised."

Chantel had never been electrocuted but in the moment understood what it felt like. "You're saying King, Mayor Richardson, is my biological father. You're lying, right?"

"No, Chantel." Jett sounded weary.

Chantel felt as though she were floating outside of her body. She stood and walked out on the balcony, then slid to the concrete floor. Terrence was there in an instant. He sat and down and pulled her into his arms without saying a word.

"King raped you?" Her voice was a hoarse whisper.

"Not exactly."

"But that's what you said! How can I believe anything when you keep on lying?"

"He denied we were ever together. It would have been his word against mine."

"That was true thirty years ago. Now there's DNA."

The irony of that statement wasn't lost on Chantel. Jett chose to ignore it.

"I thought not knowing was better than not being wanted. But whoever is trying to blackmail us evidently knows what went down."

"Exactly what did happen?"

"You're a grown-ass woman with a child of your own. I'm sure you're familiar with how babies are made."

Chantel ignored Jett's smart-aleck quip in favor of getting the facts. "What is he going to do?"

"Try and get the call traced. Hire a PI."

"Sounds like a good idea."

"I don't have to tell you how critical it is that we put an end to this bullshit. He was just elected mayor. My single drops next month. The show debuts in September. We cannot let this get out."

"I couldn't agree more, but how do we stop it?"

"Have you questioned your friends again? Especially those in some kind of financial crisis who'd stoop this low to try and solve it?"

"I can't be any clearer with you than I've already been. This isn't the work of my friends, or anyone that I know. It's more likely the leak is from your former friends. Someone you went to school with or dated or, I don't know, has held a grudge from something that happened back when you were fifteen."

"After all these years, I can only think of one person who'd hold on to that that kind of vendetta."

"Who?"

"The bitch who harassed me at Mama's funeral. Brenda Moreland."

There's probably some jealousy there . . . she took my man.

Chantel closed her eyes and suppressed a groan. *Shit!* She had yet to tell Jett about their interactions. It had to happen. The timing sucked.

"Hang on a minute." Chantel muted the call and said to Terrence, "Can you help me up?"

Terrence stayed on the balcony. She returned to the room and lay across the bed.

"Okay, sorry about that. I was on the patio. Had to get off the concrete. I need to tell you something. I met Brenda."

"What do you mean you met her? How? Why?"

Chantel relayed what happened in the clothing store, and their exchange at King's celebration. "She didn't try to hide her animosity but said at one time y'all were friends."

"Did we look like friends at Mama's gravesite?"

"She said you slept with her boyfriend."

"She's a liar."

"She said you did it to be spiteful and then dumped him after that."

"Sounds like you two had quite the cozy conversation about me. What else did she say?"

"Basically, that she was very jealous of you. Because you were everything she'd never be."

"She actually admitted that."

"Yes, Jett, she did."

"Well, I'll be damned."

"That's not all. We spoke this week."

"So, what. Y'all are friends now?"

"No, but she's always been friendly. Just like that day at the store. When we saw each other at King's party, she gave me her number. The day after my article appeared in *The Call*, she sent a bouquet of flowers congratulating me. Because of your beef it took me a while, but I finally called to thank her."

"It's that bitch."

Chantel's brows scrunched. "Do you really think so?"

"Who else? Don't be stupid, Chantel. What better way to cover up blackmail than to befriend the very person you're black-mailing?"

What Jett said made a whole lot of sense.

"Your naïve Midwestern ass got played."

Chantel digested Jett's comment, compared it against the Brenda she knew. Then she did what her mama Anna told her and went with her gut.

"We're both from the Midwest, and I'm not naïve. I'm actually a fairly good judge of character, and I don't think Brenda's our blackmailer. What was the postmark on your envelope?"

"Los Angeles, but that doesn't mean anything. It would take a person five minutes to reach out to someone they knew here and call in a favor."

"She's a logical suspect, but I don't feel it."

"You didn't get the feeling King was your daddy either and you've worked with him for months."

"You know what, Jett? You throw the word *bitch* around quite a bit, but you might want to look in the mirror." Chantel sat up and saw that Terrence was back in the room. She eased off the bed. "Look, I'm done with this conversation. I've had enough of diva and daddy news for one night."

She walked over and directly into his arms. "Did you hear all of that?"

"I heard enough."

"Do you think King's my father?"

"I don't see a resemblance, but he hooked up with your sis-ter . . ."

"I feel like I'm in some sort of Twilight Zone. I mean, you cannot make this up."

"What are you going to do?"

Chantel looked into Terrence's gorgeous brown eyes. "That's the million-dollar question for which I don't have a dime."

The anonymous blackmailer called twice in one week. Jett had gotten another call, too. The blackmailer—one week and counting. By Thursday afternoon Chantel was a wreck. She hadn't decided on singing at the club, wasn't sure she could sing at the Diplomat and chance running into King. Not that she was 100 percent convinced about what Jett had told her. When it came to Chantel's parentage, Jett had lied more than she'd told the truth. Yet after her big reveal, Chanel had gone online and read everything she could find about King Richardson. Had squinted at every pic of him she found online. There was nothing that stood out to make her think they were related. If anything, he seemed too light and distinguished looking to be her dad. He also looked like someone who didn't have to go around raping girls for sex. There hadn't been many interactions, but the times they'd engaged in brief conversations, he'd been respectful and kind. He'd even noticed her being preoccupied after finding out that Jett was her mother and had asked Terrence about her.

Wait. Was he concerned because I sang at his club, or because Jett's telling the truth and I really am his daughter?

Chantel left the office fifteen minutes early and was on the phone to Terrence before she'd reached the parking lot.

"Hey, beautiful."

"Hi, Terrence."

"The appropriate response is 'hi, handsome.'"

Chantel didn't respond.

"I'm just trying to make you smile, babe. How are you feeling?"

"I've been better."

"Worried about tomorrow night and whether or not King will be there?"

"Bingo."

"Yeah, I kinda thought that might happen."

"You did?" Chantel reached her car, popped the lock, and slid inside.

"Of course. It would take hella nerve to chance singing in front of someone who just might be your daddy and not know it."

"Thank you for ensuring that I most definitely won't be at the club tomorrow!"

"When I told you I gotchu, I meant it. Don't worry. I've got somebody to cover."

"Damn, Jasmine is about to have my job." Chantel started her car and eased out of the lot.

"Not her. This young dude from Olathe who's been blowing up on social media. He'll be good for business and bringing in a younger crowd."

"Here I'm worrying about Jasmine and it's you trying to replace me."

"Never that. I just got your back, that's all."

"What does he sing? What about the band?"

"Let me worry about the club. You talk to Jett about those calls you got?"

"She got them, too, along with instructions on where to wire the money."

"Damn, somebody is serious. You think that chick Brenda would do all this?"

"Maybe I should call and ask her."

"I don't know, Chan. You might either get answers or give her ideas."

"True."

"Look, don't worry about the club or King. I'll handle King. If you decide you want to sing, then cool. We can maybe have Black Satin do a song or two in your sets."

"Did you say Black Satin?"

"Yes, and believe me, he lives up to the hype."

Chantel ended the call feeling even more conflicted than before. Thanks to Jett, she had a reserve in the bank but nothing close to what the blackmailer demanded. Jett said without knowing who was behind it, she'd be damned before she came off a cent. What if the blackmailer went through with the threat and ruined Jett's comeback? What if she lost her singing gig and then found out Jett lied and King wasn't her father? Chantel drove home on autopilot, barely remembered picking up Artani from daycare, and was somehow not surprised to see Rita's white Kia Soul parked in front of her house. Rita had obviously been watching for her in the rearview mirrors because her door opened as soon as Chantel turned into the driveway.

"What are you doing here?"

"Good afternoon to you, too."

"Good afternoon. What are you doing here?"

Artani raced in front of the two women as they all headed toward the front door.

"Sean's brother's church gave him ten tickets to that new movie with the Black kid as a superhero. It's showing over in Sedalia. He's taking the boys. I came by to see if Artani could go."

They'd entered the house and were standing in the hallway.

Artani overheard and started jumping up and down. "Ooh, yes, I wanna go. Say yes, Mommy! Please say yes!"

"You couldn't have called with this question?" She nodded toward her son. They continued into the living room.

"I was over at High Five. It made more sense just to wait."

"Are you trying to buy stock in that place or what? You're over there almost every day."

"I like browsing the aisles. They've got good stuff." Rita looked at her watch. "The movie starts at seven, so if Artani's going we need to leave."

"Does he need money or anything?"

"No, but you might want to get him a jacket. They always keep those theaters cold."

"Get your jean jacket, Artani. Hurry up!"

"I know it's a little late for a school night, but Sean should have him back by ten."

"That's cool."

"Ready for your show tomorrow?"

Chantel's face dropped. "I'm not going."

"Why not?"

"You won't even believe it when I tell you."

"Try me."

Artani ran into the hall. "Call me later."

After Rita left, Chantel called Art and asked if he'd watch their son that weekend. She had some serious thinking to do, and needed the whole house to herself to do it.

Chapter 21
How Can I Ease the Pain

After Chantel left work on Friday, she picked up Artani from daycare and drove to Kansas City. They ate dinner together before she dropped him off at his father's, then drove through the streets of Kansas City with no particular destination. Thirty minutes later, she found herself in front of her mother's house. She pulled to the curb and turned off the engine. Her mama's rose bushes were fuller than the last time she came here. The blooms swayed as if in welcome. Their scent traveled along the breeze. The feeling of missing Anna came over her suddenly like a thick, woolen blanket. For a second, she found it hard to breathe. She rested her head against the steering wheel and tried not to cry. Anna Scott would have answers on how to handle the situation. Her mother would know just what to do. She looked up to see Miss Blanche standing in her doorway, waving her in. Chantel wasn't sure whether or not she was ready for a convo with the neighbor. But she'd already been seen, and there was no way she'd ignore her, so she reached for her purse and stepped outside.

"Hi, Miss Blanche."

"I thought that car looked familiar."

"I'm not going to be here long," Chantel said, after stepping onto Blanche's porch and giving the older lady a hug. "Was just missing Mama and ended up stopping by."

"That's totally understandable, child. Come on in."

"I only have a minute."

"On the porch or in the house, it's sixty seconds either way." They stepped inside. "Have a seat!"

Chantel hid a smile as she sat on the love seat. Blanche sat on the sofa. "What brings you to the city?"

"Artani's spending the weekend with his father."

"That's good. You got plans for all that free time?"

Chantel shook her head. "I thought about maybe doing something up here before driving back, but I couldn't really think of anything."

"You're too young to be sitting home on a Friday night. That's for people like me. Hold on, I thought you sang at the mayor's club on the weekend. That's what it said in *The Call*."

"I took this weekend off."

"But everything's okay, though."

"Yes, ma'am. Everything's just . . ." The tears started before she could get out the lie.

"Oh, child." Miss Blanche heaved herself off the couch to come sit by Chantel, who she then pulled to her bosom as she would a child. "Go on and let it out, honey. Whatever's hurting, the tears can help wash away."

Chantel didn't just cry, she had an all-out boo-hoo, probably because it was the first time since losing Anna that she'd felt safe enough to let it happen. After several minutes she sat up, reached for a Kleenex in a holder she imagined Blanche had knitted, and blew her nose. Blanche reached for her hand, patted it, and rubbed her arm. It went this way for several minutes.

"Sorry. I must have needed that." Chantel wiped her eyes, then blew her nose again.

"Ain't nothing like a good cry every now and then. Sometimes we women ask too much of ourselves. Feel like we've got to be strong, holding it together for everybody else. I say that's a bunch of malarkey. If we shed more tears, there'd be less heart attacks."

Chantel leaned over and hugged Blanche. Kissed her on the cheek. "I sure do miss my mama, Miss Blanche, but tonight you were a pretty good substitute."

"You're Anna's child. I'm glad to do it. Don't try and carry burdens by yourself. Use my number. Anytime you need a shoulder, I'm here."

Chantel figured tears must be heavy because she felt lighter going down Blanche's steps than when she went up them. So much so that picking enough of Anna's roses to make a bouquet brought more joy than sorrow. She decided not to stay in Kansas City. Instead she bought fish dinners from Saltwater for her and for Rita's family, then back on the road, welcomed the quiet, drove without music so she could recognize the endless thoughts crowding her mind. She tried not to examine them too closely to judge or correct, but simply allowed herself to feel however she felt. She thought about Rita and her comment after the initial shock from the news about King.

"You better hope he is your father. The Richardsons have bank!"

She thought about Jett, and almost called her. Thought of Art, her ex. Artani. Her own childhood. King Richardson. Miss Blanche. She thought about Brenda and a lot about Anna. She thought about Terrence, and finally acknowledged how her feelings for him had deepened. It surprised her that the reality wasn't scary. She'd known him and his family forever. Knew he was a good man. Life was a straight-up trip right now. Chantel knew for sure that he was the only one she'd want along on this journey.

Once in the house Chantel drew a bath, poured a glass of wine, and pulled up old-school R&B on her streaming service. She retrieved her eReader from the bedroom, the one with over two hundred novels downloaded and almost none of them read. She dimmed the bathroom lights and lit her favorite cashmere vanilla candle from Joe + Monroe. After several minutes of luxuriating in the atmosphere she'd created, she scrolled through the titles on her eReader until she found one that resonated. It was by another one of her favorite authors, Donna Hill—*Confessions in B-Flat.* Soon she was out of Marquette and transported to Harlem in the 60s, before she was born, and the challenges Blacks faced in that era. Only a writer like Donna could create a love story in the midst of civil, social, and racial unrest. Chantel read until the water had turned cold yet again and her skin likely resembled a raisin. She took time pampering said skin with oils and lotions, shaved her legs and arms, and considered getting a bikini wax. It was only eight thirty when she finished, but she brewed a pot of tea, pulled on a pair of burgundy silk pajamas, and curled up in bed with her book.

A loud knocking on the front door startled Chantel out of sleep. She looked at the clock. A little past ten. Then at her phone for missed calls. There was one. King.

Please don't let him be here without calling. She looked out the window, saw a late-model Jaguar, and knew that's what he'd done.

She hurried to the end of her hall. "Just a minute!" Then she went back to slip on a robe and house slippers. On the way back she redid her topknot, then took a few seconds to gather herself before opening the door.

"King?"

"I know. I apologize for coming over so late and without permission. I called, twice, and when there was no answer, I became concerned. May I come in?"

"Sure."

It was her first time around her boss outside of the club. Chantel felt vulnerable and nervous, which she hid behind a smile. She was thankful to be wearing the silk pj's and matching wrapper instead of her well-worn "period pajamas" or a cotton granny gown.

They reached the living room. "Please, have a seat." She indicated a pair of wingback chairs that flanked the fireplace, noting King's impeccable style as he made his way to the chair. He was tall, over six feet, with a body that suggested he worked out regularly. Maybe had a gym in his home. He was almost sixty, and even though there was a streak of gray here or there, he emitted vitality and power, like he could take on any opponent in any way, and win. He wore a charcoal gray suit that was obviously tailored. If forced to venture a guess, she wouldn't choose Payless as his source for shoes. The merest hint of jasmine and cedar wood lingered behind him. He was more alpha than metrosexual; however, his nails were manicured, his hair, mustache, and goatee expertly trimmed, and if he said his skin hadn't experienced a charcoal, Dead Sea mud, or some kind of facial, Chantel would call him a bald-faced liar straight to his face.

"Can I get you anything?"

"I'm fine, thanks."

She sat on the side of the sofa nearest him, rested her hands in her lap, and waited. All while not trying to stare at him as if he were a biology experiment, trying to tell if she showed up anywhere on his face.

The silence didn't seem to make him uncomfortable. In fact, his commanding presence gave off the vibe that he was the one who owned the house and she was the guest.

"This is my first time in these condos. I remember when they were built."

"Yeah, I think they're around twenty years old."

"That sounds about right." His eyes roamed the living room. "It's a nice place."

"Thank you."

"Do you live here alone?"

"With my son, Artani. He'll turn four in the fall."

"I was a rascal at that age."

Chantel crossed her arms and, before she could think, said, "You're probably a rascal now. Wait! Did I say that out loud? I'm sorry!"

His laugh was deep and full, from his gut. "No worries. Tamela would probably agree."

"Your wife is always so put together when I see her. Is she at the club?"

"She had a dinner engagement with her sorority sisters. My brother-in-law accompanied me down."

"Oh."

"I want to make it clear that my intentions for this visit are honorable, and very specific."

"I had no doubt."

"Good. I'm sure Jeanetta told you about the call I received at my office."

"Yes, she did."

"She said that both of you received similar calls, and threatening mail?"

"Yes."

"About Jett being your mother?"

"You knew?"

"I talked to Jett. As I shared with you previously, Jeanetta and I knew each other back when we were younger . . . and fooled around."

"Is that what you call assaulting someone?"

King's demeanor changed three times in two seconds—from shock to anger to disappointment. "Chantel, I swear to you, our intimacy was consensual."

He looked her dead in the eyes. Chantel felt he told the truth.

"I had no idea she wasn't eighteen. She carried herself as someone older, as an adult."

"How old were you?"

"Twenty-four, twenty-five. We were only together a couple times. Several months later she told me she was pregnant, and that I was the father. I knew that was not true and told her so. The next time I saw her was from my television screen. I did inquire among our mutual associates, discreetly of course, if Jett had had a baby. Not one person could corroborate her story. I went on with my life."

"Since you were so sure about not being the father, why did you want to know?"

"Jeanetta and I weren't exactly close but she was a cool girl, even back then. I cared about her and wanted her to be all right. When she reached out a while back, I was glad to hear from her."

"And now?"

"I'm concerned. What she eventually shared about the black-mailer took me aback, I can only imagine its impact on you."

"It's been shocking, to say the least."

"I have every intention of getting to the bottom of who's behind this sick attempt at money extortion."

"Jett said you hired a private investigator?"

"Yes. Lee Rivera is one of the best."

"Any luck so far?"

"Not from the phone call tracing. The routing number given to Jett for the money drop is connected to an account of a questionable check-cashing establishment in Gary."

Chantel raised a brow. "In Indiana?" King nodded. "Do you know anybody from there?"

"Only the Jackson 5."

A bit of much-needed levity came into the room.

"Is that legal?"

"Not really, but enough money will get some people to bend the rules. The management there were very tight-lipped, conveniently hiding behind privacy laws, in my personal opinion. Lee contacted Jett, who overnighted the note and envelope she'd received. Do you still have your paper?"

"Unfortunately, no. I thought I'd kept it but must have accidentally thrown it away."

"That's okay. Lee gave specific instructions on how to package the evidence to preserve any potential fingerprints or DNA. Hopefully, there will be something on it that the lab can use."

"Is that why you came over, to get whatever evidence I had?"

"I came, Chantel, because I was concerned about you. I also want to allay any fears or worries you may have about me or our professional relationship. You are a beautiful singer and lovely young woman who any man, I'm sure, would be proud to claim. However, I am not your father."

Once again, Chantel felt a wave of emotion. She wasn't sure bawling could be prevented if she opened her mouth. She simply nodded.

"I'm sorry."

Finally, control. "There's no need to apologize."

King cleared his throat. "I asked Terrence if he knew . . . Excuse me." He coughed, cleared his throat, and coughed again, louder this time.

Chantel stood. "Let me get some water."

She left without waiting for a reply and returned with two cold glasses of water from the fridge.

She handed one to King, placed a coaster on the table beside him, then returned to her seat. "It's filtered, just in case you don't do tap water."

"Not if I can help it." In a long swig, he downed half of the glass. "Thank you."

"Better?"

"Much. Does Terrence know about this?"

Chantel didn't hesitate to tell the truth. She took a sip of water and set down her glass. "We happened to be together when Jett called me. Honestly, I'm glad that I wasn't alone."

"As am I. That revelation would be jarring under any circumstances. Doubly so considering our working relationship, and, though limited, my past with your sister."

"She seemed positive about being with you when she conceived."

"I know." King raised his hand and slowly rubbed his goatee, perplexed. Chantel noted the sparks from the carats on his pinkie ring.

"I'm not sure why she said it."

"This is a sensitive topic to discuss with a young lady, but my father drilled in his boys to always use protection. When Jeanetta and I were together, that was the case."

"Hey," Chantel said somewhat teasingly, raising her hands. "You don't have to convince me. I believe you."

He smiled. His body relaxed. "I hope you find your father, Chantel. If that's what you want."

She nodded. "I'll try."

King checked his watch. "I should get back to the club, but I have a few more questions."

"Okay."

"Are the contents of the threat I received why you aren't working tonight?"

Chantel dropped her eyes for a second, then met his gaze. "Yes. It seemed so awkward. I . . ."

"No worries. I completely understand. Now that we've had this conversation, however . . ."

"I'll be there tomorrow night."

"Beautiful. Lastly, the inaugural celebration on Wednesday. Will you still do me the honor of singing a couple numbers?"

"Given that someone is trying to blackmail you with a lie about me, are you sure that's a good idea?"

"You have a point. Let me think about it."

"Okay, but I'm fine if you decide to make another choice."

King drank the rest of the water, then stood. "Thanks for the water, and for your time."

Chantel stood as well. They headed to the door. "You're welcome. I appreciate you coming over."

"Again, my apologies for the late hour." He extended his hand. She shook it. "It was no problem. Thanks again."

Chantel closed and locked the door. She returned to the living room, retrieved the glasses, and headed to the kitchen. She deposited them in the dishwasher, turned off the light, and walked toward her bedroom. Halfway down the hall she stopped, thought for a moment, and turned around. She turned on the kitchen light, pulled out two large storage bags, took the glasses from the dishwasher, and secured King's DNA. He was as confident that he wasn't her father as Jett was that King was her bio daddy. One thing about DNA: It didn't lie. So if for any reason it turned out Chantel needed irrefutable proof, she had a way to get it.

Chapter 22
Unpretty

They didn't send the blackmail money. In a hastily scheduled video call on the PI's secure line, the pros and cons of doing so were weighed, along with conducting a sting to nab whoever came to pick up the cash. In the end, it was decided that without involving the local authorities, such a move was too risky. The last thing either Jett or King wanted was the press getting wind of what they were dealing with. Was being blackmailed worse than having news of a secret daughter splashed across the headlines? Neither was desirable, but King refused to be bullied and Jett reluctantly went along. That they hadn't uncovered who was behind the threat bothered her, too. Everyone hoped calling the asshole's bluff was the right move. Meanwhile, Jett had to put on her big-girl thongs and go on about the business of being a star.

With the first season taping wrapped and the *Star Searchin'* single set to drop in August, her schedule picked up with a round of meetings—manager, agent, publicist, stylist, record company and *Seeking Stardom* execs. Her career felt as hot as the Fourth of July fireworks that had recently flashed across the nation's skies. In addition to the LA photo shoot for *Melanin Magic*, there was a photo shoot and video in New York for the single. The photographer was a young Asian phenom, just twenty-two, but creating

major buzz in the industry. Jett liked that he was young and ener-
getic, and grew even more excited after the conference call to
kick around ideas with Myles and the record execs. One idea involved her covered in nothing but star-shaped plexiglass cubes.
Another was to have her embody Mother Earth by giving the illu-
sion of her growing out of a tree that reached the stars. All she
could think of was her audience being reminded of *Roots*. She
was quick to ixnay that idea. There were a few others, but her favorite involved her dressed in a ball gown, hanging from the landing skid of a helicopter as it hovered over a nighttime New York
skyline. Securing insurance to cover that type of shot could make
it cost-prohibitive, but Jett was ready to battle for it. A pic like
that would be classic, and totally badass. The production team
shooting the video were some of the best in the biz. Her earlier
recordings had been mixed down. They'd handle overdubs, fills,
ad libs, or whatever else the producers felt was needed. Their last
appointments would be a round of *Seeking Stardom* promotions
on the morning talk show circuit, which would also provide the
chance for her to drop a few teasers for the show's theme song.
Everyone believed it possible for the song to hit Billboard Top 10.
Maybe even #1. As the showbiz whirlwind spun around her, Jett
was calm and confident. She was born for the lifestyle and exactly
where she was supposed to be.

With all of the hobnobbing, designer fittings, and near-
genuflecting people at her beck and call, it was easy for Jett to almost forget about her little blackmail problem. Every day without
Zola receiving crazy mail or her not getting a phone call, brought
Jett closer to believing that calling the chump blackmailer's bluff
had been the right idea. The idea of a threat further decreased the
bigger her entourage and bank accounts grew.

The first photo shoot took place in Malibu, on an estate Jett
quickly dubbed "Wow." According to Myles the home was
owned by an Arab sheik, who purchased it for a modest $125 mil-

lion as a vacation spot for him and his family, who visited from November through January. Three months! *Wow.* The rest of the year the property was maintained by a house manager and staff, and rented out for A-list parties, million-dollar weddings, and extravagant photo shoots by studios who could handle the daily rental price of one hundred grand. Myles explained this as she, the stylist, designer, photographer, and assistants were given a tour of the home, the immaculate grounds, and the private beach just steps below a black-bottomed infinity pool. Outside the mansion were gardens, palm and bright orange Madagascar trees, and a wraparound patio. Inside, for *Melanin Magic*'s December issue, it was Christmas. The stylist dressed Jett in leather, wool, silk, and satin. She draped her in diamonds on loan from Vanleles. There were tiaras and politically incorrect animal furs. The shoot lasted a grueling seventeen hours. Jett had the time of her life!

There was barely time to recover before she boarded a customized Zenith Gulfstream G700 for her stint in New York. For Jett it seemed like a day that lasted three hundred plus hours, with bits of sleep snatched here and there. The studio experience? Brilliant. Morning shows for *Seeking Stardom*? Superb. Jett's worst experience—that she'd never describe as such—was the photo shoot she wanted, being suspended over the New York skyline. Because she wasn't careful of what she asked for, she almost died. Her hands ended up raw and bleeding from her death grips on the helicopter's landing skids. She hadn't been afraid of heights until looking down from the equivalent of forty-five stories with thin "grips," a stunt jump bag for falling and a director whispering "trust me." Due to the long hours, freezing rooms (to keep her makeup fresh), and blistering wind from the helicopter blades, she developed a cold that almost turned into pneumonia. Did the photos justify Jett's near-death experience? If asked, she would answer, "absolutely!"

She arrived back in LA with just enough time to recover and

prepare for the *Seeking Stardom* cast party and premiere of the commercials that would run nonstop until just after Labor Day when the show debuted. Another smashing success. Later that week she got a call from Randall. He'd seen some footage of the tapings and congratulated her on what he was sure would be a success. It was the first time they'd spoken since she'd fired him as her personal trainer.

"Let me take you out."

"No, Randall. That's not a good idea."

"Not as a date. Just a friend. Hey, I helped you get that body everyone is raving over. You can spare a brother an hour or two to have breakfast, right?"

It was true. Randall was 100 percent responsible for helping her get her body back. He also was a lot of fun, before he became a pain in the ass. Plus, she was feeling generous. Randall wasn't a bad guy. Why not enjoy the pleasure of his company and a free meal to boot?

"I can do Thursday. Early. Text me where and what time."

"You're on."

Thursday morning, Jett popped the top on her Maserati GranCabrio for a meandering street route to Beverly Hills. She pulled up to the valet stand for the quaint French bistro Randall had chosen, waved away the hostess's services, and joined Randall, who she'd spotted at a sidewalk table. They caught each other up on their lives over petit pastries and chocolat chaud. He told her about his new client/lover, a soap star from Alabama he'd met on the lot. She told him about her trip to New York and almost dying to get the shot. He insisted on getting the check, then suggested they window-shop to walk off the meal.

Thirty minutes later they reached a newsstand on the corner across from the bakery and stood waiting for the light.

"I really enjoyed seeing you, babe," Randall said, and turned to hug her.

Jett returned the embrace. "I'm glad we can be friends."

"Always." Just as the light changed, Randall said, "Hey, isn't that you on the cover?"

"Where?" Jett's publicist had told her she'd be on several covers during the first weeks of the talent competition. She ignored the green light and walked to where Randall stood, his mouth slightly agape.

She looked over his shoulder. "Which one is that?"

He handed it to her, silent. Jett saw Chantel's face and then the caption:

"Jett's Secret Daughter!"

Her heart dropped to the concrete on Melrose.

Chapter 23
Love Calls

Unlike Jett, Chantel was not convinced that they'd dodged a blackmail bullet. Terrence became her rock and helped save her sanity. They became a couple. Serious. Exclusive. It wasn't something they discussed, planned, or intended. From the night they stayed together in Kansas City, and the next day when they'd picked up Artani and spent the day at the zoo, it began to evolve into what they now had. He called her every day just to say good morning and at night to ask how her day went and share what he'd done. That Monday after the comedy show, when Chantel got home from work, he was parked in front of her condo. The next night he showed up with tacos and large tubs of refried beans and rice. She called him later that night and after jokingly calling him a stalker explained her concern about their whirlwind love situation and how it would affect Artani if and when he no longer came around. She hadn't dated anyone since divorcing Artani's father and didn't want him getting confused. Terrence assured her that while she might be undecided and tentative about where they were headed, he was clear that this was forever. He confessed that he'd wanted to pop the question that night in the hotel but Jett's "who's your daddy" phone call had killed his Romeo plans.

She'd asked him, "Don't you're think we're moving kind of fast?"

He'd given her the type of patient look a dad would give a child. "Girl, we've been dancing around destiny for twenty-five years. Come on, now."

Shortly after that conversation, Terrence surprised her with a trip to Sedalia for a picnic in the park. During a break from throwing a Frisbee, Chantel watched the two favorite males in her life having what looked to be a heart-to-heart. She didn't know what all was said, but when Artani came running back talking about how Terrence was "cool" and Artani didn't mind if he came over every day, she suspected the discussion involved a bribe of video games and chicken nugget dinners. To his credit, Terrence, who had no children, was great with her son. Seeing Artani's eyes light up when the black SUV pulled into the driveway told her it was okay for Terrence to keep making regular appearances on her doorstep. The final sign—not that she needed another one—was when he applied for and was hired as the building manager at Sedalia Super Sports. The former warehouse had been transformed into a giant fitness, sports, and recreation center offering five floors of activities for every age. The ground floor also housed an athletic store, café, video arcade, and mini-bowling alley. One of the perks of his new gig was unlimited family passes that in Artani's eyes toppled Black Panther, his former idol, from the superhero throne and gave Terrence the undisputed crown.

Between work, weekends at the Dip, and Terrence, Chantel's days flew by. Which was why as she sat having lunch with him at Marquee, a restaurant housed in the town's former theater, Terrence's question caught her off guard.

"Why don't we do something special this weekend?"

"What's so special about this weekend?"

"Your birthday, woman. Where have you been?"

"The Twilight Zone."

Terrence chuckled. "I know that's right. That nightmare might be over, though. You haven't gotten any more weird letters or phone calls from people talking all distorted and shit."

"No, thank goodness."

"What about Jett?"

"Haven't talked to her."

"Still?"

"Not because she's still mad. We've texted back and forth. Sounds like she's been on a crazy schedule. Right now, she's in New York. I think. I can't remember. Too much going on."

Terrence picked up his cell phone and began to scroll. Chantel ate the last bite of her salad.

"Who are you calling?"

"I'm googling your sister." Chantel sipped her tea and watched. "Looks like she's been on several talk shows." He continued scrolling. "Her single is about to drop. Looks like they shot a video to go with it."

"Really?"

"You should find out from Jett when it debuts so we can have a watch party at my house. I just got a new TV. Seventy-five inches."

"Are you sure that's big enough?"

"I thought you women liked 'em big."

She almost spewed out her drink. "You're stupid. You just started at the sports center. How'd you get the weekend off?"

"I didn't. I work Saturday and Monday, but I get off at six. Matter of fact, y'all should meet me at my house to get your birthday party started. You haven't been to my place since we crossed over."

Chantel shook her head. Lately, Terrence had started coming up with all kinds of terms to describe their situation. Including *situation*. Neither liked the terms *dating* or *relationship*. Cuddle combo. Two-for-one. Paired up. Twins. All interchangeable. Her favorite was *entanglement*. Of course, she'd been a Will Smith fan ever since *Fresh Prince*.

"I don't want you to make a big deal for my birthday. I still don't quite feel like celebrating it without Mama."

"I hear you. We can just chill."

"We can do that at my house."

"Ms. Scott, that would be a negative."

"What would we do at your house that we can't do at mine?"

"Sit on *my* sofa. Sleep in *my* bed. Cook food in *my* kitchen. Watch *my* brand new seventy-five-inch TV. You get the drill. It really doesn't matter. I'm getting ready to buy a house anyway."

"Seriously? Since when?"

"Since getting the job at the sports center. I've been riding around Sedalia, checking things out."

"It makes sense that you would move there. Close to your job. A little bigger than Marquette but still a small town. Would you keep working at the Dip?"

"Probably. At least for now. It's only a fifteen-minute commute, even less if the law isn't around."

"How long have you been thinking about buying a house?"

"About a month."

As long as we've been paired up. Hmm. Chantel didn't know whether that was a hint or coincidence. She didn't ask for clarification. Her mother believed that sometimes it was better to hold your hand, wait and see how the cards play out.

Terrence reached for a napkin, wiped his hands, then tossed the crumpled paper on his empty plate. "That's one thing we can do this weekend."

"What's that?"

"Go house hunting. You ready?"

"Not really." She looked at her watch. "But my hour's up. Time to get back to work."

Their cars were parked behind each other. They stood near them and shared a quick hug.

Chantel kissed his cheek. "Thanks for lunch, babe."

"No problem." He leaned in. "Later, I'm having you for dinner."

Chantel didn't know whether it was because the July heatwave had broken or next week's rain forecast, but on both Friday and Saturday nights, folks were ready to party and the Diplomat was packed. Nothing like performing in front of a crowd. Their enthusiasm gave her extra energy. The musicians played their fingers off! Except for Papa passing out in the middle of the dance floor during their take on Mary J. Blige's "Family Affair," the shows passed without incident. No major arguments. No drunken brawls. From the band to the servers to security to the patrons, everyone had a good time.

On Sunday, Terrence invited Chantel and Artani over for a casual birthday brunch delivered with a kiss and a card. No presents, per Chantel's request. Wanda's grandson Kaleb was with her for the weekend. She brought him, too. While the boys played video games, Terrence and Chantel surfed online real estate. After printing out the specs on five houses with potential, they piled into Terrence's SUV and drove to Sedalia.

The first two homes, both three-bed, two-bath, were disappointing.

Backing out of the drive of the second one, Terrence commented to Chantel, "Those pics were misleading."

"I agree. Why are the houses so old?"

"The town's old."

The next two stops were better than the first two. Terrence was still not impressed.

"I could see potential in that last one," Chantel said.

"Nah, too small."

"There's only one of you. How much room do you need?"

Terrence gave her the patient parent-to-child look and remained quiet. The home on the last printout had stirred the greatest debate between them. Chantel thought it was too big and too far from the town's main hub. For Terrence, it was his favorite. *Figures.* Ten minutes later they pulled up to a brick house with tan and white trim that had been described as a five-bed, four-bath at 3,924 square feet.

"This is what I'm talking about!" Terrence gave Chantel a smug look as he pulled into the driveway.

"It does have curb appeal. I like the brick."

"I'm digging the red door."

They piled out of the car. Chantel issued a warning. "Boys, don't break anything."

Terrence entered a code into the key box, opened the door, and stepped back for Chantel and the boys to enter. Chantel was immediately impressed, but kept her feelings off her face.

"I love that it has an actual foyer. And coffered ceilings . . . nice!"

Terrence entered the living room and looked up. "What are they called?"

"Coffered. Do you like them?"

"Um, let me think about it." He turned in a circle. "I like the space."

"This place is big! Look, Terrence. I can't even touch it." Artani made grunting noises as he made multiple attempts to get his four-foot-seven frame anywhere close to the ten-foot ceiling.

"It's huge!" Kaleb added, doing the same.

Chantel shook her head. "Come on, boys."

They entered an adequate dining room that flowed into a semi-galley style kitchen with stainless appliances. Upstairs they saw four bedrooms, including the master, and four baths.

Back downstairs, Chantel said, "I thought it said five-bedroom."

"The fifth one is downstairs." Terrence led the way. One look at the finished basement and he shouted, "Man cave!"

The boys were equally thrilled.

Finally, Chantel admitted, "Whoever buys this could live here forever."

Back on the highway, Terrence asked her, "What was your favorite thing about that house?"

"The kitchen," she responded, without hesitation. "The size of the laundry room and the master. And, of course, that basement."

"That was my favorite area. The bar, separate bedroom and living area for guests, and a sauna in the bathroom? That sold the house!"

"That and the deck."

"Man, I could almost smell the 'cue on the grill. Still think it's too big?"

"Clean it up one day from top to bottom and I bet you'd agree with me."

The conversation flowed from houses to cars to video games. Terrence introduced the boys to the age-old highway game of count the cars. Made it a competition to see which boy could count the most. Since they were in one, they chose black SUVs. Soon the boy's faces were glued to the window, with them yelling, "There's one! There's one!"

Terrence turned up the music, the fast rap blasting as he sang along and danced in his seat. Back in Marquette, they stopped to get ice cream. While Terrence helped the boys make what they acted like was a life-or-death decision between Chunky Monkey, Brownie Batter, or Tropical Taffy with real pineapple chunks, Chantel checked her phone. She'd missed eight calls and five texts.

"I didn't hear my phone ring," she murmured, growing slightly alarmed.

She tapped the call log and saw four names—Rita, Jett, Brenda, Miss Blanche. Phil. *Phil? What the hell is going on?* Instead of checking voicemail, she pulled up the text messages.

Jett: *Where are you? Have you seen it? Call ASAP.*

Brenda: *Girl, I just left a voicemail. Are you okay?*

Brenda, second text: 911. *Chantel, where are you? Call as soon as you get this.*

Rita: *Chantel, call me.*

Rita (second text): *It's been an hour. Do I have to drive over there?*

She walked over to Terrence. "I need to return a phone call."

"Everything all right?"

"I don't know." She stood under the awning and tapped Rita's name.

"Chantel, girl, where have you been? I've called, texted, been by your house . . ."

"We're with Terrence. Who died?"

"You haven't seen it."

"Seen what, Rita?"

"*Celebrity Gossip.* Don't freak out, but you're on the front page."

Chantel freaked out. "What?" Asked with the emphasis of a hundred question marks after the word. "That's crazy! King's celebration was over a month ago!"

"It's not about King's celebration."

Only then did Chantel hear the pain in her best friend's voice. Her stomach flip-flopped.

"What is it about?"

"Jett's on there, too."

"Oh, no."

"Yes, and I'm so sorry. That you are her daughter is on the cover in big, bold print."

"Shit!" Chantel's knees almost buckled.

"Where's Terrence?"

"Getting the boys ice cream. I've gotta call Jett."

"I'm here if you need me."

Next thing she knew, Terrence was beside her. "Babe! What's going on?"

"I've got to get to a convenience store. Jett's secret is out."

"Damn. Get in the car." Terrence held up his fob, unlocked the doors, and started the engine. "I'll get Artani and Kaleb."

Chantel tapped her sister's number with shaky hands.

Jett picked up on the second ring. "Did you see it?"

"We called their bluff and they played the joker. We don't even know who it is!"

"I have a damn good idea. First, I'm going to hire King's PI and have him prove it was Brenda. Then I'm going to give that greedy tramp a beatdown that's long overdue."

Chapter 24
I Wanna Know

After the tabloid story broke, the press had a field day. Jett's phone blew up. The story led every entertainment show. Zenith studios were flooded with calls. The execs demanded an emergency meeting.

Jett played the part of victim, used by someone trying to make some bucks on her fame. When asked for the truth, if Chantel was indeed her daughter, Jett flat-out lied. What else could she do? She employed the most frequently used tactic of those who were guilty—deny, deny, deny. So far, the studio stood behind her. Their PR departments worked overtime to back Jett's "innocence" and put out a positive spin. Luckily, the public's insatiable appetite for celebrity drama instantly heightened Jett's profile. Internet searches went through the roof. In the midst of all this hoopla, *Star Searchin'* dropped. Undoubtedly due to the #JettsSecretBaby scandal, it debuted at #1.

The success of the single pleased Zenith Records and calmed the show execs. Jett finally got a break in her crazy schedule. Forty-eight hours. That's all the time she had, and all that she needed for what had to be done. She chartered a plane to Kansas City. It had cost a grip but to bypass airport security, paparazzi, and judgmental fans made it worth every penny. Once she ar-

rived, she'd call Chantel. By then it would be too late for her sister to try and talk her out of the trip.

After landing just after midnight, she spotted the limo King
had arranged parked not far from the plane. The driver, dressed
in a black suit stood near the bottom of the airstair. He introduced himself, helped her into the limo, then retrieved her bags.
Jett sent a quick text to King letting him know she'd arrived. The
limo driver was a typical Midwesterner—polite, friendly, eager to
chat. But after a few one-word responses to his questions, he got
the message that she wasn't up for conversation and turned the
radio to an easy listening channel instead.

She rested her head against the seat, caught bits and pieces of
the burgeoning metropolitan landscape that came into view when
he exited on to Twentieth Street and a part of Kansas City Jett
didn't remember. A few blocks later, he turned and drove up a
fairly steep hill. At the top were three houses spaced an adequate
distance apart. The driver pulled into the driveway of the one re-
sembling a block of cement with huge windows closest to the
hill's precipice. While the driver gathered her luggage, she punched
the code King had given her into the keypad on what looked like
a solid steel door. It opened automatically, silently, into a space
that starkly contrasted with the home's cold exterior. The driver
placed her luggage just inside the door and waving away the tip
she prepared to give him, headed back into the night. The door
closed and enveloped her in a silence complete and absolute.
After a brief glance around what looked to be an open-concept
masterpiece, she mounted the floating staircase and walked down
the hall into the master suite. After removing her shoes, she placed
her phone on its charger and took a pill left over from her last trip
to the dentist. She climbed fully clothed onto a shimmering cop-
per raw silk spread, gazed at the lights twinkling from the outlines
of downtown, and fell asleep.

The sound of chimes began in the distance and slowly became

louder. Roused out of sleep, Jett realized it was her ringtone. She blindly reached for her cell phone, squinted at the face.

That it was King produced a flicker of a smile. "Good morning."

"Yes, in California. But here in Kansas City, it's almost one o'clock."

"Seriously?" Jett eased into a sitting position. "I can't believe I slept so long."

"Your body obviously needed the rest."

"Most definitely."

"How's the house?"

"I don't know. So far I've only seen this room and the staircase." She turned toward the windows that covered almost the entire wall. "From here on the bed, it's a very nice view."

"Are you hungry?"

"No, but I probably should eat."

"I was hoping you'd say that. How about I grab us both lunch and see you in about an hour?"

"Perfect."

When King arrived, Jett was wide-awake and ravenous. A brief walk outside, a long, hot shower, and a professional-tasting macchiato whipped up in the home's fancy espresso machine had revived her. She wore a pair of ivory-colored yoga pants with a matching midriff tee. Her mane of silky Indian tresses cascaded freely down her back. She walked barefoot across the colorful slate tile and opened the door.

"Hello, handsome."

"Hello, Jett." They hugged. "You look beautiful, as always."

"You smell good," she replied, as they crossed the foyer toward the dining room. "As does whatever you have in those bags."

"I hope you like it." He placed the bags on the table and began emptying the closest one. "It's lunchtime but you haven't eaten breakfast, plus I didn't know if there were any dietary restrictions, so I brought several dishes."

"Dietary restrictions?" Jett peeked into the second bag and reached inside.

"Vegan, vegetarian, pescatarian, all the arians . . . you Californians are choosier than the rest of us."

"No vegetarian here," she said, removing the lid from a quiche dish. "I love meat."

King didn't bite on the sultry double entendre. *Duly noted.*

"Do you think you brought enough?"

"I figured none of it would be wasted. There's probably enough here for two or three meals."

Jett eyed the various containers. "At least."

"With all of this, I still forgot something."

"I can't imagine what."

"Drinks."

Jett walked from the table. "Let me check."

"Not sure there's anything in the fridge, but there might be a bottle of wine."

"Yay, there's Perrier!"

"Perfect."

Jett brought in plates and silverware. They sat down to a table of quiche made with Italian sausage and caramelized onions, a ten-veggie salad, teriyaki meatballs, glazed chicken drumettes, lemon pepper linguini, roasted asparagus and brussels sprouts, and whole wheat rolls. Plates were fixed. Small talk exchanged. The first few minutes were all about food. Then Jett changed the subject.

"Whose place is this?"

"Ballplayer friend of mine." King swirled a healthy bite of pasta onto his fork.

"Nice. It has the feeling of being secluded even though we're next to downtown."

"That's what he wanted. Convenience and privacy."

"A guy after my own heart."

"I'm sure being hounded twenty-four seven can take its toll. Is that why you came here? Try and get away from California's relentless paparazzi?"

"That's one reason."

King paused. "There's another one?"

Jett nodded. Her eyes narrowed. "I need to take care of some unfinished business."

"Sounds serious."

"It is."

"Does it have anything to do with the article?"

"It might."

"I'm not sure I like how you sound." King sat back and crossed his arms as he eyed Jett keenly. "I assume Chantel knows you're here."

Jett shook her head. "It was late when I got here."

"But you are going to call her."

A beat and then, "Of course."

"I'm sure she'll be thrilled to see you." King stood. "Well, lady . . ."

Jett wiped her hands with a napkin and stood, too. "Leaving so soon?"

"Lunchtime flies when you've got a city to run." He pulled out his phone as they walked to the door. He turned to hug her. "Take care of yourself, okay?"

"I'll do my best. Thanks for everything."

"Anytime."

Jett headed back to put away the food, her mind in overdrive. Lee hadn't been able to connect Brenda to anything—the notes, the calls, the article printed in *Celebrity Gossip*. To Jett, that only meant one thing. With age and cunning masked as wisdom, snakes slithered more discreetly. She retrieved the glass of water on the dining room table, walked to the large window with a view of downtown Kansas City, and thought back to her and Chantel's last conversation. The reason she hadn't called her yet.

"You should call Brenda."

"Hell, no," Jett snarled.

"I knew that would be your reaction," Chantel replied.

"Then why are we having this conversation?"

"Because the two of you need to talk. I thought you might hate the person who jacked up your life even more than you hated her."

"It's the same person, which is why I now hate her twice as much."

"Brenda didn't do it, Jett. I called and asked her point blank. She wants the chance to share something with you that will help prove she's not lying."

"I told you not to trust her. Nobody readily admits to being that low-down."

"She gave Lee a copy of her cell phone records."

Jett paused. Lee hadn't told her that.

"If this news is so valuable and will help uncover the trash who sold the story, why didn't she tell you?"

"I guess it's rather personal."

"This sounds like fish bait. I'm not biting."

"What do you have to lose? She also volunteered her finger-prints. Wanted me to see that she had nothing to hide. Maybe something she says can help change the awful narrative that *Gossip* created, and help you tell your own story."

"A PR team is handling all public responses."

"Did these publicists know you when you were pregnant with me? The way Brenda did?"

Jett had no comeback for that.

"She might be able to help you figure out who sold the story to the tabloids. Considering what it's done to both our lives, I'd think you'd want all the help you can get."

"I have a feeling that Brenda has helped enough. I hope she enjoys this childish payback for shit that happened before we were grown."

"Then you probably won't take her other suggestion, either."

"The next time you see Brenda, tell her to kiss my ass." Jett hung up without waiting for Chantel's reply.

With Chantel she'd been dismissive, but Jett had thought long and hard about what her sister shared, had gone back to those high school days when she and Brenda were friends and to the incident that ended the friendship. Jett sleeping with a guy that no longer mattered to either of them was nothing compared to what that bitch had done to her life. It's why Jett changed her mind and with it her tactics. Brenda being so willing to help was perfect for the trap Jett planned to set. She picked up her phone and clicked on Lee's text message that included Brenda's phone number. Her blood boiled at the mere thought of hearing that witch's voice. Still, her fingers were steady and calmed as they punched in the number from a burner phone boasting a KC number she'd purchased before leaving Los Angeles. She retrieved her now flat glass of sparkling water and took a sip.

The other line engaged. Three rings. Four.

Jett didn't want to or plan to leave a message. *Come on, Brenda. Answer your phone!*

"Hello?"

"Brenda."

"Yes, who's this?"

A second of thought before Jett answered, "Jeanetta."

"For real?"

"Yep."

"Ooh, girl, I'm so glad you called. Chantel give you my number?"

"She didn't have to. Lee did. There's no such thing as privacy anymore, as you probably well know."

"Yeah, girl," Brenda replied, her tone pacifying. "Don't I know it. That article was messed up."

"Yes, it was."

"I feel so bad for both of y'all. And a little guilty, too."

Now we're getting somewhere. Jett clenched her fingers into a fist, forced herself into a calm that was hard to feel. Now wasn't the time to go off. If Brenda knew she was Jett's primary suspect, she'd never come over.

"Why's that, Brenda?"

"Because, well, I've been wracking my brain to figure out who could have done this underhanded bullshit. It had to be somebody from back in the day, and probably somebody we know."

"Uh huh. Tell you what? Why don't we get together and talk about it?"

"You're here, in Kansas City?"

"Yes, but not for long. I know there's bad blood between us, but Chantel says the two of you have become friendly. I thought that if for no other reason than to help her, you and I could meet."

"You know what, Jett. I'd really like that. Chantel said it was a shame to still be harboring bad feelings after all these years. I totally agree. Where do you want to meet?"

"With all the press still hounding me, somewhere private. I'm at an AirBnB near downtown Kansas City. Will you meet me here?"

"Hold on so I can write down the address."

"I can text it to you."

"Cool. I have to pick up my grandson from work in an hour. After dropping him back off here, I'll be on my way."

Jett went to the en suite bath upstairs and retrieved a scrunchy from her luggage. She pulled her hair into a tight ponytail, and removed the hoop earrings from her pierced lobes. Jett would bet her *Seeking Stardom* paychecks that Brenda was behind the mess she now found herself in. Today Jett would get the truth out of her . . . one way or another.

Chapter 25
I'll Be There

Overnight, Chantel's life had gone from a sleepy Hallmark drama to a crazy reality show. Twenty-four hours after *Celebrity Gossip* hit the stands, paparazzi had descended on Marquette en masse. They parked in front of her condo, camped out near her job, screamed for interviews, invaded her space for pictures, basically tried to record her every move. When they found out that she sang at the Diplomat, King hired extra bouncers to keep them from harassing her. It got so bad that she took a break from performing. Phil finally suggested she work from home. When she saw one of them try and snap a picture of Artani, she almost snapped. Had it not been for her neighbor Wanda she would have caught a case. After that, they mostly stayed with Terrence. One time after work, they'd followed her there, too. Bad career move. He'd stormed outside and made an announcement to the photographers camped out by his building, informing them that the next time he came out it would be with a baseball bat to break all of their equipment. He hadn't yelled. He hadn't cursed. But he told Chantel that his eye kept twitching and he was pretty sure they thought he was missing some screws. They hadn't seen a strange car since.

Chantel reached for her purse, the fast-food bag, and the files she'd picked up at the job—by surreptitiously slipping through a backdoor entrance—and entered Terrence's apartment. She sat at the bar counter, turned on a game show to fill her mind with nothingness and was half-way through a lackluster salad when her phone rang. Terrence probably, she surmised. He usually called during the lunch hour. She pulled out her phone to see an 816 prefix. Not recognizing the number, she answered anyway.

"Hello?"

"Chantel, it's King."

"Hi, King." She set the phone on the dash and reached for her soda. "You calling to see if I'll be working this weekend?"

"This isn't about the club. Has Jett called you yet?"

"Jett? No, not lately."

"So you don't know that she's here, in Kansas City."

The hand holding Chantel's soda slowly lowered from her face. *Jett came to town without letting me know?* "No, I didn't."

"Somehow I didn't think so."

"But she called you?"

"Yes. She said she had some business to handle and asked if I knew of a private residence where she could lay low. When I saw her a short while ago, I was surprised to learn that she hadn't contacted you."

So was Chantel. "She's probably here as part of her promotional tour and just hasn't had time."

"If that were the case, I believe she would have said so. Or that the network would have handled her travel plans. Call it instinct or a sixth sense or whatever but . . . following our conversation I didn't have a good feeling. She told me she'd call you. But since she hasn't, maybe you should call her. I'm sure the two of you will want to meet up."

"For sure. Thanks for reaching out, King. I'll call her right now."

Chantel immediately hung up and called Jett. The call went straight to a voicemail already full. Not able to leave a message, Chantel sent a text.

I just talked to King. You're in KC? Your VM's full. Will wait to curse your ass in person. Text me where you're staying. Will come up after work.

Chantel finished her salad and opened her laptop. Fifteen minutes went by and Jett still hadn't called. That made sense if she were at a radio or television station being interviewed. But why had she flown into town without a word to her sister? And what kind of vibe had King picked up that led him to call Chantel? King's feeling of discomfort soon rubbed off on her. She tried Jett again. Still no answer. When she didn't pick up on the third try, Chantel picked up her purse and car keys and headed back out the door. Something didn't feel right. She didn't overthink her actions or second-guess the emotions that spurred them. Once in her car she called King for the address where Jett was staying. After plugging it into the GPS she called Terrence, then Rita, and told them where she was headed and why.

"Why didn't you call me?" Rita demanded. "I would have come with you?"

"You should have called me before leaving town, babe." Terrence said, sounding both worried and disappointed.

Chantel assured both of them that she would be fine, and suggested they all ride together and meet her in the city. Sean, too, she'd suggested, and the kids. Then she put on some music and tried to calm the butterflies soaring around in her stomach, and tried to believe the assurances she'd given her family were true.

Instead of the doorbell, Jett heard a light tap. She glanced at the clock. Brenda told her she'd be there in an hour. Almost two had passed. She forced the frown off her face but when opening the door didn't go for a fake friendly expression.

"Brenda."

"Hey, Jeanetta."

The two women stood and stared at each other. A second passed. Two. Five.

"Are . . . you going to invite me in?"

Jett stepped back. Brenda entered with curious eyes, taking in the swanky setup. "This is nice," she said, mocking the line Tiffany Haddish popularized. "I might need to rent this place myself, get away from the grandkids driving me mad."

Brenda turned to see Jett still standing by the doorway.

"Why are we acting all stiff and formal. I know at times we've both wanted to kick the other's ass, but that's over. Come here and give me a hug."

She crossed back over to where Jett stood and embraced her. Jett allowed it for a second before stepping around her and entering the living room. The thin veil on her anger had been rent with Brenda's touch.

"Bitch, I've agreed to speak with you but let's not act like we're friends."

"The only way you'll see a bitch is to look in the mirror." Brenda, nonplussed, dropped her purse on the couch. "You can drop that tough act. If I was scurred"—she paused for affect—"I wouldn't be here You forget, darlin, I knew you when. All that fame and money and you still haven't changed.

"This view is amazing." Brenda sidled over to the window, but Jett noticed didn't fully turn her back.

"Chantel believes you're innocent. I think you're full of shit." Jett crossed her arms, her tone turned frosty. "Whatever the fuck you think you can say to prove otherwise, say it. Quickly. Then get the fuck out of this house."

Brenda turned slowly, her eyes widening with each f-word. "Okay, now hold on, sistah. I understand you're upset. You've been through a lot. But what you're not going to do is talk to me like I'm a piece of shit on a sidewalk for you to step on. I'm here because I want to help your arrogant ass. And not even for you. For your daughter, Chantel. The one who I'm sure is the beautiful person she is because your selfish, whorish ass didn't raise her.

"You know what?" She walked over and snatched her purse off the couch. "I came over here to do your ass a favor. And to help Chantel. But I'm not going to put up with this bullshit. I'll take my Black ass home right now."

For a woman more than a few pounds overweight, Brenda was fast on her feet. She was almost to the door when Jett reached her, grabbed her arm and swung her around.

"Don't put your muthafuckin' hands on me again," Brenda warned, her voice low and deadly.

Jett invaded Brenda's personal face, besting her former friend's height by several inches. She felt empowered, ready to avenge a horrible wrong. "Or what?"

"Fuck you, Jeanetta." Brenda turned again, placed a hand on the knob.

Jett pushed her away from the door. "You sold that story."

Brenda stumbled against the wall but recovered her balance. "Didn't I tell you not to touch me again?"

Jett's comment was cut off by a hard purse to the mouth.

"Aw! Bitch!"

Jett put a hand to her mouth, tasted blood, and saw red. She reached for Brenda's collar with an eye toward her roly-poly neck. Brenda bent down and slammed her head into Jett's stomach. They both stumbled back against the wall. What old girl lacked in height she made up for in weight. Jett struggled to get the advantage. Brenda lifted her head. Jett saw her chance. She grabbed Brenda's hair and yanked, hard.

"Let go of my hair, bitch," she huffed.

"Not until I finish kicking your ass," Jett snarled.

"I don't think so," Brenda growled. She lifted her leg and stomped on Jett's foot. Jett released Brenda's hair. Brenda grabbed Jett's ponytail, wrapped it around her right hand and delivered a left hook that would have impressed Mike Tyson. Neither heard the constant pounding on the front door.

"Jett! What the hell? Let me in!"

Jett was too busy trying to prevent getting in a headlock. Her face was smushed into Brenda's arm. Nothing to do but open her mouth and bite the fleshy appendage.

"Got dammit!" Brenda yelled before charging into Jett like a bull. They crashed into the table holding a stunning flower-filled vase. At least it was before it crashed to the floor.

"Brenda? Are you in there? Jett!" The pounding grew louder. The women continued to tussle on the floor.

"If this door doesn't open in ten seconds, I'm calling the police!"

"You ready to stop fighting," Brenda panted. "Or do I have to put my full weight on your ass."

"Get the fuck off me."

"Jett! Brenda!" Chantel had run around to a window and could now see inside. "Open this got damn door!"

After entering the house and remanding each "boxer" to her "corner"—Jett using the upstairs bathroom while Brenda regrouped in the half-bath downstairs—Chantel surveyed the room. Aside from the destroyed vase and flowers, the damage was minimal. Most of the destruction had been inflicted on each other. Brenda exited the bathroom with her hair still in disarray and a hand covering the long scratch on her cheek.

"Your sister's crazy. I come to offer help and she attacks me. I'm going to press charges and then sue her ass."

"Brenda, I am so sorry." She made a move to hug Brenda, who stepped back.

"Uh-uh. Not right now."

"Okay. I understand. I'm really sorry. What happened?"

"Your sister acted like the bitch that she is. She started the fight. I finished it."

From her vantage point she would have called it a draw, but that's an opinion Chantel chose not to share.

"Did you guys get to talk at all? Did you share what you wanted to tell her?"

"Hell, no, and now I never will."

Chantel's heart dropped. She reached for Brenda's hand. This time the older woman did not pull away. Chantel looked up to make sure they were still alone and inched closer to Brenda.

"Does what you know have anything to do with me?" she asked in a hushed whisper. Chantel took Brenda's looking away as a yes. "Is there any way you tell me what you know? I don't ask for Jett's sake, but for mine. Whoever leaked that story might be able to help me know more about myself."

It took a long time for Brenda to answer, so long in fact Chantel doubted she would. Finally, Brenda reached up grabbed her neck and worked her shoulders. "I don't want to see your bitch sister ever again," she said, with a nod toward the stairs. "But out of respect for Miss Anna, whom I loved dearly, I'll tell you."

It didn't take long. Less than twenty minutes. But when Brenda left, Chantel had been told quite a story. And she'd been given a name. With a sigh, she headed up the stairs. She didn't relish the upcoming conversation with Jett. But it was one they had to have.

Chapter 26
Unbreak My Heart

The flight back to LA was brutal. The plane, quiet.

Jett sat stock still, alone with her thoughts. Broken fingernails from the fight with Brenda. A broken heart if what Chantel had told her was true. She wanted to not believe it. But she couldn't deny the possibility that what she heard might be true. There was only one person who could either refute or collaborate what supposedly happened. Back in LA and once safely ensconced within the walls of her home, she called King.

"Jett! I'm glad you called me. My friend said some of the items in his home were broken?"

"Yeah, King, I'm sorry about that. I'll pay for the damages, whatever they are."

"Fine, but that's not what I'm concerned about. Was there an accident? Are you okay?"

"We had a fight."

"You and Chantel?"

"No, me and Brenda."

"Brenda Moreland?" She heard a deep sigh on his end of the phone. "What happened, Jett?"

"That's a story for later. But there's another one I just heard and want to share with you."

"Okay."

"That night when I saw you and your friend and came over with Yvette, did you leave at one point?"

"Maybe."

"Were you gone the whole night?"

"I can't remember, Jeanetta," not realizing he'd reverted to her childhood name. "You're asking about a random night more than thirty years ago. Why do you ask?"

"Turns out it wasn't so random for me. According to what Yvette supposedly told Brenda, that's when Roy raped me."

"What?" Jett could tell King's incredulity was for real. "Brenda said Roy Simpson raped you?"

"*I'm* saying he raped me because I damn sure didn't consent. He must have put something in my drink because I remember waking up feeling really groggy. My clothes were off. You were nowhere around. I blamed it on the alcohol," she finished, with a humorless snort.

"Damn. I'm so sorry that happened to you, Jett. Honestly, there were so many guys in and out of the house all the time that I can't say for sure whether or not he was there when I left, or even if I left. It was so long ago, I just . . . wait a minute. Maybe that's why that motherfucker reached out to me!"

"Did you know that Roy was the cousin of Yvette's boyfriend at the time?"

"No idea. Do you think he's . . . could he have fathered . . ."

"It'll break my heart if it's true, but yes. He could be Chantel's father. I found a couple pics of him online, mugshots actually, and there is a slight resemblance." There was a long silence. "There's another thing."

"I'm listening." King's voice was strained.

"His family is from Gary, Indiana."

When King finally responded it was only to tell her, "I've got some business to handle."

* * *

A week had passed and King hadn't called back. Part of Jett was actually relieved. She wasn't sure she wanted to hear whatever he might have done or found out. When Myles phoned to set up their first meeting since a tabloid story upended her world, she wasn't sure she wanted to hear him, either.

Jett could count on one hand the times she'd been to Myles's office. They usually met at one or the other's home. With sex involved. Today's atmosphere was decidedly different. There were no winks or sly glances. No casual touching or deep French kisses. No blatant declarations from Myles that he was going to "fuck that weave off her head." No, today felt more like a corporate board meeting than one between a manager and his almost A-list star client. When he'd left a message for her to come in for a meeting, his tone was all business, no bullshit. Jett had dared not consider what that meant.

Instead, on this Monday morning, she'd dressed as impeccably as someone about to rock a Fashion Week runway in Paris or Milan. The dress was an Ace Kouture ruched midi in bold sunshine yellow paired with London Drake stilettos covered in Swarovski crystals and pearls. Her ears dripped with gold Tiffany earrings courtesy of Oliver. She'd paid more for the Patek Philippe & Tiffany diamond watch on her wrist than most folk paid for their cars. Her Indian human hair weave was swept up in a high ponytail that brushed her behind. The style emphasized the slant of her eyes and her high cheekbones and pouty lips. She wore little makeup, just mascara and gloss. Her look in one word? Flawless.

Myles, on the other hand, compared to Jett, looked almost unkempt. On any other body the jeans and simple black tee he wore would have looked casual but on his tall, toned frame came off as *GQ*. But his eyes were bloodshot as though he hadn't gotten much sleep and his five o'clock shadow was heading toward a twelve o'clock beard. He sat with his elbows on the desk, the fingers of both hands pressed against each other, a copy of *Celebrity Gossip* featuring Jett and Chantel on the cover opened to the centerfold where their article covered two pages.

Other than perfunctory greetings, no words had been said.

Myles dropped his head and rubbed his fingers across his forehead. He rested his chin between his thumbs and forefingers and looked intently at Jett.

"Congratulations on a number one hit."

"Thank you. They say all publicity is good publicity. I guess that's true."

"Somewhat." He eased back in the chair. "Were you as shocked to see this story as I was?"

Jett crossed her legs. "Probably more."

"Is it true?"

"Some of it."

"You're a mother?"

"I can't exactly claim that title. But I did give birth to someone."

"Thirty-four years ago."

"Correct."

"How old are you?" The way he emphasized the third word of the question made it sound like an accusation.

"Old as a dinosaur," Jett spat back, offended. "Older than dirt!"

He raised his arms, palms up, a sign of surrender. "That came out all wrong. What I meant to say is I can't believe you have a daughter in her thirties."

"I was two when it happened," she deadpanned. "A medical fucking miracle."

The F-word was said with such force, a spray of spittle shot out.

Myles shot back in his chair. Jett tittered, then laughed. Myles managed a smile. Also miracles. He picked up the tabloid. "Says here you were a teen mother."

"I got pregnant at fifteen, had her at sixteen."

"So you're forty-nine, not forty-five as it says in your bio."

"I knew you were smart, and before you even ask, if that number comes anywhere near any of my bios, I will fire you on the spot."

"I'm afraid it's not up to me, sweetheart. With your legal name out there, your entire life can be found. It's the twenty-first century. There's no such thing as privacy anymore. Not even secrets, for long."

"So, what's the verdict? What's going to happen?"

"I don't know."

"Didn't you call me in for a meeting?"

"Not just me." He looked at his watch. "A conference call is set up for nine thirty. The Zenith execs, both TV and music, will be on the line."

"A simultaneous firing squad. Fucking. Great."

"Let's not automatically anticipate the worst-case scenario. Sometimes what looks like career suicide can make the person a billionaire. Look at Kim Kardashian. The whole family has eaten off the video of that bitch sucking dick for the last twenty years. And the quality was horrible!"

He went back to the paper. "She's a singer. Your daughter."

"My sister."

"Okay. She sings." Jett nodded. "Is she any good?"

"I don't know. I've never heard her sing."

Jett couldn't read the look Myles gave her. She wasn't sure she wanted to.

The conference call lasted two hours. She didn't come out of the discussion unscathed, but Jett knew it could have been worse. Since *Seeking Stardom* had debuted to great reviews and high ratings, the network was willing to wait and see how the public reacted. The general feeling was that with the right spin, they could salvage the season, and maybe the show. If the story had a negative impact and ratings dropped, Jett would be replaced. If the residual of her scandal continued into the second season, she'd likely be blackballed from the network, Zenith studios, maybe Hollywood. No one said this, but it wasn't Jett's first rodeo. She knew that unless she could turn this scandal around, her career was effectively over. The guys at Zenith Records weren't as optimistic. Scandal didn't fit with the brand they'd planned to build around her. Even though the single had gone to number one, they cancelled plans for an album. Myles had remained optimistic, saying, "They could always change their minds."

By the end of the week, the team had come up with a game plan. With her publicist Cindy largely in charge, the plan was made for Jett to take control of the narrative and steer the public in a sympathetic and compassionate direction. The consensus was that in the present climate, that could best be done by focusing on topics that would impact the largest swath of society. The first was teen pregnancy, a trend that had declined in recent years but was still a relevant issue impacting communities of color in greater number than the total population. The second was date rape or teen sexual assault. With the sick irony that the lie she'd initially told Chantel turned out to be true, Jett had pushed back against this one. The team argued back that the accuracy of an assault description didn't matter. They were going for pity and spin. It happened thirty-plus years ago. Who'd remember? Who could refute her? Who cared? Bottom line,

#MeToo was still a trending hashtag that could get her story on major entertainment and news outlets. She cursed, argued, said the accusation was a straight out lie. She was outvoted. And because it could mean the difference between one or five seasons on *Seeking Stardom*, making a million or paying back two, and more accurately, because right now Zenith owned her, Jett went along with the program. Life wasn't always fair. Hollywood, almost never.

It was only noon when Jett left Myles's office for the second time in as many weeks. Jett was exhausted as though she'd gone ten rounds. A romp with Oliver would definitely revive her. Then she remembered. He was out of the country—a private chef gig in Costa Rica for a ten-day retreat. A couple other guys came to mind but were quickly dismissed. She didn't really know them. If she'd learned anything from these past few months, it was that you needed to know the people around you, and even then, be slow to trust.

Jett reached her car and pulled out into Ventura Boulevard's heavy traffic. Randall crossed her mind. She was surprised at how good it was to see him and how she'd genuinely enjoyed his company. No doubt if she called, he'd come running. But she didn't. Lovers were plentiful. True friends were few. As good as he was in bed, she liked him better in the latter category. She slid her hand down the wheel to turn on the music but stopped when her phone rang. Seeing the name of the caller, she considered not answering but thought better of it.

"Hello, King."

"Afternoon, Jett. Where are you?"

"Heading toward the 101 Freeway. Why, you in LA?"

"I'm in Lee's office and need you to pull over and park as quickly as possible. He's sent a video conference link to your phone but for security purposes it expires after five minutes."

"Damn. Hang on." Jett whipped around a Toyota and took a right on to a side street, stopping her Maserati beneath a No Parking sign. She put the car in park, pulled out her phone, and tapped the text message icon.

"Okay, I see the link."

"Just tap on that," Lee replied. "It will connect you directly to my computer system. Let me know when you see us."

Jett did as instructed and was soon looking at a very clear picture of Lee's office, with King leaning against the credenza behind Lee's chair.

"You look very Californian," Lee said dryly.

"You look very, um . . ."

"Watch it!"

King chuckled. Jett smiled. "All right guys. What's up."

"We found Roy."

The news should not have been unexpected but still gave Jett a jolt. "Okay. And?"

"He admitted to everything, Jett. The two of you being intimate."

"Intimate? There was no—"

"Calm down, Jett. That's not all."

"But we weren't intimate. He raped me!"

"He's the blackmailer, Jett. He sent the letters. Made the phone calls."

"Roy was behind all this? How did he know . . ."

"Apparently the details Brenda remembers Yvette sharing are true. I did leave the house. Roy admitted stopping by. He denied giving you any drugs though and said the sex was consensual. All these years later there's no proving it either way."

Jett was reeling, in a state of shock. "Does he believe he's Chantel's father?"

"I don't think so, otherwise he wouldn't have threatened to reveal your secret. I'm sure he thought I was her dad. But that's a question we can get definitely get answered. Lee collected a sample of his DNA. Jett, are you there? Say something."

"I will ruin him."

"According to his brother William, he's done that on his own. Got addicted to crack in the late 80s, early 90s. Did prison time behind possession, robbery. Got out about five years ago and stayed clean for a while. Met a good woman. Had a little girl. Unfortunately, she was killed in an accident two years ago."

Jett knew she should have felt sympathy. But with all of the anger she was feeling right now in her heart, there was no place for it.

"Guess she was riding her bike on their block when a car came out of nowhere. Baby girl died in his arms. William said that shortly after that he got back on drugs, even worse than before. Took to stealing, robbing, anything to feed his habit. One day he came across a magazine article about you. I guess that's when the wheels started turning. That call to me was probably to gauge the temperature, see if I suspected anything and try and find out if his plan was working."

"But why even involve you?"

"You were taking too long to pay up. He figured threatening to tell me would be added pressure. Obviously, since never mentioning another daughter in decades of bios and press releases, he figured I didn't know."

Trying to process so much in so little time nearly took Jett's breath away.

"I know this is a lot to lay on you. But I wanted you to know everything as quickly as possible. I also wanted to tell you that you don't have to worry about Roy ever bothering you again."

"Is he—"

"Alive? Yes. But he understands if he ever pulls another stunt like this, that status will change."

It took a while for Jett to pull it together, and twice as long to call Chantel. In fact, she was back at her home in Toluca Lake before gathering enough nerve to dial her.

"Chan, it's Jett," she said simply. "I've got news. Are you sitting down?"

Chapter 27
Livin' La Vida Loca

Chantel spoke with Jett for almost an hour. When they finished, every part of her was numb. Mind, soul, spirit. She could feel no part of herself. She felt as though her entire life had been a series of lies and deception. Forced to deal with so much truth in so little time could easily drive her crazy.

Anna not being her mother but her grandmother. Jett not being her sister, but her mother. King not being her father, just an employer. Then there was the stress of living under a national microscope during fifteen seconds of unwanted tabloid fame, and the irony of Jett's lie about being raped being closer to the truth than either realized, and the story of how Chantel was conceived. All of this without the woman who'd been her rock, her foundation, for all of her life. She thought losing Anna would be the worst that happened this year. It still was, but the event had stiff competition.

So lost was Chantel in her thoughts, it didn't register that the doorbell was ringing until Rita's voice and the sound of knocking came through the open window and broke her trance.

She went to open the door. "Hey, Rita."

"Why haven't you returned my calls or answered my texts?" Rita asked Chantel, who'd already turned and headed back into the living room. "Had me worried to death about you. I came over to make sure you were still alive."

"I am. Barely."

"I cannot even imagine. Your life has been pure insanity, girl." They reached the living room. Rita caught Chantel's arm before they sat. "You need a hug."

Chantel didn't know how much she'd needed one until her chin was on Rita's shoulders. It was one of those good ol' sistah-girl hugs. One of the mama, grandmama hugs. One of those church ladies in the white dresses kind of hug, where you rocked back and forth and got your back patted. Had there been any more water in her tear ducts, Chantel would have cried.

They finally parted. "Thanks, sis. I needed that." She started to sit down and then asked, "Can I get you something?"

Rita waved away the offer as she eased into one of two new accent chairs. "I'm good. I see those photographers aren't parked on the street the way they'd been the past couple weeks."

"Jett told me they'd soon be on to the next story. I hope that's true."

"I still waved a third-finger greeting around just in case somebody wanted a picture."

Chantel smiled as she went into the kitchen. "Believe it or not, those guys are the least of my worries."

"I can't tell. Between you hiding out and hooking up with Terrence, I've barely seen you." Rita sat back in the chair. "Catch me up. What's been going on?"

Chantel came back with two glasses of wine.

"I told you I didn't want anything."

"With all the stuff I'm about to tell you? Trust me, you'll drink it."

Chantel gave Rita the rundown, starting with the flourish of Jett and Brenda's combination boxing/wrestling match and ending with the news that she might finally have the identity of her bio dad. By the time she finished, Rita's glass was drained along with the blood from Rita's face. In recounting it, Chantel saw the humor and ridiculousness of it all.

"It's not funny," she said, after surprising herself by joining Rita and laughing out loud.

"I would have paid money!" Rita exclaimed, wiping her eyes. "Your sophisticated sister-mother trying to hand out a beatdown while the other woman channeled somebody from the WWE and tried to take your girl to the mat!"

"It was straight mayhem."

"Okay, on to the next scandal." Rita sobered. "Is King your daddy?"

Chantel side-eyed Rita. "Only you."

"Hey, you're in the midst of multiples and I've only got so much time!"

"According to the private eye working with King and Jett, the man's name may be Robert Simpson. In three or four days, I'll know for sure."

The following Thursday, Chantel opened the overnight package sent by Midwest Health & Diagnostics, and one of biggest mysteries in her life had been solved. King told the truth. He wasn't her father. Robert Simpson had lost one daughter and gained another one that due to the circumstances surrounding her conception he'd likely never meet. After putting Artani to bed and having a long conversation with Terrence, Chantel made the call she'd put off for far too long. It was time to call King.

"King Richardson."

"Hello, King. It's Chantel."

"I thought I recognized the number. I've been meaning to give you a call. How are you, Chantel?"

"I've been better, but life could be worse."

"That's a good attitude. I always say it's not so much what happens to us as how we handle it. Have you spoken with your sister lately?"

"She's next on the list. This call won't take long. I just wanted to call and thank you."

"For what?"

"For locating Roy Simpson. Getting his DNA tested. I just received the results back earlier tonight. It's him."

"I'm sorry, Chantel. How are you feeling?"

"I'm not."

"You've had a lot to process."

"Almost too much."

"Yet you can hopefully find some solace in knowing the truth."

"I will. I do. There's something else I need to tell you, King. I should have said something sooner and have too much respect for you to keep what I did a secret."

"What's that?"

"Remember the night you paid me a visit? We were talking. You began coughing, and I offered you a glass of water?"

"Yes." The word was dragged out in a way Chantel believed King knew where the conversation was heading.

"You can probably guess what I did with that glass?"

A beat and then, "Had my DNA tested?"

"I apologize for not being forthright from the beginning. But I couldn't risk you saying no. When you came over the weekend I didn't show up at the club, you left what I needed on the rim of a glass."

"Damn. I need to hire you to work in my law office. I should be upset, but considering everything that's happened, I can completely understand why you did what you did." He paused for a second. "Are you sure you're not mine?"

They both laughed then. Chantel's was one of relief.

"I can tell you with absolute confidence. You are not my father. But you are a good, upstanding man that I truly admire. That's why I decided to tell you the truth. Jett swore up and down that you were my father. I felt you deserved to know just in case there were doubts."

"You didn't have to tell me, but thanks. I appreciate that you felt that you could." He paused for a moment. "Customers miss you at the club. Where are you performing these days?"

"Ha! Nowhere. The paparazzi isn't as bad as a couple weeks ago but I still feel like a prisoner in my house."

"May I offer some advice?"

"Sure, counselor."

"Stop hiding. Own your story, Chantel. You have nothing to be ashamed of and no reason to run. One of the best lessons I've learned both as an attorney and now as mayor is the power of a positive perspective. I've learned to look at a situation, no matter how bad or wrong or negative it seems, and find the silver lining. It's always there. For you, it could be the chance to advance your career."

Chantel was taken aback. "How? By recording a remake of 'Mother' by Ashanti?"

"Might not be a bad idea. I was thinking more along the lines of the publicity that could be generated by you coming out and telling your own story. How this whole situation has affected you. To share your mother, Anna, with the world and what a blessing it was that she raised you. That's a positive that came from a seeming negative, get what I mean?"

"I think I do," Chantel replied, unexpectedly getting emotional.

"No matter how crazy our situation is, there is always someone out there going through the very same thing, or something similar. Think of all the children raised by grandmothers. The thousands, millions of those who've grown up without knowing their dads. Your story is different, but if you share it, you might learn that it's not as unique as you think. You might be surprised at the support you receive, and who you might help."

"I am almost speechless right now. Thank you, King. Seriously, I would have never looked at what I'm going through from the perspective you just gave me."

"Well, now you know why I can charge the big bucks!"

She appreciated the levity as much as his honesty.

"One more thing."

"Sure."

"Jasmine is a beautiful and talented lady. But if you ever want to return to the Diplomat, that spotlight is yours."

"Okay, King, you're about to make me cry."

"Don't cry, Chantel. Sing! And tell your story. It'll bless someone."

Chantel would need a minute to process all that he'd shared. Jett was just the person to help her do it. Chantel's story was Jett's story, too.

Chapter 28
Spread My Wings

After another long talk with Jett, Chantel emailed a popular Youtube vlogger, Kasha Tay, who replied that very same night. She wanted to do the story as an exclusive. Jett needed to consult the team, inform them of this change of events. The irony that the narrative the studio had wanted to push actually happened might be a game changer, make everything that went wrong during the last meeting right again. In the meantime, she lined up the backup plan. The agreement from *A Day with Tay* was sent to her attorney. If Zenith wasn't interested, Kasha would be ready to roll. Either way, Jett's story got told.

The next step Jett took to control her story was to not charter a return flight home. It was time to straighten her spine and face the public. She had nothing to be ashamed of and nothing to hide. It was time to start acting like it. Kansas City was a good place to make a soft entry. Though not equipped with a VIP lounge, the airport was rarely crowded or busy. Midwesterners for the most part were respectful and polite. Those who recognized her smiled or waved but kept their distance. It probably helped that once inside, she kept her shades on, along with an expression that translated as "bitch, not today." When an agent recognized her, she was discreetly pulled out of line, quickly processed, and allowed down the Jetway to her first-class seat for an uneventful flight.

Navigating Los Angeles International Airport was a different story. There were more looks, comments, and people asking for pics. She had on her game face and, of course, the shades. Long, determined strides took her quickly to baggage claim, where thankfully the car service—most likely at the request of her personal assistant—had two people waiting. One escorted her directly to the car. The other stayed for her luggage. While waiting, she called Myles.

"Hey, you."

"Hello."

"You're still my manager, right?"

"I don't know, Jett. You've pissed off some major players, and you know how this town gets down."

"Unfortunately, I know it all too well. I was in that meeting, too, remember?"

"I'm sorry, darling. This isn't personal. You know that."

"I do. I also have potentially good news. There may be a way to salvage the Zenith partnership."

"I'm listening."

Jett gave Myles the short version of what she'd learned and finally remembered.

"I didn't want to play the rape card just because it trended," she finished. "Especially regarding a Black man. The last thing I wanted to do was play into the age-old oversexed Negro stereotype. You guys get maligned enough. But now that I know everything that really happened, I can come from an honest place. I think that makes all the difference."

"Whew! Damn, Jett. That's some story."

"Stranger than fiction. The mind is incredible. I'd effectively blocked out a memory for almost forty years. But when the protective layer around it was punctured, the entire scene rushed in, as though it took place yesterday. What do you think the execs will say? Both here and New York."

"Hard to tell. But if I had to guess, I'd say the chance of them going back to the original two-year with a third option contract is fairly strong. The record company, that's going to be a tougher sale. Even though you're the victim, we're talking about rape here. Sexual assault. That's right up there with murder and may-hem, all the stuff they want to avoid. But I'll give it all I've got. At the end of the day, you deserve it. That album is fire and needs to be heard."

"Thanks, Myles. You saying that means a lot to me. There's one more thing."

"More than you've already told me?"

The way his voice rose octaves made Jett laugh out loud. "In case Zenith plays hardball and don't change their minds, I have a backup plan."

They talked pretty much from LA to the Valley. She told him all about the vlogger, Kasha Tay. He listened. Asked questions. Gave his opinion. Told her he'd continue to help her, albeit dis-creetly, until the hoopla died down. That was more than most would have done. Hollywood was a cutthroat town. She called her publicist next. It was a much easier call because not only had she heard of Kasha's show, she was a fan.

"What do you think Zenith is going to say about this?"

"I'm off the show after this season. My album's shelved. They're not going to say anything because I'm not going to ask."

"You're still under contract. Do you think that's wise?"

"This isn't just about contracts. This is about me. My life. My journey. My truth. It's my story. No one gets a say on whether or not it gets told."

"She's got a great audience, and a very loyal following. Plus, she keeps it real and seems like a genuinely good person. If you're going to do it, I'd say she's an excellent choice."

"Thanks."

"No problem. Just keep me posted. I want to tune in live."

Three weeks later, as ratings for *Seeking Stardom* soared, Jett sat on her plush Italian sofa, professionally lit, miked and ready to do her first live YouTube show. Kasha Tay was a beautiful chocolate drop of a woman, with a warm and caring personality and a brilliant smile. She was also down-to-earth, a real sistah-girl, which is why Jett agreed to do the show in the first place.

"Are you ready?" Kasha asked her from the fifty-inch screen set up on a table before her.

"I guess so."

"Don't be nervous. You'll do fine. I'm going to do my intro and then bring you in."

Jett took a sip of water, during the short musical intro. In less than a minute, Kasha was back.

"All right ladies and gentlemen tonight we have an exclusive. And when I say exclusive, I mean that shit."

Tasha laughed. Jett smiled, and relaxed more.

"Everybody in the country is watching *Seeking Stardom*. That muthafuckin show has got the spot on lock. They're number one in ur-thang right now. And I have the extreme pleasure of having one of the main reasons the show is number one, in my studio tonight. Oh, yeah, baby. Y'all are the shit. Y'all, my wonderful viewers, is why everybody is open to having a day with Tay. Tonight, that guest is none other than the woman who only needs one name. I'm talking about the glamagirl, the diva, the one and only Jett. Welcome to the show."

"Kasha, thanks for having me and with that intro, making me feel right at home."

"Oh, that's how we do it over here, girl. Now, let's give that one person who's been living under a rock, a little background on the scandal that helped shoot your single, *Star Searchin'*, to the top of the charts and make *Seeking Stardom* a number one show."

262 / LUTISHIA LOVELY

For the next ninety minutes, Jett shared her incredible journey of a story. From being unknowingly date raped to getting pregnant. From leaving a newborn behind to chase success to coming to full circle. There was laughter and tears. Questions and answers. But most of all, there was raw honestly. By the end, over a million viewers were tuned into the chat.

"Wow," Kasha exclaimed as the show neared its end. "There are so many lessons, so many pearls of wisdom, so many topics that we've covered that can literally help so many women. Out of all that you've shared, what is the one piece of advice you'd most like the viewer to leave with? Or is it even possible to break it down to one single thing."

"I don't know," Jett drawled. "We've talked about a lot. But if there was one thing to pass along, one thing I've learned, it would be to live in your truth. Ain't no future in faking. A little fact trumps a big lie any day of the week."

Chapter 29
Spread My Wings

It was liberating to challenge the boogeyman and discover he wasn't real. When Chantel spoke with Jett after her interview on *A Day with Tay*, that's what Jett had said. Chantel understood. Not that the all-powerful entertainment company known as Zenith wasn't real and their actions ineffective. Before Jett decided to rip off the mask she'd carefully cultivated during three decades in the industry and be her authentic self, before Kasha asked the right questions and Jett gave her real answers, no one in Hollywood was looking for her. No one was calling Myles or her agent about a potential booking. Zenith hadn't had a change of heart, revised hers to a multiyear contract or taken the completed album containing Jett's best work off their shelves. For Jett, the boogeyman had been fear. It had been the assumption of what would happen if she looked back on her past and stared it dead in the face. Jett had always imagined the worst. That her life would be over. Today she knew for sure that even without Zenith or upcoming work in the industry, she would be okay because the people had spoken. No, she wasn't perfect, and that was perfectly fine. She was accepted. She was supported. She was loved.

For the small part she played in Jett's coming-out party, Chantel was very grateful. They would never have a mother-daughter relationship. For the first time ever, they had sisterhood, and a friendship. Chantel imagined Anna was thrilled. That was more than enough.

Watching Jett's unfolding transformation had caused Chantel to examine her life. Who she was, where she was, where she wanted to be, and how she would get there. After a second followed by a third visit, Terrence had bought the five-bedroom house. He'd invited Chantel and Artani to live there. She'd agreed to move to Sedalia and made another decision. One that was not without risks, and was a little bit scary, but felt absolutely right.

She walked to Phil's office and tapped the open door. "Hey, Phil. Got a minute?"

"Always got time for a star."

"Stop with that."

She walked in and sat down. He leaned back in his chair and laced his fingers behind his head. "What can I do you for?"

Chantel smiled, gathering her nerve as she deeply inhaled. "I'm leaving the paper and moving to Sedalia."

Phil's carefree mood ebbed like the tide. He slowly sat forward. "Come again?"

"It wasn't an easy decision to make. But it's the right one. I'm willing to give a thirty-day notice and help train my replacement. I've enjoyed being a part of the *Monitor* family, but it's time to move on."

"Sedalia doesn't have a paper, so I know they didn't steal you. Last I heard, South Cass isn't hiring. Kansas City, Jeff City, Columbia are all thirty-minute commutes. So what are you going to be doing?"

"I'm going to start a blog."

"A blog," Phil deadpanned. "You're moving to Sedalia to start a blog? You don't have to relocate for that. Darn it, Chantel. If I'd known you wanted to be a writer, I could have sent you out on assignment, given you a column or let you write a few articles at least. You're a solid editor and a dedicated worker. That's not an easy combination to find. Plus, I'm still hoping to snag a date with your sister. If you leave, I won't be able to play the boss card and heck, my chances were already slim."

"I hate to tell you, but even with the boss card . . ."

"Yeah, I know. I know."

"I'll have to work outside the industry for a while, until I build up a following and develop my writing chops. But time goes fast, and before you know it, life is over. Sometimes the ending comes with no warning. It's just bam, and you're done. I don't want to be sixty, seventy years old and wish I'd tried this or made an attempt to do that. I have the opportunity now. I am going to take it."

"What about the singing career? You know I have yet to see you perform."

"I'm going back to work part-time at the Diplomat. Every other Friday and Saturday night. You're always welcome."

"It takes a lot to leave something fairly stable and jump into the unknown. Kudos for having the nerve."

Chantel stood and extended her hand. "However I can help with the process, let me know. I'll go write up a formal resignation letter effective thirty days from now." She turned to leave.

"Chantel."

"Yes?"

"Does this move have anything to do with the rumor about a boyfriend floating around?"

"As a matter of fact it does, Phil. His name is Terrence. He also works at the club. When you visit, I'll be sure and introduce you."

That weekend Terrence, Chantel, and Artani moved into their dream home. A month later, they invited a few folks down to help break it in. At the height of it all, when most of the guests were lounging in the massive back yard, Terrence walked up the stairs to the back deck and yelled.

"Hey! Can I have everyone's attention?"

The talking slowly died down as everyone turned and looked up at him.

"Chantel, can you come up here? You too, Artani?"

Chantel's brow creased as she looked at him. She put a hand on her hip. "What do you want?"

"Woman! Come up here and find out!"

Since a summons often meant another toy or video game, Artani didn't need any encouragement. He was already halfway up the stairs when he stopped and said, "Mama, come on!"

Murmurs began as Chantel mounted the stairs. When she reached him, Terrence grabbed her hand and turned to the crowd.

"We just want to thank everybody for coming down to celebrate us moving into our dream home. And now, I'd like to," he turned to Chantel, "ask you, if you'd be my dream wife."

Chantel's jaw dropped as Terrence pulled a ring from his pocket and dropped to one knee.

"Will you marry me, baby?"

She wanted to be sassy and say "maybe," or "let me think about it," but when her mouth opened only one word came out. Actually, two.

"Hell, yeah!"

Applause, yelps, and whistles rang out. Among the happy faces were Rita and her family, Chantel's former neighbor Wanda and her grandson Kaleb, the guys from the band, friends from Terrence's job, Ulla, Phil and some of Chantel's co-workers, along with the neighbors from across the street she and Terrence had just met days before. Jett couldn't make it, but she'd had a painting delivered, a large, stunning William Tolliver original that now graced a living room wall. Of course, Blanche made the trip down, driving an SUV packed with the ladies from the church who'd showed up at Anna's house the day when Chantel was there. Later, after a flurry of congratulatory hugs, Blanche pulled Chantel away from the crowd and led her out to the driveway.

"I want to give you something."

"I don't know if I can take another surprise!" The ladies laughed. "Plus, I told you this wasn't a housewarming, Miss Blanche. You didn't have to bring anything."

"It's not from me. This is from your mama."

Blanche opened the back door. Seated on the floor of her car were two large cuttings from Anna's beloved rose bushes. Chantel didn't try and stop the tears.

"Thank you," she said, giving Blanche a big hug. "These will frame the steps so nicely. No one could have brought me a more perfect gift."

"Your mama is always with you. Seeing these will just be a reminder."

Chapter 30
Exhale

Jett gazed out at the turquoise-blue water, gleaming as a sparkling jewel next to the white sand. Views like these underscored the Caribbean as paradise. When was the last time she was here? She rested her chin in her hand, watched boats rock lazily with the waves and seagulls glide on the breeze of the wind. Four years ago. His name was Edwin. One of her Caribbean cuties, a flavor of the month.

Now it was Chantel getting a second chance at love. As if their lives hadn't already gone through all kinds of crazy, her sister/daughter getting engaged had been totally unexpected and, from what Jett heard, a whirlwind affair. The joy she felt ran deeper, was stronger than that of a sister. For the first time, Jett believed she understood what it felt like to be a mom.

Chantel Scott was her sister, and her child.

She only vaguely remembered Terrence from Anna's funeral and had only spoken to him once over the phone, shortly after the tabloid revealed their secret and their lives were forever changed. Chantel's happiness overshadowed any doubts or reservations she may have had about gaining a new family member. As their mother used to often say, "if you're happy, I'm tickled pink!"

Jett had been sitting at her dining room table. Her house was at an elevation that provided an impressive view of the valley below. She could see part of that from where she sat, but after reaching for the glass of juice she'd been nursing, she walked through the patio doors just beyond the dining space. It was a cool night. She welcomed the chill. Her thoughts were all jumbled up. The cold seemed to jolt them into a semblance of order and helped her gain clarity about where she was right now. All that had happened in the past few months had given Jett a very clear picture of who she'd been to that point, how the decisions she'd made had shaped her life. They'd shined a light on what she'd prioritized and how she felt about the results of making those moves. She tried to live without regrets, but to say she was totally happy with the way things were would be to tell a big fat lie. In the crisp night remarkably devoid of smog, where the twinkle of the stars matched the city lights below, she was able to not only admit some things she'd previously refused to acknowledge but to also stand in her truth.

Jett was evolving and ready for change.

The wind blew, planting goose bumps along Jett's bare arms. She rubbed them and shivered but wasn't ready to go inside. Leaning against the balcony railing, she watched the limbs from the oak tree that anchored her small backyard. When people think about trees in California, palms are usually the ones that come to mind. Jett appreciated the beauty they brought to the landscape, but the oak tree reminded her of the Midwest and the people who lived there—steady, solid, dependable. There was a type of wisdom that exuded from its wide, gnarled trunk, some-thing searching about the branches reaching up toward the heav-ens. What would it have told the fast, frightened fifteen-year-old who fancied herself attracted to an "older man" and as a result had a childhood that ended too soon?

The ringing of a distant phone pulled her out of her reverie. She walked back inside and to the bar counter where she'd left her phones. The call, from a private number, had come in on her private phone, not the wider-known number she gave out for strictly business contacts. Frowning slightly, she tapped the phone icon. She figured it was someone she knew.

"Hello?"

She detected the slightest of pauses before hearing her name. "Jett. Hey, it's King."

With everything that had or hadn't happened, something about the sound of his voice still affected her. The goose bumps were back even though her place was warm and cozy. She quickly regained control of her reaction by picturing Tamela, his wife of twenty-five years.

"Hey, King. What's up."

"I may have a gig for you."

Jett's expression changed to one who'd smelled a pile of dookie. "At your club in Marquette?"

"Ha! You sound offended. I understand. No, dear. You're entirely above the Diplomat's budget. This gig is near the Bahamas, on a private island." He waited a beat. "Still frowning?"

The smile that came from hearing *private island* grew bigger. "What made you think I frowned?"

"You didn't?"

"Are you kidding? I practically snarled. Give me the five w's— who, what, when, where, and why."

"Colleague of mine."

"Politician?"

"Attorney."

Her heart fell, but only until she remembered her vow to take a break from relationships with men and nurture a relationship with herself. There were still many layers to uncover and get to know.

"It's the second weekend in December. They'll be there all

week. He can put your crew up for two days. You and a guest for five."

"Those are generous accommodations. Whoever this is must be loaded."

"He's done well for himself. More than that, though, is why he's doing it. This is going to be a surprise party for his wife. She's been through it the past few years. Two bouts of cancer. Lost her mom."

"Geez."

"It's her sixtieth birthday and he wants to go all out. She thinks the trip itself is the gift, but he's enlisted her best friend to invite all the people in her circle and who are special in her life to surprise her on Saturday night. We were talking, and somehow your name came up. I casually mentioned that I knew you, that we both grew up in Kansas City. Turns out his wife, Gloria, is a big fan, both of shows like *Seeking Stardom* and of you."

"Ah, that's sweet."

"When he understood that I really knew you and there was a chance you could sing for his wife . . . there was no hesitation. For you to sing 'Happy Birthday' would be the cherry on top of her birthday cake."

"What's your friend's name?"

"Davis, and yes, that is his first name."

"That was going to be my next question. Tell Davis I'd be honored to join his celebration and sing 'Happy Birthday' to Gloria."

She'd given King her agent's number. Less than a week later, she'd deposited the check. Since she'd dismissed her casual boyfriends, including Oliver, she invited Myles to join her. They were both in first class. She'd perform to a soundtrack but invited Zola along to basically be her assistant everything and Zola's boyfriend Paul to run tech.

They arrived on the island. A variety of water recreation equipment dotted the shore—surfboards, Jet Skis, kayaks, boats. The grounds were magnificent, full of lush tropical plants and shrubbery. Brick roads created a deep red swath through the vibrant green vegetation. There were several homes of different sizes and shapes. Jett saw tennis and basketball courts. A pool and pool house. Golf carts for guests to get around. In the distance, two large tents had been erected for the gala. Everyone quickly realized that the idea of returning home was overrated. The decision to stay there for the rest of their lives was unanimous.

Jett and the crew were housed in a four-bed, five-bath home of white stone with a red tiled roof. There were lots of indoor/outdoor spaces and a view of the ocean from almost every room. The home also came with a chef, butler, housekeepers, and, for Jett, a lady's maid. That evening, King brought Davis to the home. Jett also met King's wife Tamela for the first time. Jett had to admit Tamela seemed like good people, with the right beauty and poise to be the mayor's wife. For two days, the crew lived like royalty. Jett had some of the best seafood she'd ever tasted. She'd never seen Myles so carefree. He and Paul raced so much on the Jet Skis she thought they'd burn out the motors. Finally, Saturday arrived. Dinner was served at six. Paul had worked with the island engineer to set up her equipment. Her performance would begin with the birthday song promptly at seven thirty. She was led around to a side entrance near the raised platform that served as the stage. She was off to the side and able to see Gloria's face when her husband made the announcement. Gloria screamed and then began to cry, a priceless reaction. Jett sang as though she were performing at the Grammys, taking the hand of the birthday girl, who refused to move from her side. After meeting everyone at Gloria's table, she freshened up in the dressing room, then came out to enjoy a glass of wine before her second set. She requested one from a waiter, then eased onto one of several rattan stools backstage. She closed her eyes for a moment, lucky and thankful. It wasn't the album release she'd planned, but she knew she was exactly where she was supposed to be.

She felt someone come near her. "Excuse me, Miss Scott."

This wasn't the same waiter she'd joked with just moments before. This guy was far more reserved. She opened her eyes and would be forever thankful that she didn't fall off the barstool.

"Mr. Steward?"

"Please, call me Godfrey. I'm not sure you remember me. We met years ago."

"In the Hamptons. Of course I remember." She cocked her head and flirted. "Some men you never forget."

Chapter 31

Giving You the Best that I Got

Las Vegas, Nevada. New Year's Eve. Jett was performing for the grown and sexy in the Encore Theater at the Wynn Hotel on the Strip and had invited Artani and Terrence to join her. Like a true bestie, Rita had agreed to have Artani to spend the time with her family so that the newly engaged couple could enjoy their first out-of-town trip together. It was as if Chantel was newly released from prison and had never been out of her small town. She was that excited. Terrence acted too cool for school, but as they gambled, ate, shopped, and people-watched, his eyes sparkled, too. They made slow, lazy love at night and enjoyed shower quickies in the morning. On New Year's Eve, Chantel treated herself to a spa afternoon for the works—mani, pedi, facial, body wrap, and pussy wax. Last week, she'd struck gold again at the same store where she'd found the white off-shoulder gown for King's celebration. Tonight she wore an emerald-green faux velvet number that looked like a flowing maxi but was actually a jumpsuit. Off-the-shoulder with an asymmetrical waistline, the dress showed off her ample girls while slimming her waist and hips. Her hair stylist had talked her into waist-length braids that she piled on top of her head and secured with crystal-covered hairpins. She was elegant and sexy.

When she walked out of the bathroom and stepped into her heels, Terrence eyed her up and down, did that sexy lip lick that made Chantel moist, and declared, "Damn, girl. You are sexy."

Sound check ran late, so they didn't get to visit with Jett before taking their front-row seats next to a debonair gentleman who Chantel had never met but knew right away.

"You must be Godfrey," she said, extending her hand as he stood. "I'm Jett's . . . sister . . . Chantel."

The slightest frown crossed his face before he regained his composure, kissed her hand, and replied, "Godfrey Steward. The pleasure is mine."

At exactly nine o'clock p.m., the show got under way with the first act, a comedian who Terrence noted was actually funny without saying the F-word or the N-word every other sentence. Jett took the stage at ten o'clock and turned it out. During a break in her second set, she chatted with the audience while the band played softly beneath her.

"I don't know you folk, but for me, it's been a crazy year. Can anyone relate to that?" She had several cosigners.

"In all of the madness, some really good stuff happened. *Seeking Stardom* aired to rave reviews. Thank you for tuning in and loving it. We appreciate your support."

The audience wildly applauded.

"A few of you may remember me from another show . . ."

"*Glamagirls!*" someone shouted. The crowd cheered again.

"That's absolutely right! Who said that? Give that person a prize." She paused as the lighting director engaged the audience by flashing a spotlight on the person who'd spoken, followed by the stage manager handing the woman a rose.

"One or two of you may even remember my very first television appearance. Anyone remember the name of that show?"

Chantel almost yelled out the name, but Terrence shushed her. It wouldn't be fair. After several incorrect answers someone yelled, "*Next Big Thing*," and received a rose.

"I was just a kid during that competition, fresh off the bus from the country—okay, technically a plane—filled with hope and ready to make my dreams come true. What very few knew until recently is that those performances happened directly after a major event in the life of my sixteen-year-old self."

Chantel's heartbeat increased. Terrence reached for her hand.

"I became a teenage mother."

The audience quieted. There was a spattering of applause.

"For a long time, I kept that a secret. The reasons don't matter now, but there were a ton, the most critical and impactful one being an obsession, an unwavering, almost blind ambition, to be a star."

Jett struck a dramatic pose. "And . . . voilà!"

The crowd clapped louder, longer this time, before quieting once again.

"The child I gave birth to was raised by my mother," Jett paused, "as my sister." She batted away tears now. Over the murmuring she added, "Yes, this could be a reality show. We could have given Mama June and what was her child's name, Honey Boo Boo, all they could handle."

That brought on the laugher and helped Jett regain her composure. Chantel managed a chuckle or two through a body almost shocked stiff as she wiped away tears. Godfrey patted her knee, a fatherly gesture that helped her relax.

"Recently, as many of you now know, I graced the cover of a magazine that's not one of our top choices. Someone knew that secret and sold the story to *Celebrity Gossip* and threw a major hitch in a sistah's career giddyup! If you watched the online exclusive with Kasha Tay on *A Day with Tay*, you know that out of that scandal something pretty amazing happened. I decided that part of my journey was a story worth telling, and no one could do that better than me. I went home. Not just the physical location, but back to my roots, to Missouri, to the place in my mind where I'd stored that sixteen-year-old self for safekeeping, while I navigated a circuitous and sometimes rocky road to success. I reintroduced myself to her and reconnected with Chantel, who'd grown up as my younger sister. Chantel is beautiful, has an amazing spirit, and is also a singer. That's right. The whole thing about the apple and falling and trees. In fact," Jett paused to smile at Chantel, "she's in the audience tonight."

Chantel gasped. Terrence whispered in her ear. "Breathe."

"She had no idea I would do this. Or the band. Or me, until this moment." She motioned to the band director. He walked over. She whispered something. He nodded and went back to directing the band.

"Would you guys like to meet Chantel? Hear us do a little duet together?"

The audience answered in an enthusiastic affirmative. Chantel was shaking her head.

"I know you can handle Anita Baker, Chantel. She was one of Mama's favorites!"

The audience encouraged her. "Chan-tel! Chan-tel!"

"Then, ladies and gentlemen, it is my pleasure, my honor, a dream come true to welcome to the stage my sister, my daughter, Chantel Scott!"

It was an out-of-body experience. The only reason Chantel could later relay what happened was because the show was recorded and she was given a copy. She and Jett had never before sung together, but with a few hums to warm up and the direction to sing every other line, Chantel made her Las Vegas debut.

Givin' you the best that I got!

278 / LUTISHIA LOVELY

Chantel and Jett received a standing ovation. When they hugged, there were tears in both of their eyes. The long overdue embrace lasted a long time. For both women, it could have gone on forever. For the first time in her life, Jett felt the pangs of maternal love. Jett looked at her with a gaze that conveyed so much—regret, sadness, overwhelming joy. Chantel's look said that all was forgiven. Each could have drowned in the love that surrounded. Both would have died happy, and whole.

Someone had a bottle of Dom Perignon delivered to their seats. Chantel, Terrence and Godfrey toasted the new year in style. Backstage there were more hugs, more champagne, lots of laughter, and a few more tears.

"Do you think Mama was here tonight?" Jett asked, as Terrence and Godfrey bonded over a love of cigars.

"Absolutely! She was right there onstage!"

Beautiful thought. More tears. Chantel didn't mind them.

"You were wonderful tonight."

"That was so much fun. I thought I'd be nervous, but once I got up there, I couldn't see anybody, so I just acted like I was in my living room and got on down."

The women high-fived and hugged again.

"I love you, sister/daughter," Jett whispered.

"I love you, sister/mom."

"If I can have your attention," Godfrey intoned, sounding like the butler sans accent on *Fresh Prince of Bel-Air*, "I've arranged a light repast in my home. Limos are waiting and I'm sure our stars would love to relax, unwind, and change into more comfortable attire."

It took twenty minutes to make it through those remaining backstage and near the side door where the group would exit. Everyone wanted a hug, a picture, a chance to thank Jett and Chantel for sharing their story and talent, and to encourage them to do a show on reality TV. Driving away from the Strip, the mother-daughter duo who would always be sisters shared their thoughts on another ambition: to honor Anna by strengthening the bonds of their family. Because one thing the past crazy year had taught them for sure. Blind ambition could lead one down a path not worth taking. Best to live life with eyes wide open, bravely authentic, and unapologetically out loud.

Connect with U s

Visit us online at
KensingtonBooks.com
to read more from your favorite authors, see books
by series, view reading group guides, and more.

for sneak peeks, chances to win books and prize packs,
and to share your thoughts with other readers.

facebook.com/kensingtonpublishing
twitter.com/kensingtonbooks

Tell us what you think!

To share your thoughts, submit a review,
or sign up for our eNewsletters, please visit:
KensingtonBooks.com/TellUs.